HEART OF A PRINCE

CAROL MONCADO

To my new bestie Melissa!

I hope you enjoy Jordan, Astrid & Sofia's story! ♥ Carol Moncado

CANDID PUBLICATIONS

COPYRIGHT

Scripture taken from the Holy Bible, King James Version.

Cover photos:

People: maximkabb / depositphotos.com

Author photo: Captivating by Keli, 2010

First edition, CANDID Publications, 2017

AUTHOR'S NOTE

The first chapter of *Heart of a Prince* begins in the summer of Summer 2016. This is approximately 18 months before the events of *Reclaiming Hearts*. For further reference, *Hand-Me-Down Princess* ends in the late spring of 2016 and *Winning the Queen's Heart* begins in October 2016.

Therefore, the events after *Hand-me-Down Princess* in the Monarchies of Belles Montagnes series and the entirety of the Serenity Landing Second Chances have not happened yet. If you have not read those books, there will be some spoilers.

I appreciate all of you!

— CAROL MONCADO

PROLOGUE

JANUARY 2013

"I do."

Crown Princess Astrid of San Majoria blinked to clear the tears from her eyes as Andrei gave his biggest grin.

Then it was her turn.

"Do you Astrid Sofia Hannah Esther take Andrei Barnes to be your husband? To have and to hold from this day forward, in sickness and in health, as long as you both shall live?"

"I do!" She did! She'd longed for this day for years, and it had finally arrived.

"Then by the power vested in me by the King of San Majoria, I pronounce you husband and wife. You may kiss…"

Astrid didn't hear the rest of the sentence because Andrei was already kissing her.

It wasn't the most intense kiss they'd ever shared, but it was the most meaningful.

The rest of the day passed in a blur. The night passed, sleeping in her husband's arms for the first time.

The first year was one filled with great fanfare for the young couple as they toured the islands of San Majoria and began to put their own stamp on the Cordovan royal family.

But then…

Eighteen months after their "I dos" reality crashed down around the crown princess.

Nearly twenty hours after the other vehicle rammed into Andrei's side of their car, Astrid stood in a hospital waiting room, her sea-foam green chiffon dress caked in the rust-red blood of the love of her life. Her family was there, but gave her the space she needed. For the time being.

Astrid stared, nearly unseeing, at the doctor in his light blue scrubs as he used phrases like "we did all we could" and "despite our best efforts" and "brain dead" and the worst of all "organ donor."

The intellectual side could understand the terms, their meaning, the life they would pass on. But the part of her that wanted to break down weeping wasn't ready for the final good-bye. To be the one who gave permission to take his still-beating heart out of his chest and place it in someone else's.

But being a member of the royal family had taught her to always look out for the good of her people – whether it was one person or the entire country. And Andrei would want to help as many people as he could, and so she nodded.

"Can I say good-bye?" she whispered, her heart rending in two.

"Of course."

Astrid followed the doctor down one corridor and then another, the beeps from assorted machines surrounding her and giving her something to focus on.

He stopped next to a curtained enclosure and motioned to the nurse bustling about inside. The nurse bobbed a curtsy but left, leaving Astrid alone.

She walked to Andrei's side.

The figure lying under the blankets and covered with wires and tubing couldn't be her handsome husband with his wavy dark hair and laughing chocolate eyes. She gently picked up his hand, still covered with dried blood. Hers. His. Mixed together like their lives had become. The small bandage on her head belied the copious amounts of bleeding she'd done.

They'd had their problems, serious ones even, but she never would have wanted this. Never would have dreamed she'd face life without him.

Astrid leaned over, resting her torso on his, his heart still beating under her cheek.

So much left to say. To do. To be. Together.

And it was her fault. Not the accident, but he'd only attended the event with her because she'd begged him to. Another chance to show off the most handsome man in San Majoria.

She'd never dance in his arms again.

Never wake up next to him.

Never kiss him.

Never share the secret she'd been saving for weeks and was finally ready to share in a couple of days – on the anniversary of their first date.

Astrid sobbed like she hadn't sobbed since she was a little girl and her favorite dog had been put down. Because once she left this room, this cocoon away from the prying eyes of the media and her well-meaning, sympathetic countrymen, she would need to be stoic. To be a member of a royal family that seldom showed emotion in public. The family who hated that she and Andrei defied her grandmother's stance on PDA and held hands and embraced openly in public.

How long she lay there, she didn't know, but eventually the doctor cleared his throat softly behind her.

"My apologies, Your Royal Highness, but it's time."

Astrid straightened, but made no effort to wipe her tear-stained cheeks. She leaned over and pressed a kiss to his forehead. Her desire to kiss his lips one last time was thwarted by the breathing tube. She turned and took a deep, steadying breath.

"Doctor?"

"Yes, ma'am?"

"Is there any way we can fudge on his time of death? He would want his organs to go to those who need them most, but I don't believe I can stand people knowing or believing they received those organs. I think he would want people to know he'd given them, to set that example, but if everyone knows precisely when he died and those who get the organs know when they were called, it would be a fairly simple thing for them to connect those dots."

The doctor nodded. "We'll do what we can, ma'am."

"Thank you."

"Your father is waiting for you in the hall," the doctor prodded gently. "It's time for us to take the duke to surgery."

She squeezed Andrei's hand one more time and laid it gently on the bed. "Good-bye, my love. Godspeed until I see you again," she whispered.

Astrid tried to keep her head high and her shoulders back like she'd been taught. Her father waited for her, opening his arms. She crumpled into them as she hadn't done since she was a little girl.

"Papa…" Her voice sounded as broken as her heart. "What am I going to do, Papa?"

If she'd been more coherent, she would have expected an answer like, "Keep your head up as all members of the Cordovan dynasty must."

Instead, he tightened his grip around her and spoke softly, "Let us love you, my sweet girl."

Behind her, men and women prepared her beloved for transport to the operating room.

And then they were gone.

He was gone.

They were no longer a they. She was now a she.

A widow.

And still a Crown Princess.

She would be expected to marry again, though how she could when her heart had just disappeared down the hall, she would never know.

1

SUMMER 2016

Jordan Haines gripped the bar and leaned his weight backwards. The wind shifted, again, and he found himself windsurfing toward an unfamiliar beach in a sheltered cove. Posted signs warned that this was a private area, but Jordan ignored them. He knew himself. He knew his body.

He knew his limits.

And he was about at the end of his sometimes frustratingly short endurance.

The time had come to get off the ocean and onto the beach for a rest, until he could call someone to pick him up or get enough of his oomph back to get back out on the waves. The former was more likely, but the latter was his preference. He'd packed some energy bars, just in case.

A few minutes after ignoring the signs, he sat on the beach, his gear dismantled for the time being. Under a conveniently placed umbrella, Jordan opened his pack to remove the protein bars and water bottles with energy drink flavoring.

Jordan sat there, mesmerized as the waves moved in then out

then in again. He loved the ocean, always had. More and more in the last two years, something about the clear blue salt water called to him like a beacon.

Especially this water.

San Majoria, halfway between Bermuda and Puerto Rico, was roughly the same latitude as Palm Beach, Florida, and had beautiful weather year round. Despite its location in the Sargasso Sea, it was often included with the Caribbean countries.

"Hey!"

He turned to see a woman walking onto the beach from a staircase a short distance away. Jordan lifted a hand in a friendly wave.

"What are you doing here? Did you not see the private beach signs? Do you know what private means?"

She came closer with each step. Slender, with wavy golden-brown hair, a gorgeous accent, and an attitude. This could be fun. Unless she had him arrested for being on private property.

Jordan held up both hands in mock surrender. "The wind got a bit out of control, and I needed a break before I could go any further. I promise I'll be out of your hair soon." One way or another, he would be.

The wind swirled her skirt around her knees as she dropped her basket next to him. "You're under my umbrella."

"So you own this property?"

"My family does, and I asked for an umbrella to be set up down here. For me."

Jordan moved to one side. "I don't mind sharing."

"It's not yours to share. It's mine."

Up close, he realized everything about her screamed money. That shouldn't be a surprise, not given her presence on a private stretch of sand. Manicured nails. Jewelry that dazzled. Way too fancy for a day at the beach.

"Are you really planning to spend the whole day on the beach with nothing but whatever you've got in that basket?" He reached over and peeked inside. A book. A tablet. Food. Water.

"Yes. I plan to do just that. I'm going to read a book or two. Eat. Spend time alone."

Was she near tears?

"Hey." His tone changed from teasing to concerned. "What is it?"

"Today is my least favorite day of the year." She sat next to him, her skirt tucked neatly underneath her. "I want to spend it alone on the beach. Without you or anyone else."

"Not even your family?"

"No. Not even my family. None of them know exactly what today means to me. They don't understand how difficult it is."

Jordan picked up a handful of sand and let it slowly trickle back to the ground. "I understand tough days. I've had more than my share."

She didn't reply but continued to stare at the waves.

"If you want to talk about it, I'm a great listener." What made him say that? Did he really care what this woman had been through?

Something deep inside told him that, yes, he did care. Far more than he should.

"I don't want to talk about it."

"Then we can just sit. I'm good with that." He took a long drink of water. "Does everyone in your life know this is a tough day, or are they going to expect you to put on a happy face for all of them?"

"Yes."

"Yes to which?"

"Both. Everyone knows why today is a difficult day. Today and tomorrow, actually. But, in my family, you put on a happy face no matter what. At worst, you are allowed to be stoic."

Jordan winced. "Ouch. That can't be fun."

She shrugged. "It is what it is."

He wiped the sand from his hand off on his wet-suit-covered leg, then held it out to her. "If you're not going to have me arrested, at least I should introduce myself. I'm Jordan."

She shook his hand without looking at him. "Sofia. And I won't have you arrested. Yet. But we are under surveillance, so don't try anything."

He chuckled. "You have nothing to worry about from me, Sofia. Do you have a last name? Mine is Haines."

Sofia hesitated then shook her head. "Just Sofia."

Jordan tried to stifle a grin. "I'm not sure I believe you don't have a last name."

"That is your choice, but it is the only answer you're going to get."

He didn't reply for a moment. "So, Sofia, what do you do?"

It took her a minute to answer that question as well. "My family is wealthy. I will never have to work a day in my life until I take over for my father. I do charity work, and look pretty, mostly."

It didn't sound like a great life. "Well, you've got the look pretty part down." Jordan tipped his water bottle like it was something to toast with. "There's that."

She glared at him. "It's not much of an accomplishment."

"If that's basically your job, I'd guess you have to look your best at all times. No one can do that without feeling the pressure and eventually cracking under it."

"I don't have the luxury of cracking under pressure."

Jordan hesitated. "You don't always have a choice. Sometimes it just happens. Don't ask how I know." He took a big swig of water. He couldn't let his thoughts go there.

Not today.

Astrid found herself wanting to know more. She should have called security and had this man removed from her beach rather than confronting him, but today she wanted to be alone. She didn't want to deal with the security teams or her father or anyone else.

But somehow Jordan managed to convince her to allow him to stay. Maybe because he didn't appear to know who she was. None of the normal deference had appeared when she was close enough for him to recognize her. He didn't question her use of one of her middle names.

"Where are you from?" She'd known from the moment she saw him that he wasn't a local.

"Canada. Little town in New Brunswick."

"That is in the eastern portion of Canada, correct?" She'd studied Canadian geography once, many years earlier, when she'd accompanied her grandmother on a trip.

He looked impressed. "It is. Atlantic Standard Time Zone. Same as San Majoria. An hour ahead of the East Coast of the U.S." After another swig of his water, he pointed toward the ocean. "I can't see whatever mega-mansion you must have on this property from here. Can you see the water?"

Astrid shook her head. "A few glimpses from a couple places, but not really."

"That's sad. You live so close, but you can't see it."

"I don't live here, not full time."

"Can you see the water from your home?"

"When I moved away from my parents, I made sure I had the best view of the water I could." She reached into her basket and pulled out her own water bottle. "It is almost my favorite view ever."

"What's your favorite view then?"

Astrid took a sip of water. "I don't know you well enough to tell you that."

"To tell me what your favorite view is?"

"Yes."

He wouldn't understand. He couldn't. Not without more details about her life than she was willing to share.

Jordan twisted the lid back onto his water bottle then leaned back on his elbows. "Tell me more about yourself."

She almost forgot he was talking about her. "What is there to tell? I was born into a wealthy dynasty. My job is to look pretty and raise money for charity. Today is the anniversary of the worst day of my life, a fact that is unlikely to ever change. What more do you want to know?"

He was unfazed by her comment. "What's your favorite water sport? Do you surf? Windsurf? Body board? Jet ski?"

"Lounging. I like to watch, but I don't participate." She'd watched Andrei kite surf many times. "I do parasail from time to time, but that's it." She hadn't in years. For all his other athletic prowess, Andrei had hated it. She hadn't gone since not long after they started dating out of respect for his fears, though he had told her he didn't mind if she did. He just wouldn't join her.

Her phone buzzed in the pocket of her skirt. Wasn't it on do not disturb? She pulled it out to see her father calling. After sending an automated text, she checked the screen. Six missed calls and a dozen text messages asking if she was okay and warning security would be there momentarily.

"Pardon me for a moment." She swiped to open her phone and typed in her passcode.

Everything is fine. He was tired while windsurfing. He doesn't even know who I am. I know you'll want to check him out though - Jordan Haines. He's Canadian. From New Brunswick.

Are you sure?

I'm sure, Papa. I know you have people watching me, but please, leave me be.

Very well.

Thank goodness.

"Security worried about me?" He couldn't have seen what she typed.

"Something like that. I gave them your name. I'm sure a background check is already underway."

"There's nothing to find."

"Then you have nothing to worry about."

He rolled onto his side, still propped on one elbow, and grinned at her. "I'm not worried."

She reluctantly admitted to herself that he did have a very nice smile.

"So you like to watch aquatic sports, and you occasionally parasail. Not to be presumptuous, but I'm sure you can swim."

"Like a fish," she confirmed.

"What else do you like to do? When you're not raising money for all those charities."

"Spend time with my family."

"The all-powerful Majorian business moguls put a priority on family time. That's nice to hear."

It surprised Astrid to realize he genuinely meant it. "What brings you to San Majoria?"

He sobered. "I haven't been back in two years. I haven't windsurfed in a little over two years, but it was time to come back."

"Why now?"

Jordan picked up a handful of sand and slowly let it flow through the opening on the bottom of his fist until it all returned to the beach. "My little sister married my best friend."

"You're not happy about this?"

"They're perfect for each other, but it came out of nowhere. Two weeks ago, they were pretending to be an item to keep a creep from hitting on her while we were in Serenity Landing, Missouri on vacation. The next weekend, they were married. They basically eloped, though we were all there." He snorted. "She even had royalty at her wedding."

Astrid's heart thudded to a stop. "Pardon?"

"We were staying in a suite next door to a couple from Mevendia. Rick and his wife. He's a prince. Betsy hit it off with the wife."

"They're from Montevaro, not Mevendia."

"Right."

She'd never met Prince Richard and Princess Ellie. San Majoria was a footnote in the story of Belles Montagnes, but San Majoria owed the Commonwealth its very existence. If any other royal family could be considered friends, it should be the Eyjanian family, or possibly Islas del Sargasso and Auverignon, though she wouldn't call any of them friends. But San Majoria and Eyjania were sister countries. Not in the same sense that Mevendia, Montevaro, and Ravenzario were sister countries through the Commonwealth of Belles Montagnes. San Majoria and Eyjania were morein the "our cities all have sister cities in the other country where our schools do the pen pal thing" sense.

Not so much pen pals anymore, of course, though there were still actual letters exchanged. Most of the correspondence was done via email or videos, including real time video chats.

"Is there a man in your life?"

Jordan's question caught her off-guard. "What?"

"A man. Boyfriend, fiancé, husband."

Astrid shook her head. "No. No one." Not any of those.

"I can't offer to take you to the kinds of places you're probably used to, but would you be interested in a date sometime?"

Astrid stared at the waves as they crossed onto the beach, but didn't answer.

How could she?

Her heart still belonged to Andrei, but something about Jordan…

Something made her want to say yes.

2

"Where are we going?" Jordan didn't like not knowing, but the yacht - one Sofia admitted didn't belong to her family - headed for an unknown destination.

"To wage a war." Sofia almost certainly had her eyes closed behind those giant sunglasses she loved. Her long legs stretched out on the lounge chair, and Jordan had to force himself not to stare.

Sofia was an incredibly attractive woman.

She'd turned down his request for a date, but did invite him to join her on her beach the next day. And the next. And the one after that.

After two weeks of seeing her almost every day, he'd arrived to find a yacht anchored off-shore. Sofia stood on the bow of the top deck wearing the black swimsuit he'd seen her in a few times with a sarong type thing wrapped around her waist as she motioned him aboard. His windsurfing equipment was dismantled somewhere on a lower level.

But now he just stared, confused. "What?"

She raised an arm over her head. "Relax, *viejo*. You won't get hurt."

"I am not an old man," he muttered.

"You know your Spanish."

Her amusement was worth it. Since that first day, he'd known he'd do almost anything to make her smile, to help clear the tinge of sadness that always hovered around her eyes. "I know enough." Not much, but enough.

"You mean you can find the bathroom?"

Jordan chuckled and stretched his own legs out onto his lounge chair. The sun beating down almost made him wish he'd go without a shirt sometimes. Maybe someday soon. He would tan easily enough so he wouldn't be pasty white long.

But the scars…

"It's not spoken much in San Majoria." Jordan closed his eyes.

"We do have some Spanish heritage, if you go far enough back. My great-great-grandfather was Hispanic, and some of it has passed down. My mother calls my father *viejo* all the time."

"How long until we get to this war?" Better to keep conversation on the innocuous and off family. Sofia didn't like to talk about her family.

"About fifteen minutes, I think. It's usually a forty-five minute boat ride from the beach."

"But this isn't your usual yacht so you're not sure," he finished for her.

"Exactly."

"Why not your family's yacht? Someone else using it?"

"No."

She didn't elaborate, and Jordan decided not to push. "Do I need my suit of armor for this war?"

"No. This war is quite civilized."

"I won't need to lay down my life to defend your honor or anything?"

"Highly unlikely."

"Good. I normally don't like to do that sort of thing until I've known a girl at least a month."

She smirked, but still didn't look at him.

He wasn't sure what to make of that. Even though they'd only spent a few hours a day together for the last two weeks, he thought he'd gotten to know parts of her pretty well. She definitely kept some things to herself and was only available for a little while most afternoons. Odd, but he'd take what he could get.

Because he liked Sofia. A lot. And not just because she was incredibly pretty. She seemed to like him, too.

But she didn't seem inclined to talk, so he did something brave. He reached over and took her hand, linking his fingers with hers.

"You all right?" he asked softly.

"Another hard day."

"Related to the one a couple weeks ago or something else?"

Sofia didn't say anything, but did curl her fingers around his. "Related. After the days two weeks ago, there was a tough day the next day and again five days later. That was a Sunday this year, and I didn't see you that day. Today is another one."

"Is there anything I can do to help?" He thought about checking the news from a couple weeks ago to see if there was anything about the anniversary of some event that might still affect her. It didn't seem likely that whatever it was had been newsworthy except to her. He also wanted her to trust him enough to tell him what bothered her so much.

"Just being here is more than I had last year."

"You were alone all four days?"

"More or less. I am rarely completely alone."

Jordan turned that over in his head. "You have security with you all the time or something? Because of your family's wealth?"

She nodded.

"Ma'am?"

A voice from behind made them both turn.

"Yes?" Sofia settled back into her seat.

"We will arrive in a few minutes."

"Thank you."

Jordan scanned the horizon as best he could from behind his own sunglasses. A small cluster of palm trees appeared in the distance but nothing else. Could that be their destination? It wasn't much of one, if so.

The engine sounds changed, though. A reduction in power.

"Is that where we're headed?"

Sofia didn't look but answered anyway. "I would imagine so. A small island with palm trees on a little bit of a hill and not much else?"

"Yes."

"That's the place." She stood, far more elegantly than he could ever hope to out of a lounge chair. After tying the sarong back around her waist, Sofia turned to him. "Are you coming?"

Jordan stumbled as he tried to stand up from his lounge chair. "This has to be the oddest war ever."

She didn't say anything but walked down the staircase to the next deck. Jordan followed.

"Can I fight this war in my flip flops?"

"If you must."

"I didn't bring my metal boot cover things from my armor so I guess I don't have much choice."

The boat pulled in as close as it could. They transferred to a smaller one to get ashore. One of the crew members pulled the small boat even closer. Jordan jumped out so he could help Sofia instead of the random crew member.

Once safely in ankle deep water, she turned back and took a bag from someone else.

She held it up by one finger and waggled her eyebrows. "Let's fight."

Astrid struggled to hide her smile. War was a bit of a

misnomer, but it was too much fun to tell Jordan everything right away.

Together, they trudged up the sand toward the small hill.

"Is that a flagpole?" Jordan stopped with his hands on his hips and stared toward the trees.

"Yes." She passed him. "Come on."

They made it a few more steps through the sand before he stopped again. "Wait. Is this like the war between Canada and the Danish over Hans Island?"

"This is actually far more peaceful than the Whiskey Wars."

"How do you figure?" He began following her again.

"Because both of those countries actually want control over the island. This island holds no strategic importance for either of us."

"Either of who? What's the other country?"

"Islas del Sargasso. This war has been going on for a century." She finished the trek through the trees and set her bag at the foot of the flagpole. "Can you help?"

"Of course." He reached for the ropes holding the other flag in place and began to lower it. "Do you fold it or wad it up in a ball?"

She had a hard time keeping a straight face. "Fold it properly. We are not savages."

"Of course not."

She couldn't see it, but a grin probably covered his face.

He gathered the flag as he unclipped it from the rope. She took one end, and he the other, working together to fold it into a triangle.

"Do you keep it or return it to Islas del Sargasso?"

"It will be shipped with no return address to Queen Carlotta. She, or more likely her assistants, will immediately know where it's from. At some point in the next six months to a year, she will send someone to replace our flag with theirs and return this one to San Majoria."

As soon as she said it, Astrid wondered if she'd said too much. Would he realize she had a connection to the San Majorian royal family? How else would she know when to come and take their turn at the war?

"It's crazy." He didn't ask why she was a part of it, just put the flag carefully in the bag and pulled out the San Majorian flag. She held it while he clipped it in place. Jordan bowed to her one arm out, clearly in jest. "As you are the native San Majorian, you should do the honors, Sofia."

Astrid smiled, and the twinge inside caught her again. She needed to tell him the truth, at least about her name. Pulling the rope, one hand over the other, she raised the flag of her homeland.

"Do you leave whiskey?"

She laughed. "No. Not whiskey. But you'll find what we do leave in the bag. There's a storage chest nearby that we'll put it in."

"Whatever they leave is still there?"

"No. The San Majorian Navy comes by and picks up whatever is left behind when the flag arrives at the palace. The Sargossian Navy will do the same when this flag arrives there."

Jordan leaned against a palm tree and crossed his arms over his chest. "I'd guess you're friends with someone who lives in the palace. One of the mail clerks, maybe?" His eyes twinkled. "Is that how you know when it's time to come fight this war?"

Astrid managed a half-smile. "Something like that."

He snapped and pointed at her. "You come from a wealthy family. We established that the day we met. I bet you're friends with the royal family. They know you've been having a rough time, so they sent you to fight this war to take your mind off whatever else is happening today."

The smile slid away. "That is much closer to the reality, Jordan. I would appreciate it if you wouldn't press me further."

"Hey." He pushed off the tree and came to stand in front of her, his hands resting on her hips. The weight of them was familiar and comforting.

And disconcerting at the same time.

Tears sprang to her eyes. *No. Not now. Just enjoy it.*

"It's okay, Sofia." His hands slid around her waist, and she let herself be pulled close. "I won't try to figure it out. Promise. When you're ready to tell me, you will."

How could he have more faith in her than she did?

Astrid rested the side of her head on his chest. Her arms slid around him until her hands clasped against his back. "There is something I need to tell you."

"What's that?"

"My name's not Sofia."

She felt his chuckle as much as heard it. "I kind of figured."

"You know?"

"Sometimes it takes you a second to answer, almost like you're not used to being called Sofia. I guessed that it might not be your name."

He surprised her when he didn't ask what her name was.

"It is my second name," she blurted out.

"I kind of figured that, too." His hand ran up and down her back.

Astrid found herself relaxing against him, a weight lifting off her shoulders. One that had been there so long, she'd become used to it. Her father and the rest of her family had tried to share her burden, but it had been hers alone.

Jordan's hold on her tightened. "I know you're not ready to tell me your whole story, Sofia, but whenever you are and whatever you want to share, I'm here."

"I know." She heaved a sigh. "I appreciate that." After another minute, she moved away from him. "It's been a long time since anyone's just hugged me like that. I needed it. Thank you."

"Anytime." Jordan grinned. "Well, anytime between one and four in the afternoon during the week." His wink told her he wasn't serious. "Which reminds me that we should hurry up fighting this war so we can get you back home."

"I've already told those who need to know that I will likely be later than usual this afternoon." She smiled. "I have another surprise out on the beach when we're done here."

Together, they unloaded the kitschy San Majoria t-shirt from the bag into the chest partially buried in the ground near the flag pole.

Jordan surprised her by taking her hand and linking their fingers as they walked back toward the beach.

And even more, Astrid surprised herself with how much she liked it.

3

Two weeks. That's how long it had taken Sofia to tell Jordan it wasn't her real name. He'd realized it within an hour of meeting her. She'd been distracted that day, but he'd noticed even more than when she didn't respond to him calling her name several times.

But now her hand nestled snugly in his, like they were meant to be there. She led him back toward the beach. When they arrived, he noticed a table had been set up and lunch set out on it.

"I know it's a little late in the day for lunch," Sofia started.

Jordan stopped and tugged on her hand until she did, too. "I had a late breakfast." He grinned at her. "You said we'd eat late, and I decided to sleep in. I didn't even get up until almost ten."

"Then it's perfect." She smiled at him, her eyes lighting up. He liked this side of her.

Their feet sank into the sand as they walked toward the table. Jordan stopped and let go of her hand before kicking off his sandals. He bent down to pick them up. Sofia rested her hand on his shoulder, bracing herself against him as she took off her shoes. He gladly let her.

She let go of him, and they resumed their walk toward the table. "Where's the crew?" Were they really alone?

Sofia ducked her head. "Well, you'll be happy to know the background check finally came back clear. I knew it would, but unfortunately, until it did, we were always watched by security."

"I know." He'd always felt the eyes on them, even when the watchers weren't visible. "I'm glad someone's protecting you."

She set her bag containing the Sargossian flag on the table. "Now that they know what I know, we can be more alone than we were before. They're all still on the ship."

Jordan could see it in the distance.

"But no one is specifically watching us."

A slow grin crossed his face. "Really?"

Sofia glanced up from where she opened the basket. "What?"

He didn't let himself overthink it. Jordan reached for her, pulling her into his arms. "No one will see me do this."

"Do what?" Her hands rested on his upper arms, and she didn't move away as he leaned toward her.

"This." Heart pounding in his chest, Jordan kissed her.

Sofia's hand slid to the back of his neck, but rather than pulling her even closer, Jordan moved away. A short, sweet, first kiss. Nothing more.

It didn't need to be anything more.

Not yet.

He let her go and pulled the closest chair out for her to sit down then sat next to her.

The pink tinge to Sofia's cheeks made Jordan smile.

"That was nice," she told him, reaching for the basket.

"I thought so." He helped her take the food out and set it on the table. "Thank you for lunch."

"My pleasure."

Over lunch, small talk continued. Jordan told her about playing hockey. She told him about horseback riding. He noticed she didn't say much about her recent past.

When they returned to Sofia's cove, Jordan took a chance by kissing her again, this time a little longer, but still soft.

"Will I see you tomorrow?" he asked.

Sofia shook her head. "I wish we could, but I have some obligations I must see to. The day after?"

"Of course." After another kiss, he took to his board and wind surfed his way back toward his home away from home.

By the time he reached the beach, the sun was setting. After disassembling his equipment, he called the nearby resort and ordered room service for dinner. Lunch with Sofia had been nice, but not as filling as he would have liked.

At least this was an almost all expenses paid vacation.

Since he wasn't going to see Sofia, Jordan slept late the next morning. Morning had nearly disappeared by the time he finished his room service breakfast and headed out onto the beach. Though his cottage was mere steps from the sand, and it was a private beach, it wasn't the same kind of private beach as Sofia's. This beach was available for anyone staying at the resort to use.

It still beat the public beaches by a long shot. Only a couple dozen people were in view, and that made what he was about to do much simpler.

Taking a deep breath, he tugged the bottom of his t-shirt up and over his head. He stood, letting the waves wash over his feet and the sun warm his chest. How long had it been since he'd been shirtless on the beach? He knew the date. It had been seared into his brain nearly two-and-a-half years earlier.

After a few minutes of soaking it in with his eyes closed, Jordan returned to the blanket he'd spread on the sand. One thing he didn't want to do was burn. It was far easier to put sunscreen on his chest than his back.

"Do you need some help?"

Jordan looked up to see a girl standing there. Girl might have been a misnomer. She was likely his age, but somehow seemed younger.

He managed a half-smile. "I've got it, thanks."

She rolled her eyes and tossed her bag on the blanket. "You've got a farmer's tan there, buddy. You're going to burn. Let me get your back." She held up both hands in mock surrender. "No ulterior motives. You just look like you could use some help."

Reluctantly, Jordan handed over the bottle of sunscreen. "Thanks, then."

True to her word, the girl just rubbed the lotion in, but didn't try to make any advances. She stood and picked up her bag. "You're all set. You might try to find someone to help you with that when I'm not around."

And she walked off, catching up to some friends a bit further up the beach.

Jordan had never been one to just lay on the beach to get a tan, but this time it seemed to be just what he needed. A day to rest, to relax, and, maybe later, do a little surfing.

Astrid slid her feet into the boring beige pumps. If she were to choose, she'd wear brighter colors and more casual clothes, but no one really asked what she wanted. Her stylist gave her options considered acceptable, and Astrid chose from among them.

Even Queen Elizabeth II had a more colorful and vibrant wardrobe than Astrid did.

Of course, Queen Elizabeth was the queen, and Astrid merely the Crown Princess. Perhaps when Astrid became queen she could insist on updating her wardrobe.

Once she was done mourning the death of her father.

Because she wouldn't become queen until he was gone. Like Queen Elizabeth, he would not step down as monarchs from other countries sometimes did.

"Your car is waiting, ma'am." Jade, Astrid's new assistant, stood in the doorway.

"Of course it is," Astrid sighed.

"Pardon?"

"Nothing."

Jade didn't know her well enough to pick up on the subtle snarky nuances that occasionally slipped through.

Astrid left her dressing room and headed for the main portico where her car waited. Jade would ride in the front seat and go over the details of the day's events with her... *again*. The events were such that Astrid could likely attend them in her sleep and no one would notice, but Jade was still feeling her way in her new role, so Astrid would let her.

Part of the reason Astrid chose her from the available candidates was because she was young enough to not be set in her ways. Some of the other candidates had already served in similar positions for other family members, such as Astrid's uncle, or some of the San Majorian nobility. They were quite insistent that they knew the best way to do things.

If she could just convince her father she needed a new stylist, too.

No. That wasn't fair to Martina. She did the best she could with what she had to work with.

The ride was far too short, but at the same time, far too long. Everything was these days. Except time spent at the beach each afternoon. That was only too short.

What was Jordan doing? She'd seen the disappointment in his eyes when she told him they wouldn't be able to see each other. She'd even convinced herself she felt it in the soft goodbye kiss he'd given her. Astrid found herself wanting more.

Not *that* kind of more, not yet, but more than just two little-more-than-pecks each day.

"Ma'am?"

Jade's voice snapped her out of her thoughts and back to the present. Someone held open her door and waited for her to exit. The hospital administrator stood to the side and offered his hand to assist her.

Because her genetics meant she couldn't do anything alone.

Maybe she'd get Jordan to teach her how to surf. Or play hockey. Wouldn't her father love that?

Once on the sidewalk, cameras clicked, documenting her every move. Questions were shouted by members of the media, both local news stations and gossip hounds.

Astrid answered none of them.

Instead, she focused on the other side of the path cleared for her. On that side were members of the community. She spent a few minutes shaking hands, posing for selfies, and accepting flowers from children.

One little boy, in particular, caught her attention, and she lowered herself down as gracefully as she could. When her weight rested solely on the balls of her feet, she was nearly eye-to-eye with the dark-haired boy.

"These are for you, Pwincess Ast'id." He held out a few tropical flowers, native to the island, and clearly not from a florist.

"They are lovely, kind sir." She inhaled their scent. "And what is your name?"

"And'ei."

Astrid forced herself to continue smiling. "Andrei?"

"Yes, Pwincess."

It was as though a knife stabbed through her heart. "That is one of my favorite names."

"Mama say she name me for Pwince And'ei. She like him."

"*Andrei*!" Two hands appeared on his shoulders. Astrid looked up to see his mother standing there. "I'm sorry, Your Royal Highness."

Astrid made her smile even bigger, though inside her slowly healing heart began to refracture. "It is fine. I liked him quite a lot, too."

"My husband and I got married the same day you did, but in Ravenzario where his family is from," the mother explained. "His grandfather's name was Andrew, but we decided we liked Andrei better." Her face colored. "We kind of felt a little connected to you both because of the wedding date, though the time zones meant our wedding day was over by the time your ceremony began."

Astrid and Andrei had both hated waiting for that evening wedding. "He would have been honored, of that I am certain." Her feet began to tingle. She would need to stand soon.

"You have been in our prayers, ma'am."

Young Andrei nodded. "My pray for you."

Astrid's smile turned more genuine, though she had to blink back the tears. "I thank you for that. It is very appreciated."

"Ma'am?"

She looked up to see barely-concealed annoyance on the face of the hospital administrator. "Of course." Astrid stood as gracefully as she could, barely managing not to wobble. She motioned to Jade, who hopefully understood her meaning. They'd been over it often enough. "I must go, but thank you again for the flowers."

Walking half a step in front of the administrator, she walked to the front door of the hospital. Reflected in the glass, she could see Jade talking to Andrei's mother. Astrid would see they were invited to something soon - the end of summer party perhaps.

Today's hospital visit was both her favorite and her most dreaded. She would spending time with children who were in the hospital for extended stays. They were always so kind and welcoming and cheerful despite their circumstances, but sometimes the reality of their situations could not be hidden, and Astrid knew their prognoses wasn't good.

By the time she returned to the palace several hours later, Astrid was worn out. Though she had her own quarters and access to any kitchen in the palace, her parents insisted she have dinner with them several times a week. Tonight was one of those nights.

It would be a long dinner filled with official business, and unofficial prying about Jordan. They knew about him. They probably knew about the kisses. Her father, at least, knew far more about him that Astrid did, thanks to the completed background check.

In her dressing room, Martina, Astrid's lady's maid and stylist helped her out of the beige pantsuit, though Astrid dismissed her before donning her new favorite pajama pants and a soft t-shirt.

She collapsed on her bed. Dinner wasn't for another few hours. The snack that had been waiting for her in the car would hold her over until then, but for the moment she just wanted to sleep.

Maybe dream that Andrei was still with her, holding her in the bed they'd shared for far too short a time.

And dream she did.

But instead of the placid dreams of living life with Andrei, when Astrid awoke, all she remembered was the laughing blue eyes of a certain Canadian.

She changed and walked to her parents' dining room with an unsettled feeling deep inside.

4

Jordan moved his oar smoothly from one side to the other as he paddled his kayak into the cove. Though his body had let him down the day he met Astrid, he'd come a long way. He'd been in shape before, but was in better shape now. The miles long trek, both ways, each day had pushed him into the best shape of his life.

He paddled right up onto the beach before getting out and pulling the kayak further away from the waves.

"A kayak?"

Jordan turned to see Sofia walking down the last few steps to the sand. "I didn't feel like wind surfing today."

"Sometimes I wish I could do some of the more adventurous things." She sighed as she set her bag under the umbrella someone always placed there.

"Why can't you?"

"My father would never allow it."

Jordan lowered himself to the blanket before leaning over to give her a quick kiss, one he wished could be longer. "You know, before I came here, my sister, my best friend, and I stayed in this little town in Missouri for a week or so. Somehow, we ended up next door to this guy from Europe and his wife."

He glanced up to see her raise a brow his direction.

"I'm getting there," he protested. "Turns out, this guy is Prince Richard of Montevaro. An actual prince. Like Your Royal Highness. His wife, Princess Ellie, was with him. I told you they came to my sister's wedding, didn't I?"

She nodded.

"This guy does all kinds of stuff. Hiking in the Andes. Everest Base Camp, though he's never climbed the mountain. Dog sledding across Greenland. You name the extreme sport, he's tried it. And he's been either first or second in line for the throne his whole life. My sister says he's always been that way."

"Your sister?"

Jordan picked up a handful of sand and let it run through his fingers. "Yeah. She's something of a royal watcher. Nothing creepy, just follows Facebook pages and stuff. They fascinate her. I can tell you about the Windsors, but that's only because I'm Canadian." He shrugged. "I know a little bit more, because I spent several hours with Prince Richard and his wife over the course of a few days, and because my sister blathers on all the time."

"I see."

He sat up. "My point is that if the heir to a European monarchy can do all this stuff, why can't you do stuff that's not nearly as dangerous?" Jordan pointed to the cove. "I've not seen the waves big enough to surf here, but you could paddleboard or kayak, or if you leave the cove even a little bit, windsurf. Jet ski. Any of that stuff. With a big enough storm off-shore, you could probably body surf."

Sofia just stared at the ocean. "Perhaps."

The conversation was clearly over. For all the time they'd spent together, there were certain things Sofia didn't discuss. Her personal life was one of those things. Oh, she shared stories of attending a private, all girls boarding school as a child, mentioned that she didn't want to send her children to boarding school someday, talked about her first boyfriend after she started co-ed school as a tween, but never anything truly personal.

She did tell him she'd been in love once. She clearly still loved the guy, whoever it was, and it pained her to talk about him, even though she never mentioned his name.

"Is kayaking hard?" Astrid stared at the water.

"Not particularly. You learn your own best stroke and pace, but otherwise it's mostly about endurance."

"I would like to try."

"Sure." Jordan pushed to his feet and held out a hand to help her up.

Once standing, she shed her cover-up. "I don't suppose a long dress is best for kayaking."

Jordan grinned. "I've never tried it, but I'd imagine not." As much as he wanted to, he didn't let his eyes linger places they hadn't been invited to go. He knew her figure would be the envy of women and the object of men's admiration and fixation - even desire - but he didn't want to be one of those men. He didn't want to objectify her.

Unless he was mistaken, she already had plenty of that.

He moved the kayak to the water and turned to Sofia. "You don't just climb in." After demonstrating proper technique, he climbed back out. "I know it seems ridiculous, but it's important to learn how to do it properly."

Sofia saluted smartly. "Yes, sir."

Jordan lifted an eyebrow. "I know this is kayaking in your cove and nothing more dangerous, but learning to do something right from the beginning is far easier than having to relearn it later."

"I know." She took the paddle from him and positioned it across the back of the kayak, just behind the cockpit. "Like this?"

"Like that." Knee deep in the water, he held it steady for her as she carefully climbed in. Once she was situated, he pulled her out a bit farther until the water reached his waist.

Standing next to her as the waves - ones that barely deserved the name - rolled in, he explained the paddle. He reached around until she was trapped between his arms as he showed her the proper way to hold it and which side was up.

"You're right handed?" he asked. He'd never seen her write anything, but she did occasionally wear a watch on her left wrist.

She nodded, the hair in her ponytail brushing against his cheek. He wanted to turn, to press a kiss into that hollow between her neck and shoulder. Though he wasn't as innocent as his mother probably wished, he'd never kissed a woman there before, but he'd seen both his father and his new brother-in-law do so. He knew what kind of relationship that signified.

Sofia turned her head, looking up at him and breaking the spell, just a bit.

It signified the kind of relationship he'd never be able to have with this woman. No matter what he wished, this would never be more than an innocent summer romance.

A week later, Astrid was getting far better at kayaking and paddleboarding, but she managed to knock Jordan in the head with her oar.

"Are you all right?" she gasped as he collapsed into the waist high water.

"I think I'll live." His grin, the one she loved, came easily to his face. "My scars have got scars far worse than that will leave."

She fingered her hairline, almost without realizing it. "You have scars?"

He snorted. "I've got more scars than anyone you know." A minute later, they were back on shore.

Jordan twisted his elbow around to show her a thin line about four inches long. "This one is dumb. My best friend had this old car. Like a 1980s Datsun or something, but it was cheap, and he could afford it. The front of the glove box was missing but there were still screws sticking out of it with a bit of plastic still on them.

I scraped it on one of those when I was getting out of the car once."

Astrid just shook her head. "I cannot imagine how painful your life has been. To have so many scars."

"And you don't have any?" he challenged.

She hesitated, then answered truthfully. "Just one, that I know of." She brushed the hair back off her forehead with one hand and ran her finger along the scar with the other.

Jordan snorted in response. "That's barely a scratch."

"It bled profusely. It's more than a scratch." Plus the loss it represented. That hurt far worse. "It was the worst day of my life." Would he ask to know more?

Would she tell him?

He lifted the side of his shirt, and pointed to another thin line on his side. She'd never seen so much of his torso. "Hockey skate." Then he pointed to a smaller scar on his abdomen. "Same hockey skate, different pick-up game with no adult supervision. I got that one first and a huge lecture from Mom about only playing hockey with protective gear. After the one on my side, I was grounded until they took up the ice and there was no hockey for months." He moaned. "My Bantam team took our Zones without me that season. And Mom lectured me daily about gear for a year. She was convinced I wouldn't make it out of TimBits alive."

Astrid didn't understand half of what he said, but understood his meaning. That one wasn't what held her attention. Astrid reached out and ran her finger down the two inches of exposed scar right in the center of his chest. It was thicker, more pronounced than any of the others he'd shown her, though not overly so. What made it different? "What's this one?" she finally asked.

Jordan did something she'd never seen him do.

Hesitate.

"I don't like to talk about that one. It happened the last time I was in San Majoria, just over two years ago."

Astrid couldn't explain why, but she couldn't stop running her finger up and down the little bit of it she could see. "I'm sorry my country left you with such a wound. What did we do to give you such a scar?"

He stepped back and stripped his shirt off completely. She saw it - and his chest - for the first time. Starting just under his clavicle, it was about ten inches long. Astrid reached out and ran her forefinger down the entire scar.

Jordan didn't flinch under her scrutiny. "It's my second chance at life scar. It wasn't anything San Majoria did. In fact, San Majoria saved my life."

"How so?" It didn't bother her to be touching another man's chest like this. The still coherent part of Astrid's brain knew it should, but it didn't.

He captured her hand and held it to his chest. She could feel his heart beating under her palm. "Nope. Not until you tell me how that little scratch was the worst day of your life? Daddy's little princess didn't like the blood in her hair?" His teasing tone let her know everything she needed to. He still didn't know who she was. And he still thought she was a spoiled snob, that she'd never known real pain.

"It was a car accident, just over two years ago, like yours," she told him, her eyes steadfastly focused on their two hands intertwined.

"And you walked away with just that little scratch? I'd say that was a pretty good day."

"We were on our way home from a charity gala. I was wearing a sea foam green chiffon dress."

"I don't even know what chiffon is." His tone had softened to match hers. "I do know sea foam, though."

"A car ran a red light." She was transported back. To the police escort. To the dark. To the screech of tires. The crunch of metal. The wet, sticky of blood.

The screaming.

Her own screams she barely recognized as she knelt over Andrei's unmoving body.

"He was on the side of the car with the impact. He'd insisted I sit against the other door and not in the middle next to him because the seatbelt wasn't working properly."

Jordan didn't say anything.

The smell of blood and antiseptic. The sounds of sirens. Of yelling. The vision of his still body on the gurney being loaded into the helicopter.

"There was nothing they could do. His body lived on for a short time, but he was brain dead at impact. Machines kept him alive until..." Astrid stopped. She wasn't ready to share with Jordan, the gut-wrenching decision she'd made.

"I was windsurfing." He seemed to know she wasn't ready to go on. To tell him the rest. "We'd come to San Majoria for spring break. Surf. Sand. Sun. Pretty girls. But I didn't feel right. I couldn't breathe very well and just felt off, so my buddies took me to Cabo Juan-Eduardo General Hospital. I didn't leave for nearly three months. My heart was failing. I needed machines until a donor heart could be found. I wasn't stable enough to return to Canada, so I waited here. This scar represents my second chance, but I'll never forget it also represents someone else's loss."

They stood there for an interminable period of time before Jordan spoke again. "Who was he? Who was in the car with you? Your father? Your brother?"

She stared at their hands, resting against his surprisingly sun-bronzed chest. The lighter scar ran beneath their hands and reappeared below them. His tanned hand resting on top of her naturally light one. "No. He was my heart. The love of my life. We'd been married eighteen months."

His hand squeezed hers. "I'm so sorry, Sofia. I can't imagine the loss."

"He was an organ donor. Even though I knew it was the right thing to do, what he wanted, the decision was the most difficult I've ever made."

Jordan reached out with his other hand and tilted her chin until their eyes met. "On behalf of those who received his gift, your gift, thank you." He grinned, breaking the somber mood. "Remember the movie *Return to Me*?"

She shook her head.

"My sister made me watch it when I finally got home. It's about this guy whose wife dies in a car accident. He donates her organs. A year or so later, he falls in love with this girl. But before she can tell him something important, she finds the letter she wrote to the family of her donor heart. She had his late wife's heart. They argue and split up for a while, but eventually, they live happily ever after."

Astrid smiled, weak. "I could not do that. I could not marry a man who carried part of my soul, part of Andrei. I will have to remarry someday, but that would be asking too much."

Jordan moved back and pulled his shirt on before wrapping his arms around her waist. "Then it's a good thing I don't have Andrei's heart, isn't it?"

And he kissed her.

5

Ten in the morning, but the umbrella was already set up on the beach along with a blanket. For the first time, Sofia had asked him to join her in the morning instead of early afternoon.

Jordan wasn't about to complain. He liked spending time with her.

While he waited, he pulled his shirt off. The tan was close enough to even he wouldn't blind her like he would have when he first arrived in San Majoria, and the sun wasn't quite high enough for him to be too worried about sunscreen just yet. He hadn't even thought about his tan when he pulled his shirt off the day before. When Sofia arrived, he'd have her help him put sunscreen on. The thought made him grin the way the girl a couple weeks ago hadn't.

With the sun warming his skin, he closed his eyes until a shadow crossed over his face.

"You're in my sun. Ruining my tan." Jordan didn't try to hide his smile.

"There's someone I want you to meet." Sofia sounded nervous.

Jordan opened his eyes to see her standing a few feet away.

In her arms, she held a little girl with curly brown hair.

He sat up and rolled to his side until he could stand. "Who's this?" Her niece? Little sister?

"My daughter."

Or that. He struggled to keep his surprise under control.

Jordan held out his hand for the little girl to give him five. "Hi. What's your name?"

"This is Sofia."

Little Sofia just stared at his hand. Jordan brushed the back of his knuckle against the soft skin of her forearm. "Hello, Sofia."

"She's pretty shy around new people."

He grinned, hiding the terror he felt inside. "Then we'll have to get to the point where I'm old people."

Before he knew what changed, Little Sofia leaned away from her mother and reached for Jordan. He reached out and took her from Grown-up Sofia. Little Sofia wrapped her arms around his neck and laid her head on his shoulder, all while not saying a word.

Jordan leaned his head against the little girl's. "Guess I'm old people already?"

Grown-up Sofia tilted her head. "She's never done that with anyone before. Usually it takes several meetings and quite a bit of time before she'll let someone hold her."

"She must know how crazy I am about her mother." Jordan leaned over and kissed Grown-up Sofia.

"Maybe that's it." Grown-up Sofia brushed Little Sofia's hair off her forehead. "Or maybe she knows her mother is crazy about you."

"I'll take it, whichever way it goes."

For the next hour, the three of them played on the beach. Jordan helped Little Sofia build a sand castle - or at least a series of bucket towers.

Clouds were starting to roll in when Grown-up Sofia told Little Sofia it was time for her to go back to the house. Grown-up Sofia carried Little Sofia up the walk and reappeared a few minutes later, just as the first sprinkles started.

It didn't bother Jordan, but he wasn't sure about the more refined Sofia.

"I don't mind a little drizzle. We've got an umbrella," she told him.

Jordan eyed the sky. "I'm afraid it's going to be more than just a little drizzle." He picked up a handful of sand and let it trickle back down to the beach. "So that answered a couple of my questions."

"What did?"

"Little Sofia. She's your favorite view and why we always meet for a couple hours in the afternoon. It's during nap time."

The drizzle turned heavier. "I'd forgotten you asked what my favorite view was, but yes." Sofia sat up. "Come on. You're right about the rain."

Jordan grabbed the blanket and closed the umbrella, tucking both under his arm as he followed her up the beach to the sidewalk. It didn't really surprise him, when she took an offshoot from the main path. She wouldn't take him to the house. Not when she didn't trust him with her name.

A minute later, they came to a gazebo. "This looks almost like the one from *Sound of Music*," he told her. "I feel like we should break out in song."

Sofia smiled at him. "No singing here."

"Not your thing?"

"Not particularly."

A wrought iron table sat in the middle of the gazebo. Jordan laid the blanket and umbrella on the bench connected to the wall around the interior.

Sofia opened a basket already sitting on the table. "Are you hungry?"

"I could eat."

She smirked. "If you're anything like my brothers, you can always eat."

Jordan managed not to show his surprise. A piece of personal information? "How many brothers do you have?"

She didn't look at him, but began to empty the basket. "Two. And two sisters. I'm the oldest of five."

"I'm the oldest of two."

"Your sister who married your best friend."

"Exactly. Any of your brothers marry your best friend?"

"No. None of them are married, or even dating. My father wishes we would all find someone to settle down with soon, though."

"Why is that?"

"Don't all parents want their children happy? They want us to find true love and begin our lives together."

"And they think you'll find someone else?" He held her gaze as he asked.

"I have to. I have to remarry sooner rather than later." The look in her eyes challenged him. Would he run?

"Will they make you? Pick a guy for you?"

"Probably not just yet." She turned her attention back to the food. "I likely have at least a year before the pressure gets too great."

"Why so short?"

Sofia shrugged. "It is the way it is. A year, even two, can be written off as grieving, but beyond that..."

"Will you at least get a say in who you marry?"

She stared past him, out the gazebo. "My parents would never ask me to marry someone completely unsuitable. More likely, they will give me a few choices they find acceptable. I will pick the most adequate of those."

"And the men will actually agree to this?"

Sofia nodded. "My family is powerful and important and wealthy, remember? Most men would give their right arm to be my husband."

That made Jordan sad, and he turned it around. "But will you find one for whom you'd give your right arm to be his wife?"

The question surprised Astrid. No one seemed to care if she wanted to marry a man.

As soon as the thought ran through her head, she knew it wasn't true. Her parents cared very much. They just couldn't do much about it.

"I would have given my right arm to marry Andrei," she finally told Jordan. "Fortunately, I didn't have to."

"Then I hope you find a guy who would give his right arm for you, but who you love just as much."

They ate the food prepared for them, though the conversation turned to less serious topics. She learned more about his brother-in-law, Dare, and the exploits that led to some of Jordan's scars.

"Did you know they were already in love before they announced they were getting married?" she asked

They were seated next to each other on the bench surrounding the interiors of the gazebo. He took her hand, and she twined their fingers together. Too bad he wasn't staying. This could turn into something.

"I heard they'd been making out on the balcony. That was a pretty good indication something was going on."

Astrid laughed. "That would do it, all right. But before that? Before you got to the States, and they pretended to be a thing."

Jordan's thumb brushed along the back of her hand, stirring things in her best left forgotten. "He asked me once a few years ago if I would be okay with him asking her out. I didn't think she'd say yes, but told him to go for it, and if he hurt her, I'd make him eat Zamboni snow. I'm pretty sure she actually laughed at him."

"Zamboni snow?" What on earth?

"The machine that scrapes the ice leaves shavings behind. Zamboni snow."

"I see. Does it bother you that your little sister married your best friend?"

She rested her head on his shoulder as he turned the thought over.

"It bothers me more that my best friend married my little sister. Semantics, I know, but it's different. I'm happy Dare's happy. I do kind of wish Betsy was happy with someone who wasn't the one person I've spent more time with than anyone else in the world. Though neither one of us have a world of experience like a lot of men do these days, we've talked about enough over the years that I wish it was someone who wasn't my best friend." He leaned his head back against a support post. "And I really don't like that he's experiencing that with my sister. If I had my way, she'd be a nun or something. It's not fair. It's a double standard. I know that, but it's the way it is."

None of Astrid's brothers had friends she was remotely attracted to, but she could imagine them feeling the same way.

"At the same time, it's nice not to have to break in some other stupid bender who doesn't fit with the family, like the one she almost married earlier this year. We invited him to play hockey with us more than once, but he never would. Dare probably would have checked him into the boards. I would have, too. Maybe he would have gone away sooner."

When Astrid asked, he told her that his sister's first fiancé had already been married and allegedly had his wife's blessing to cheat as long as it was far enough away.

It struck almost a little too close to home. "Cad."

Jordan chuckled. "That's far nicer than what Dare and I said when we found out. All we knew until we were in the States was that the wedding had been called off a few days before the big day."

"I'm glad she has him. I wish I could meet her sometime." Too bad things would never be able to go any further.

"Maybe the next time I'm in San Majoria, I'll bring them with me. And we'll show up on your beach together. We'll have to bring jet skis though. Betsy doesn't do the other stuff much."

And by the time that happened, she'd likely already be married to someone acceptable to her family and Parliament. Jordan would only ever be a nice summer memory.

She couldn't dwell on that.

She needed to be in the here and now.

With Jordan.

A man she could easily fall for, if only he would meet the expectations of her society.

Suddenly, she didn't care about the rain.

She stood and grabbed his hand, running for the beach. "Come on."

Laughing, he followed her down the path to the beach. She pulled her sundress off, revealing the swimsuit underneath. Less risqué than many she'd worn on this very beach, she still didn't love the way she looked in it.

But she didn't care.

If all they were going to have was a few days, a few stolen moments on the beach, she wasn't going to waste any of them.

They ran through the waves that almost deserved the name, much bigger than her normally quiet cove experienced.

They were even big enough to do a little body surfing.

But when she took a wave Jordan wanted, he vowed revenge.

He came in behind her as she raced up the hard-packed sand of the beach.

"I'm gonna get you!" His yell followed her. "You'll regret taking my wave, princess!"

For a split-second, she wondered at his use of the title, then realized he still thought of her as a spoiled rich girl. Even as she twisted away from his grasp, she knew he didn't think her spoiled.

Nor did he know she was an actual princess.

Astrid squealed as his arms wrapped around her waist.

"You're about to get wet," he growled.

"I'm already soaked." Her giggles were unfamiliar, but welcome.

"Yeah. Well, I'm going to drop you in the surf..."

Whatever else he was going to say cut off when a wave caught them at the knees, knocking them to the sand.

It left as soon as it came, leaving Jordan stretched out, his body pressing hers into the sand.

Before she could stop herself, Astrid reached up and grasped the back of his neck, tugging him toward her.

It could never be more than a few stolen kisses on their private beach, but she wasn't about to give up the chance to show him she wished it could be more.

"Hello?" Jordan barely managed to get the word out through his cotton-filled mouth.

At least that's what it felt like.

"Why didn't you tell me?!" His sister's voice hit him like a rogue wave.

"Tell you what?" He rolled over onto his back and stared at the ceiling.

"That you're dating a princess."

He blinked a few times as he tried to bring that statement into focus.

"And not just any princess, a *crown* princess."

"What are you blathering about? Does Dare know how hard you hit your head?"

"She didn't hit her head." His best friend's voice came through the phone. "She's barely awake and checking her Facebook. And there you are."

No. This couldn't be happening. He couldn't be talking to his little sister *and* his best friend while they were in bed together.

Even if they had been married almost two months. "Would you mind never, ever calling me, ever, from your bedroom?"

"Forget about that. We're both fully clothed," she protested.

"Fully pajama'd anyway," Dare interrupted.

"I don't even want to know." Dare never slept with a shirt on, ever, and now that he was married to Jordan's sister, it was more than Jordan cared to know.

"Forget us. How could you not tell us you're dating Astrid, Crown Princess of San Majoria?"

"I'm not dating a princess." A feeling of dread began to fill the pit of his stomach. "I don't think I am."

"What's that supposed to mean?" Dare asked.

Jordan blew out a breath. "Dare, remember a few weeks ago how I told you I went windsurfing and needed a break?"

"Yeah. You knew you couldn't go any further so you stopped at a private beach."

"Forget the princess," Betsy jumped in. "Is your heart okay?"

"Yes. My heart's fine. I was just tired. I'm healthier than I've been in years."

"Good."

Dare chuckled. "And that's why you didn't mention it to Bets."

"Exactly. If something that little worries her enough to forget about royalty, she doesn't need to know." Jordan reached over and grabbed his tank top, pulling it over his head.

"Fine." Betsy's huff made Jordan smirk. Dare probably did too. "Whatever. You're not dying. I'm glad. But now back to the business at hand. The pictures are all over the Internet. You're making out with Princess Astrid, rolling around in the surf with her, Jor."

He swung his feet over the side of the bed and groaned. They'd rolled around in the surf for all of twelve seconds after the wave knocked them over the Friday before. He'd kissed her for maybe two of those then they stood up.

But was she right about Sofia's identity?

He had to ask. "Is this one of the families you follow, Bets?"

After turning on the speaker phone, he set the phone on the side table.

"One of them. I started following the Belles Montagnes families because of a paper I had to do. I hadn't followed San Majoria, Islas del Sargasso, Eyjania, or Auverignon until we were there. I watched Princess Astrid and her husband the whole time we were there waiting for your heart." She hesitated. "I'm sure you don't remember, but her husband died the day after your transplant."

"Two years ago," he said softly. "Two years the day after I met her."

"They were in a car accident the night before your surgery. I was watching the news and saw your hospital on the screen. I probably saw the helicopter land with him in it because I could see the landing pad from where we usually waited," she said softly. "All I could think about whenever I saw them take someone out was how lucky you were to still be alive, and would this be the moment, would that be the person, to save your life. And how incredibly hard that would be on this person's family. I'm sure I thought that when they brought Prince Andrei in. But he didn't pass right away. It wasn't until a couple of days later that they told everyone he'd died the day after the accident."

Jordan buried his face in his hands. "What's her full name?"

"Astrid Sofia Hannah Esther."

He couldn't stop the groan. "I knew her name wasn't Sofia. She told me that much, but I had no idea she's a princess. It's a summer fling while I'm here. That's all." He'd avoided thinking about any of it too deeply because he'd known he would go home.

He'd also known, without asking, that she couldn't leave.

"Playing with her daughter?" Dare's voice drifted to him. "A woman doesn't introduce her kid to a summer fling."

"I've only met Little Sofia twice. Once the day after Grown-up Sofia, that is Princess Astrid apparently, told me about her husband, and I told her about my heart. Then yesterday morning." Odd to get together on a Sunday, but Jordan hadn't complained.

"That's it. I've spent a total of about an hour and a half with Little Sofia."

"You mean Her Royal Highness, Princess Sofia Andrea Estelle Brigitte?"

What a mouthful. "Apparently so." He ran his hands down his face. "Sofia's gonna be livid. She told me she's from a wealthy family, and that there's always pictures of her around, but that her beach was safe."

"And you didn't try to figure out who she was?" Dare asked from thousands of kilometers north.

"I wanted her to trust me enough to tell me."

Even though his cottage was on a secluded section of the beach, he could hear voices outside. Odd. He needed to take a shower and get to the beach early. He needed to talk to Sofia. No. Princess Astrid.

Jordan glanced down at the board shorts he'd fallen asleep in. Why bother? He was just going back out into the salt water. Maybe he'd rent a jet ski this time. It would be faster. As soon as one of her guards saw him near the cove, they'd let her know.

He picked up the phone, but before he could tell them his plan, there was pounding on the door.

"Jordan Haines! His Majesty's Royal Security. Open up!"

More pounding.

Jordan hurried across the room and opened the door. He wasn't a small guy but these two intimidated him, and it wasn't just the serious expressions or the sunglasses.

"You need to come with us," the one on Jordan's right said.

"Just let me change." He turned back to the room and held the phone to his ear. "Dare, Bets, I gotta go."

A hand on his arm stopped him. "I need your phone, and we're leaving now."

One of them took the phone and turned it off while the other gripped his arm just above his elbow and hurried him out the door.

He didn't even have shoes on.

6

Astrid walked into her father's office with a spring in her step. "Good morning."

He glared at her.

"What?"

"I've let this little fling with the Canadian go on longer than it should have."

Fling? She and Jordan had never discussed where the relationship was going, if anywhere, but fling? *Yes.* That probably was the right definition, though it saddened her to realize it. "What about Jordan?"

He tossed a tabloid paper on his desk. "Look for yourself. This comes out in two hours. It's already online. Security has been sent to pick him up."

Astrid picked up the magazine and felt her breakfast roil in her stomach.

Princess Astrid's New Duke blared the headline. In smaller letters, a statement proclaimed, *Princess Sofia already loves her new daddy.*

"No," she whispered, trying to take in the pictures. The largest was of them laying on the sand where the wave had knocked them. They'd been there seconds at most. Whoever had taken the pictures had to know that.

The first of two smaller pictures was of Jordan carrying Sofia as her head rested on his bare shoulder. One detached side of Astrid's mind noted it was a very father-daughter looking picture. The other one was of her in her swimsuit with her arms around Jordan, wearing only his board shorts, as he kissed her.

"How did they get these?" The only times they'd been out of the cove was when they fought their war and had lunch and the day it rained, and she took him to the gazebo.

"We're dealing with that, but it's too late to matter." He held out another paper. "This one, too."

It was a bit less tabloid-y, and the cover of it held only two pictures. One of Jordan catching her from behind when he'd chased her to get the kiss after she stole his wave. The smiles on their faces could light up the room.

A circular picture showed a close-up of a ring.

Her great-grandmother's fiftieth anniversary ring.

The one Astrid had slipped onto her ring finger the day after she'd told Jordan about Andrei - when her finger felt particularly naked without Andrei's ring on it.

She looked up at her father, certain she'd gone pale. "They think we're engaged?"

"With the family's blessing, given the ring."

Astrid sank into the chair. "Now what? I just felt like wearing it."

"You know what," he told her gently.

This time he wouldn't hold her and let her weep and mourn in private. This time he would expect her to have that stiff upper lip and do what was expected of her. "Grandmother is already planning the wedding." It wasn't a question.

"Three weeks," he confirmed. "Your mother tried to convince her six or even eight weeks would be better. Three weeks was the compromise. She wanted it this weekend."

"So fast?"

"You're lying on the beach making out with him, Astrid." He passed over the insides of one paper. Four pictures - Astrid underneath him where she'd fallen, kissing, then after he rolled them onto their sides but still kissing, and after the kiss.

"From the first picture to the last is less than thirty seconds," she pointed out. "It's not like we..." She felt the color rushed back into her cheeks. "...right there on the beach. And even if we had, it's private property, and no one should be able to see what goes on without our knowledge."

"There are always people watching you outside our homes, Astrid. You know that. Even after you marry, that kind of activity on the beach is unacceptable."

She slumped back in the chair. "I know. That's not the point."

"The point is, you have nineteen days to plan the wedding. Mr. Haines will be here shortly. He and I will have a discussion. After that, the four of us and my mother will have a planning session. A press conference is being set up for this afternoon."

Tears filled her eyes as she stared at the picture of Jordan with Sofia. "I'm not ready, Papa." The ache in her chest intensified. "I like Jordan a lot, but I'm not ready to be a wife again." One hot tear spilled down her right cheek. "I knew it wasn't going to be anything long term. It was safe."

"You don't *have* to marry him, Astrid."

Surprised, she looked up to see her father had aged a decade in those few seconds. "I don't?"

"No. But given the scandal, you will likely have to give up your place in the line of succession. You and Sofia will be removed from the line, and your brother will become my heir. Unless Parliament changes it, you would both be exiled immediately upon my death."

"This isn't fair."

"Life rarely is. You know that better than most."

"And if Jordan says no?"

Her father sighed. "I don't know. I will do what I can to protect you."

"I know you will."

He looked at his phone and read the message there. "There are two more papers with the photos. You're trending on Twitter."

"Andrei didn't trend when he died," she whispered. "Even with the gift he gave others."

"I know." Another message came in on his phone. "Mr. Haines has arrived. I would like to talk to him alone. Then we will find you."

Astrid nodded as more tears slid down her cheeks. "Thank you, Papa." She knew he hated forcing her into this as much as she hated being forced. Once outside of his office, she headed to her mother's sitting room. That's where she always was this time of morning.

Sympathy shown from her mother's eyes as Astrid walked into the room. Her mother held out her arms, and Astrid crumpled into them, tears streaming down her cheeks more forcefully than before.

"I can't do this, Mama. I'm not ready."

"With God's help you must be, sweet one."

"How can God be in this?" Astrid asked, bitterness lacing her tone. "He took the man I loved more than my own life, and now I'm being forced to marry a man I barely know."

"Everything will work out all right, love. Watch and see."

Astrid just wished she could believe that.

"Have a seat."

Jordan walked into the king's office as the security closed the door behind him. The leather wingback chairs didn't look inviting or comfortable, but you did as the king asked.

He just wished he was better dressed for it. Board shorts and an exceptionally loose tank top - the kind with arm holes big enough for a family of triceratops to wander through and "eh" written on the front - weren't exactly "meet the king" clothes.

They weren't even "meet the girlfriend's normal father" clothes.

Bare feet really weren't appropriate either.

But when two security guards who were probably named Guido dragged you out of your hotel room, there wasn't much choice.

"I'm sure you know a very thorough background check has been done," the king started as he took his own seat.

"I would have been surprised if there wasn't. I didn't know until an hour ago who Sofia..." He corrected himself. "...Princess Astrid really was, but I knew she was someone pretty important. I would have expected no less of those charged with her security."

"I haven't actually seen the report," the king went on as though Jordan hadn't said anything. "I told my men that I wanted Astrid and you to be the ones to tell me what I need to know, unless there was something in there that affected her health and safety."

"There isn't."

He didn't seem to notice. "Since you and my daughter are clearly something of an item, I want to get to know you a bit better myself."

"What do you want to know?"

The king's eyes took on a hard look. "What are your intentions toward my daughter?"

He would start with a tough one. Jordan could only be honest. "We haven't discussed the future, sir."

"That wasn't my question."

"I like Sofi... Princess Astrid. I like her a lot, but I've known since we met that she is way out of my league. I'm a moderately-extreme adventure loving Canadian. Until today, I thought she was *just* a wealthy heiress. On one level, I always knew she'd never end up with a guy like me, but I didn't want to think about it, because all I wanted to do was make her smile more and laugh occasionally."

The king stared at him for a long moment. "She has seemed happier in the few weeks than I've seen her in quite some time."

"Two years?"

"Something like that." The king stared him down. "Sofia seems to like you as well. There are pictures of you with her."

"And I like her, but I barely know her."

"Are you willing to be her father in every way that matters? You would never be allowed to legally adopt her."

The king was about seventeen giant moon steps ahead of anything Jordan had even considered. "I never thought that far ahead. I never thought we'd be more than a summer fling. I'll be returning to Canada at the end of the month."

If he didn't know better, Jordan would swear the king snorted. "The photo of the two of you standing on the beach with her hand on your chest. What were you discussing?"

He hadn't seen it, but it could only be one thing. "My heart transplant."

The king's eyes widened. "Pardon?"

"I know her late husband was an organ donor. I can't imagine the strength it took for her to stand there and give the doctors permission to take those parts of him and send them off to others who needed them. On behalf of those who received those gifts, I thanked her. And I thank you for supporting her in that decision. I want to live life to the fullest, for myself and for whoever it was that gave me the gift of life. In less than a month, I was on a private plane provided by a benefactor here in San Majoria and headed home."

The king's face blanched. "When was your transplant?"

Jordan told him the date. "My sister is the one who called me about the pictures. She's a royal watcher from way back. Nothing creepy. Just keeps up with the news about lots of the families all around the world. She started following your family while I was waiting for a heart. This morning, Betsy told me my transplant was the day before Prince Andrei passed."

"But you had a private jet home?"

"Yes. And basically unlimited access to the small cottage on the beach where I've been staying. I was told the same benefactor left instructions that I was welcome any time, as long as I wanted to stay. I've never been until now."

The king sighed and leaned forward, his forearms resting on his desk. "The publicly stated date of death for my son-in-law is inaccurate. He died twenty-four hours earlier. Astrid couldn't bear to think that those who received the organs might try to capitalize on the fact they came from her husband. I know the laws surrounding organ donation, and I did not violate them. I *did* ask for updates, without identifying information, on the recipients. All were locals. Except one. The young man who received Andrei's heart was a Canadian here on vacation."

Jordan felt the blood leave his face. "No."

"I'm afraid so. I told them I would take care of all medical expenses for all of the transplant recipients, including any others around that time, though they were told it was a memorial grant in Andrei's name..."

"For all transplant recipients that month." He remembered the details all too well.

"And I wanted the foreign recipient to fly home as quickly and easily as possible."

"My family and I appreciated that." It had made traveling much simpler. "I sent a thank you letter."

"I received it, but anonymously. I never knew your name."

Jordan ran a hand over his face. "So now what? I care for your daughter, sir, more than I could have imagined given the relatively small amount of time we've spent together. But she told me she could never be with the man who had Prince Andrei's heart."

"It's too late for that. Much of our country is extremely conservative, especially when it comes to the royal family. My mother has already started planning the wedding."

Jordan felt his eyes go wide in shock. "She what?"

"The wedding. There are pictures of the two of you, quite literally, rolling in the surf, making out."

He started to protest, but the king held up a hand.

"I know nothing more happened than a few nearly out-of-control kisses. I also know my daughter will never be queen if you don't marry her and soon. When I pass, she and Sofia will be exiled."

Rapid eye blinking was the only response Jordan was capable of giving for the first minute. Marriage? The thought had occurred to him, in more than just passing, but not like this. Not this soon. Not this seriously.

And the consequences?

No pressure.

"She likes me, sir. I know that. And there's undeniable chemistry between us that has nothing to do with the DNA of my second heart." Jordan stood and walked to the window overlooking the bay. "But if she finds out that I have Prince Andrei's heart, we'll never be able to get past it. Not until she and I both know that she loves *me,* Jordan. Because right now, she likes me, but she's still in love with Prince Andrei."

"Can you live with that?"

Jordan sighed. "The real question is can I live with knowing what walking away would cost her?"

7

Astrid perched on the edge of her seat in the White Drawing Room, hating her chocolate colored suit. Better than beige, though barely, it wasn't exactly how she'd envisioned meeting Jordan for the first time for real.

If she was honest with herself, she'd have preferred their relationship be limited to the beach for the foreseeable future, and then he'd return to Canada.

She and Sofia would never see him again.

At least her daughter's heart hadn't become as intertwined as Astrid's had. Sofia liked him, had taken to him like she never had anyone else, but they'd spent a couple of hours together, no more.

With her legs tucked to the side and her back straight like a proper princess, Astrid waited.

A moment later, the door opened.

Though generally her family followed protocol when outsiders were present, this day Astrid, her mother, and her grandmother didn't stand when the king entered. Perhaps because Jordan would soon be family.

If he didn't take the first plane to anywhere.

Astrid's eyes widened when Jordan walked in. His tank top, board shorts, and bare feet would not endear him to either queen.

But the first thing he did was bow to her grandmother, then her mother, and then her. "Good morning, Your Majesties, Your Royal Highness. I apologize for my attire. I was given about three seconds' notice that I would be leaving my hotel. However, it is a pleasure to meet all of you."

Her mother tried to hide a smile, and Astrid's grandmother, the Queen Mother, actually smirked.

"Have a seat, young man." Grandmother waved a hand at the chairs across from them.

Jordan took a seat, but his eyes remained focused on Astrid. In them, she could see questions, but also concern. Depending on how much her father had told him, his concern was well-founded.

He spoke first, something odd given who else was in this gathering. "I understand a wedding is being planned for three weeks from now?"

Astrid stood. "Before this discussion goes any further, I would have a word with you in private, Mr. Haines."

He looked at her father who nodded. A minute later, she and Jordan were alone in the wide hallway that ran the length of this section of the palace.

"You don't have to do this," she told him. "I don't expect you to."

"And what will it mean for you if we don't get married?" he asked gently.

She stared out the window and over the bay. "I will never be queen." He didn't need to know about the exile. "There are worse things in life than not inheriting the throne."

He stood behind her, his hands resting on her shoulders. With a gentle tug, she found herself leaning back against his strong chest. "Losing the love of your life?"

"Giving birth to his child without him six and a half months later."

"Watching them wheel him away to take parts of him and give them to others?"

Astrid nodded. "Our relationship was far from perfect, but that was probably the hardest thing I've ever done. I knew it was right, but it was so hard. I didn't have much time between finding out he wouldn't make it and watching him roll away."

"You are an exceptionally strong woman, Princess Astrid. That has nothing to do with the dynasty you were born into."

"I wish we could just be Sofia and Jordan."

"I know."

"I still don't expect you to marry me."

"Will you look at me?"

Reluctantly, Astrid moved away then turned and looked up into his eyes. "Yes?"

"I know you still love Andrei."

Astrid closed her eyes as he reached up to brush the hair back from her face. "I likely always will."

"I would expect nothing less, but do you think there's a chance you could love me? Maybe not as much, not the same way, but could you love me the way a wife should love her husband? Or will Andrei always come between us?"

She bowed her head and struggled to get her emotions under control. Her fingers curled into fists until her nails dug into the palms. "I don't know," she whispered. "I wish I could say I would love you the way you should be loved, because you are a man worthy of it, Jordan, but I don't know."

Taking a deep breath, Astrid reached for Jordan and slid her arms around him. She could feel the heat of his skin through his thin tank top as he held her close. "I want to. I never thought I'd remarry until I knew I was capable of loving a man that way again, and that I would already know this when he asked for my hand."

He tightened his hold on her, but didn't say anything.

"I would marry you if you are willing, and I will do my best to learn to love you. Maybe not the same as Andrei, but just as deeply. I pray he would not always come between us."

But there was something else.

"Can you live with knowing your children won't carry your name? Because there will have to be more children. In fact, it will be expected that there will be a child within the first year to eighteen months. Andrei and I defied that expectation, but I could not do it again. If we were to ever break up, you would not be allowed to have custody of your children. They would never be allowed unsupervised visits to Canada."

"When I say my vows, Astrid, they'll be forever. Until death do us part. I know yours will be, too, no matter the circumstances."

With a finger under her chin, he tilted her head back until she looked directly at him again. For a second, Astrid thought he was going to kiss her, but he didn't. "If another heir must be produced in eighteen months, then we have nine months to get comfortable enough around each other to engage in those kinds of activities."

Not strictly accurate, but Astrid appreciated his willingness to forgo his marital rights for an undefined period of time.

"Thank you," she whispered.

"Then I think it's time we went and told all their majesties that the wedding's on."

"Hello?" Jordan glanced at the clock in his hotel suite, a very different one than his first few weeks in San Majoria.

"Mr. Haines?"

"Yes."

"This is Jade, Princess Astrid's assistant."

Was this how she broke up with him? Via her assistant over the phone? "What can I do for you?"

"Princess Astrid woke up with a headache. She was to have taken Princess Sofia to an event at the turtle sanctuary. Princess Astrid asked if you would be willing to take her instead."

Jordan sat up in his bed and ran a hand through his hair. "Um, sure. I can do that." Of course he could. How hard could it be? Never mind that, with less than a week before the wedding, he still hadn't spent much time with the little girl, and never alone. "What time do you need me where?" His lessons on how to behave when around the San Majorian upper crust would have to wait. Apparently, being polite and following the Golden Rule didn't always cut it.

A minute later, he'd hung up. When he went out to the living area of the suite the king had insisted on, Jordan found his new assistant waiting for him along with another man.

"Good morning, sir." The guy didn't bow, though Jordan suspected that would change after the wedding.

"Morning, Thomas. I'm sure you've heard about the change of plans." Jordan poured himself a cup of coffee.

"Yes, sir. You also have a new member of your staff. This is Adam, your valet."

Jordan took a sip of his coffee. "What exactly does a valet do?"

"I'm in charge of your wardrobe, among other things, sir."

"Does that mean you'll tell me what to wear when I go to fancy shindigs?"

"I'm not certain what a *shindig* is, sir, but I would imagine so." Adam seemed to have the same personality Thomas did - not much of one. Humorless was the best word he could think of to describe them. Maybe they'd either loosen up, or he'd eventually be able to hire someone else.

"What does one wear when escorting a young princess to a turtle sanctuary?" he asked Adam.

"Today, casual slacks and a collared shirt, along with loafers."

"It's a little warm for slacks, isn't it?" That hadn't stopped Thomas from making him wear them the last few days, but he hadn't been outside either.

Jordan missed the outside... He hadn't been in the water since the day before the pictures came out.

"Members of the San Majorian royal family do not wear shorts unless they are involved in a sporting event of some kind."

All right then. Of course.

"I don't suppose there will be swimming at this turtle farm." Because then board shorts would be appropriate, right?

He could see the frustration pass over both of their faces.

"Sanctuary. Not farm. I will check," Thomas told him. "Meantime, you will discuss wardrobe with Adam."

Jordan hadn't gone many places so far. He'd been in this new suite and visited the palace almost daily, often eating dinner with the royal family then spending time with Princess Astrid. He hadn't needed much of a wardrobe, though the two pairs of slacks he'd been wearing on alternating days were getting kind of worn. They weren't exactly new to start with.

The door to the suite opened and two young women walked in pushing a rack of clothes. Jordan thought he'd seen at least one of them working with Princess Astrid before, but he wasn't sure.

"What are all these?"

Adam just gave him a look. For someone who couldn't be over thirty, he had that look down. Jordan had previously only gotten that look from his mother.

"This is part of your new wardrobe, sir."

"I haven't tried any clothes on. How could I have a new wardrobe?" They had taken his measurements though. He thought it was for a tuxedo for the wedding. Apparently, it was for every piece of clothing he'd wear for the next year.

Adam selected a pair of pants and a shirt from the rack. "These will do for today."

"And for swimming?" Jordan wasn't going to let him forget about that. "Is this gathering a casual, take the kids to see the turtles thing? Or is it a formal, we can't get excited over sea turtles because we're too proper thing?"

Jordan could almost hear the snort of derision. "I believe it's more the former, sir."

"And will Princess Sofia be wearing a swimsuit?"

"I believe so."

"Then I think board shorts are the way to go. I can't take her in the water in those pants."

"You can change there."

"And who will watch Princess Sofia while I change?" He knew moms and dads the world over managed, but he was a first-timer.

"Nanny Gretchen will be there, should you need her."

"I won't actually be alone with Princess Sofia?" That was something of a relief, and maybe a little insulting.

"Security will be with you the whole time, as well. Nanny Gretchen will stay in the background unless you need her."

With a sigh, Jordan took the pants and shirt. "Fine. When do we leave for this thing?"

"The car with Princess Sofia will pick you up in approximately an hour. Nanny Gretchen will arrive in thirty minutes to go over what you need to know about the young princess, then ride in the trailing security vehicle. Princess Sofia will be your responsibility, from getting her out of the car and into her car seat, to anything else she might need."

Jordan took another sip of his coffee. "I haven't changed a diaper in my life."

"That will be taken care of. However, unless you are in dire need, the rest of the time, for all intents and purposes, it is just you and the girl who will grow up with you as her father."

Way to put pressure on a guy. Jordan had thought about it before, even considered it over the last few weeks, but this would be his first practical experience as a father.

To a princess.

In full view of the public.

This could either go very well or very poorly.

Jordan wasn't sure which one he thought it would be.

8

"Father, can this wait?" Astrid sank into the chair in his office and wished the day were already over.

"The wedding is in less than a week."

"I'm aware of that. I'm also aware of the pounding in my head. I gave up a trip to the turtle sanctuary because of it. Jordan is taking Sofia for me."

"I know, but it still needs addressed."

"I'm not asking Jordan to sign a prenuptial agreement." She slumped back in the chair and covered her eyes with her forearm. "I can't deal with this right now."

"Why?"

"For one thing, the wedding is less than a week away. Would he feel able to say no if he wanted to? How does one negotiate a prenup on such short notice? San Majorian law dictates what he can't get should the marriage end. Besides, neither one of us is going into this with anything but 'till death do us part.' If either of us went into it thinking divorce was an option, it might be different, but we aren't."

"I know you don't plan on it..."

"No, Papa. I'm not asking him to sign one." No matter that Andrei had. No matter what she'd suspected later.

"Very well."

She moved her arm and squinted his direction. "What?"

"I'm not ignoring the validity of your arguments. I'm saying you have assets that could need protecting."

"Like what? I actually own very little. Most of all this is owned by the family or trusts or someone who is not, and never will be, me."

"That's not entirely accurate. You have the trust from your grandmother that you will gain full control of when you turn thirty. It's not a small amount of money."

"True, but I'm still not asking him."

"Very well."

"I'm glad you're not arguing with me about this."

"Why would I? Your mind is clearly made up, and we have far more important things to deal with."

Astrid heaved a sigh. "Like what? And can't it wait?"

"No. Benjamin isn't coming for the wedding."

"So? Is that bad?" She, literally, could not care less if the king of Eyjania was in attendance.

"Maybe, maybe not. His uncle exerts far more influence on him than I'd like. He's old enough to stand on his own two feet, but he hasn't started yet."

"Isaiah wasn't his regent was he?"

"No, but I would like you and Jordan to visit Eyjania on your honeymoon."

Astrid hadn't even thought that far ahead. "I'd rather stay here. I don't want to leave Sofia that long."

"She will go with you."

"You're planning our honeymoon for us?"

Her father's chuckle caused her to open her eyes a bit. "Have either of you planned one?"

He had a point. "No."

"Then it's a good thing I'm around. You can stay at Aberswythe

Hall. I would like for you to spend some time with Benjamin if possible, just an afternoon or maybe dinner. See if you can get a read on him or what's going on in the Eyjanian family. If you can't, I may have to send someone to live there for a while, and I'd rather not."

"Very well." As long as the headache had abated. "Meantime, I'm going to take some medicine and lay down."

"We do have some more things to discuss later, but I hope you're feeling better soon." He walked around his desk and folded her into his arms. "I love you, daughter."

Astrid let herself sink against him, grateful she didn't have to hold herself up for the moment. "Thank you, Papa. I love you, too."

When she left his office a minute later, Astrid nearly groaned as Jade jumped out of a chair. "Yes?"

"Your dress fitting has been moved up, ma'am." Jade shifted her weight from one foot to the other, clearly uncomfortable. "It's in ten minutes."

"No. It needs to be moved back."

"It can't. The head seamstress has a family funeral to attend this afternoon."

Astrid left her father's outer office and started for her quarters. Martina would know to keep the lights dimmed.

"Ma'am?"

She stopped at the sound of Jade's voice behind her. "Yes?"

"You're meeting them in the Green Room."

One of the brightest rooms in the palace. "No. I'm not. I simply cannot handle the Green Room today. The appointment will be moved to the sitting room off the quarters next to mine." No one had lived there since she moved out not long before Sofia's birth, and the curtains could be drawn blocking out the sunshine.

"Yes, ma'am."

Astrid could tell Jade wasn't happy about her decision, but Astrid didn't much care.

The walk took far longer than normal with Astrid taking

smaller, slower steps to combat the ache in her head. It wasn't the worst headache she'd ever had, not even close, but bad enough. Jade must have let Martina know the change of plans, because the curtains were tightly drawn and the furniture had already been pushed back.

"There you are." Martina knew to use her calming voice. "What don't you lie down for a few minutes, ma'am?"

"No. Getting back up will make it worse." The throbbing would increase, and Astrid didn't think she could handle that. "How long until this is over?"

"They should be here in about fifteen minutes. It will take an hour."

Astrid nodded and considered the chair, but decided to lean against a column instead. "I'm going to stand here with my eyes closed. In forty-five minutes, I want to take my medicine. They'll have another fifteen to twenty minutes before it kicks in. If they're not done, you have my permission to make sure I'm out of the dress and back in bed by the time it's fully in my system."

"I'll take care of it." Martina's sympathetic tone soothed Astrid. Her lady's maid would take care of her. She had been for years.

Loud noises in the hall caught both of their attention. Martina hurried to the door, muttering under her breath about some people not knowing how to be quiet.

Astrid managed a half smile. Martina's mothering could be overbearing sometimes, but at other times it was a blessing.

By the time the seamstress and her associates came in, the volume level had decreased. At least she loved the dress. Astrid never thought she'd love a dress more than the one she'd worn for her wedding to Andrei, but she did. It left her conflicted, while at the same time recognizing it was probably a good thing.

Andrei was her past, Jordan her future.

No turning back now.

Someone opened Jordan's door for him, but he was too busy trying to unbuckle Princess Sofia's car seat to climb out. Once the little girl stood on the floor, he got out then turned to reach for her. When he held her in his arms and turned back around, he realized he should have opened the stroller first. They'd brought it up to his room so he could practice. Allegedly, it could be opened one-handed...

In the not-far-enough-away distance, he could see cameras recording his every move. With his thumb, he slid the button on the handle of the stroller and twisted to release the catch. Sure enough, it popped open with a click. After testing it a couple of times to make sure it wasn't going to fold and putting the brake on one of the wheels, he went to the front.

Princess Sofia slid her legs into the openings and Jordan squatted down in front of her. "You and me, okay, baby girl? We got this," he whispered as he snapped her seat belt in place.

He slid his sunglasses into place as he went to the back of the stroller and flipped the brake up with his foot. The dreaded loafers weren't as bad as he'd thought they might be. Maybe because they clearly cost more than the rest of his wardrobe combined. The soon-to-be husband of a princess couldn't walk around in discount store shoes.

A security guard whose name he didn't remember motioned for Jordan to follow him. He needed to learn the names of people like this who he'd be seeing a lot of in the future. The small crowd of other parents and children streamed toward the entrance.

Princess Sofia's finger came into view over the canopy. *"Tur-too!"*

Jordan pulled the canopy back so he could see her face. Sure enough, it sported a huge grin. "You got that right, Miss Sofia. A turtle." It felt weird in his head not calling her by her title, something his sister had pounded into him was the appropriate address no matter the age, but he wasn't about to be caught on a microphone calling his almost-step-daughter "Princess Sofia." He was supposed to be closer to her than that.

An official met him as he walked through the archway into the turtle sanctuary proper. "Good morning, Mr. Haines."

"Good morning." Was he supposed to know this guy's name? "Thank you for having us."

"Our pleasure, sir. If you and Princess Sofia would come this way..." He gestured then started walking.

Jordan glanced at the security guy again. His face remained impassive but didn't seem to indicate they shouldn't follow the guy, so Jordan did.

They went through an office area and emerged back into the sunshine in a roped off area near the rest of the small crowd. After a brief introduction to the park, they were all walked to an enclosure where everyone would have a chance to hold a baby sea turtle. Jordan wasn't sure which species they were.

"Mr. Haines? Would you and Princess Sofia like to be first?" the guide asked.

Jordan felt like a deer in the headlights, but nodded. He unbuckled Princess Sofia and picked her up. He stood her on the concrete wall, one arm locked securely around her waist. "Would you like to hold a turtle?" he asked her.

"*Tur-too*!" She pointed to the man standing in the knee-deep water. Everyone within hearing distance laughed.

Jordan kept his arms as tightly around her as he could and still hold the turtle. "Can you help me?"

"*He'p*!"

More laughter sounded around them.

Princess Sofia clamped one hand around the edge of the turtle's shell and reached for his head with the other.

"No, sweetheart. You can't pet the turtle's head."

She stopped.

"Turn him around," the man advised.

Carefully, Jordan did. The flippers went a little frantic, but he kept a tight grip. "Can you pet his shell?"

Sofia ran a hand along the shell from near his head down to his tail. "*Tur-too*!"

After a few more seconds the man took the turtle back. Jordan set Princess Sofia down and used the offered hand sanitizer on his hands before helping her with it. He continued to hold her as they stood off to the side and let the other families hold the turtles. She pointed at every turtle she saw. What would she think when they got to the huge ones?

Jordan made sure to put Princess Sofia back in her stroller and feed her the snack in her bag while they waited. Before long, everyone was released from the group tour to do as they pleased. He'd been told there was an area for little children, but that as long as he used extreme caution, he could take her in the larger lagoon.

Like he'd do anything to hurt her.

As much as he wanted to go snorkeling in the lagoon where the fish and adolescent turtles lived, that was a bit much. He left Sofia with the nanny and security guard while he went in one of the changing rooms. At least he could wear his usual board shorts. Adam must not have considered a new pair, or Jordan would be wearing the San Majorian colors.

He took Princess Sofia, now without the dress that had been covering her swimsuit, from Gretchen. "We're going to the lagoon swimming pool thing," he told her. "I'll take it slow. Princess Astrid said she'd never really been in the water much." They'd gone over it repeatedly at the hotel, but he wanted to make sure Gretchen knew.

She nodded and took the stroller while Jordan carried Princess Sofia to the lagoon nearby. The other families were staring while trying not to make it too obvious. Pictures of his chest, complete with scars, would be out there for all to see before long.

Jordan should have thought this through a bit more. If he'd worn one of his wetsuit shirts, his heart scar wouldn't be visible. He didn't care as much in general as he had when he first arrived in the country, but if the press realized what it was and Princess Astrid found out when his transplant was, she'd know whose heart he had.

He wasn't ready for that.

She wasn't ready for that.

And if she found out before the wedding, all of this was for nothing.

9

"He's not her father yet, but Jordan Haines, fiancé of Princess Astrid, seems to have the love and trust of Princess Sofia."

Astrid stared at the screen as the picture changed to Jordan standing behind Sofia as they held a turtle. She missed seeing that look on her daughter's face in person. At least the pounding in her head had mostly dissipated.

"The pair spent the morning at San Majoria's Turtle Sanctuary along with several dozen other children, invited because of their parents' work in conservation."

Jordan-on-the-screen carried Sofia in front of his chest as he walked into the lagoon. Several other pictures followed it on the screen. Astrid frowned as she rewound the scene. Was he hiding his scar? Did he not want everyone to know he was a heart recipient? Or did he not want them to know *now,* like this?

But the next picture showed Sofia laughing as she splashed in the water. Good. She seemed to love it. Jordan was the perfect person to introduce her to more than just the tub.

A couple more pictures showed them eating lunch with another family with a little boy about Sofia's age. The woman didn't appear to have any inappropriate interest in Jordan, so that was good. It wasn't always that way.

Astrid didn't actually see Jordan when Sofia returned to the palace. In fact, he might have been dropped off at the hotel first.

She hadn't seen him in a couple of days. That would change soon enough. In a few days, she would be with him for a week straight. Then every day for the rest of her life.

It had taken her and Andrei time to figure out how to live together. The same thing would happen with Jordan. Eventually, they'd figure it out.

The rest of the day was quiet. Gretchen took care of Sofia, including putting her down for a nap and her dinner. Astrid nibbled on simple food from a tray brought to her by Martina.

The next day, Astrid's stomach was upset for a whole different reason.

Jordan's family was due to arrive any minute. Their flight, provided for by her father, had already landed. She wore another light tan suit, with the same beige pumps. "How much longer?" she asked Jade.

Jade looked at her phone. "Mr. Haines met his family half an hour ago. They left the airport approximately ten minutes ago."

She had another ten minutes until the car pulled through the gates and up to the portico. Maybe she should walk down there so she could greet them when they arrived. Probably just inside the doors where she couldn't be seen by cameras on rooftops of nearby buildings. She didn't want to meet her in-laws in full view of the public.

She started for the door when Jade's voice stopped her. "Your father has asked your family to meet in the Reception Hall in five minutes."

"Thank you." Astrid took a different set of stairs than she'd planned. Her next younger brother arrived as she did.

"Good morning," he said with a bow and flourish. "How art thou this morning, dearest sister of mine?"

It took all of Astrid's self-control to keep her hand to herself and not smack his shoulder. "I'm fine."

"Thou does not have flocks of seagulls in thy stomach at the prospect of meeting the parental units of thy intended?"

Astrid glared at him. "I'm fine. I handled meeting Andrei's parents, didn't I?"

He sobered. "But you'd been dating Andrei for almost six months, and you were still a long way from getting married when you met his family. You've known Jordan less than two months, and the wedding is in four days."

"I'm aware of all of that."

Kensington put an arm around her shoulders. "And you're really all right?"

"I don't have a choice, do I?" She shrugged his arm off and squared her shoulders. "You know that as well as I do."

"As glad as I am not to be taking over the next in line duties, you're more important than whether I become king or not."

"I know." She took a deep breath. "I will be fine. Jordan is fantastic. I'm sure his family is, too."

Wisely, Kensington kept his mouth shut as they walked through the enormous doors into the Reception Room. Her parents were already waiting, along with both of her sisters and her other brother, the youngest of the siblings.

"They will be here in a few minutes." Her father buttoned his suit coat and started for a different door.

Everyone else fell in line behind him. They knew where to be when they arrived at the door to the portico. Astrid and her mother both stood slightly behind the king, Astrid to the left and her mother to the right. Her siblings all stood a bit farther back, Kensington and Jacqueline Grace to Astrid's left with Harrison and Esther to her mother's right.

They stood far enough back from the doors that the cameras wouldn't be able to see them, though her father would likely walk forward, and they'd get a glimpse of him greeting Jordan and his family.

Sure enough, the car glided to a stop. One of the footmen opened the door. There would be no formal announcement this time. That was generally reserved for visiting foreign dignitaries on official missions, not family visitors.

Jordan led the small group up the stairs as Astrid's father took several steps toward them. Jordan bowed then shook her father's hand before stepping to the side to introduce the rest of his family.

He motioned to his parents. "These are my parents LeeAnne and Chris Haines."

His father bowed while his mom curtsied then shook hands with her father.

"And this is my little sister and her husband, who also happens to be my best friend. Betsy and Dare Weaver."

His sister performed one of the best curtsies Astrid had seen in quite some time, while Dare bowed. They both then shook hands with her father.

Her father turned. "My turn. I'm Edward. My wife, Miriam, and my children - Kensington, Jacqueline Grace, Esther, and Harrison." By leaving off their titles, he was trying to convey to Jordan's family that they were among friends and could be less formal. Then her father smiled at her. "And, of course, my oldest daughter, Astrid, soon-to-be Jordan's wife."

Astrid gave them the best smile she could muster. "Hello. Welcome to San Majoria."

Jordan felt more relaxed than he had since he was dragged out of his beachside cottage. He sat in the corner of a couch, legs stretched out in front of him. Astrid sat to his right, leaning slightly against him with his arm around her shoulders. Dare and Betsy mirrored the position on another couch, though Betsy was far closer to Dare and kept putting her hand much higher on his thigh than Astrid would ever dream of. Not inappropriately high, but they were far more comfortable together than they had been the last time he saw them.

As it should be. They'd been married for two months.

All of Astrid's siblings had drifted off to do other things, but both sets of parents remained. All four of them shared stories about Jordan and Astrid growing up. Dare and Betsy joined in with a Jordan story or two of their own while Jordan just smiled and laughed occasionally. Astrid smiled and laughed, too, but still seemed more reserved than she had been those last few days on the beach. It had taken him weeks to get her to loosen up. She'd withdrawn back into her shell.

"Why don't we leave these four to do something without us old folks?" the queen stood, followed by her husband. "Why don't we show you the Portrait Gallery we were talking about?"

Jordan and Dare both stood as both sets of parents left the room. Jordan started to sit back down but Astrid popped up.

"Why don't we go for a walk through the garden?" Her smile seemed a touch too bright to Jordan, but he didn't push her on it.

"That sounds great." Jordan let his hand rest on the small of her back as Dare held out a hand to Betsy.

Betsy asked Astrid a question about her engagement ring - the one Jordan had never actually proposed with - as she led the way out of the room. The two of them were talking like old friends by the time they reached the garden.

Dare stopped Jordan with a hand on his arm, letting the girls walk further away.

"What?" Jordan asked.

"Are you sure about this?" Dare let his hand drop. "I mean, really sure? This is forever."

Jordan crossed his arms over his chest. "I know. I'm familiar with marriage and what it entails."

"You've known her two months. Most of that you didn't know who she really was or that she had a kid. You spent a couple hours a day with her most of those days and some you didn't see her at all. Yet you're going to marry her?"

"Exactly how long did you date my sister before proposing? Two days?"

Dare glared and started down the steps away from the door and into the garden itself. "I've known her most of my life. It's different, and you know it."

Jordan stopped a couple steps from the bottom. "I know it is, but this is still the right thing. I know it seems sudden, but I've prayed about a lot of things over the last few months, even before the pictures came out. Before we left for the States, even. Not specifically about whether to marry Astrid or not, but about the next step in my life. I have a very generic business degree, but no business aspirations, really. Nothing I'm just dying to do with my life. I don't want to start my own business, except maybe as a photographer, or work for my dad." He sank down onto the stairs. "Face it. You were always more likely to take over for Dad, even before you married my sister." The transportation logistics company had never been Jordan's thing.

Dare sat next to Jordan. "You know I appreciate your dad, both of your parents, and everything they've done for me since we were kids. I'd never want to take your spot, though."

"And if I wanted the spot, that would be one thing, but I never did." Jordan leaned back, so his elbows supported his weight and his legs stretched out in front of him. "I've been pretty aimless and living on the rest of the college fund that I didn't use." Living at home helped, too. As did the free cottage, which meant he could travel to San Majoria in the first place. "You and Dad work well together. I'm not saying I wouldn't have ever come home and tried to fit in there, but I've prayed long and hard about where my life was going. I asked God to make the answer abundantly clear to me, and He did."

"And marrying a Crown Princess is the right answer?"

Jordan looked to where Astrid and Betsy were looking at a

tropical plant he couldn't identify. "If I don't, or if we ever divorce, she'll never be queen, and they'll both be exiled."

"There are worse things than that. Like an awful marriage."

He felt the expression on his face soften. "I know, but I don't think it will be. We both just need some time to get to know each other so we can make it work. We will make it work."

Dare smacked Jordan's shoulder with the back of his hand. "Then I bet I'm an uncle before you are."

Jordan groaned. "I really don't need to know anything about you and my sister and your reproductive plans. Besides, in just a couple days, I'll have a daughter which will make you an uncle."

"You know what I mean. We saw the pictures of you with Princess Sofia at the turtle farm yesterday. You looked smitten with each other."

"I like her a lot. I'm growing to love her." Jordan pushed up until he was seated and rested his elbows on his knees. "I don't know much about being a father."

"You'll figure it out. You had a great example, and the king seems like a good guy."

"He is."

"One thing we noticed, though."

"What's that?"

"You weren't wearing a shirt."

"I know. I wasn't in some of the pictures with Astrid either."

"But this was in public." Dare leaned closer. "I'm glad you're okay with the scar, but you seemed to be hiding it behind Princess Sofia or something else the whole time. What's going on?"

Jordan made sure the girls were still off in the distance and glanced around to make sure no one else could hear. "I know you're married to my sister, and it's not fair of me to ask you to keep a secret from your wife, but this is something even she can't know."

"I'm not sure I can do that."

Jordan shook his head. "Then I can't tell you."

Dare stared at Astrid and Betsy. "Fine, but if I think you're being ridiculous, I'll tell you and override the decision."

"You won't. She can't know this."

"What is it?

Jordan let out a deep sigh. "I have Andrei's heart, but if Astrid finds out, there's less than no chance she'll ever love me for me."

10

Astrid tucked her hand in her father's elbow. "Let's get this over with."

"Not exactly the most ringing endorsement of a wedding."

She didn't look up but heard the frown in her father's voice. "I don't have to look forward to the wedding for the marriage to be a success." The enormity of all of it overwhelmed her. She needed it over with.

"Fair enough."

"The comparisons started weeks ago. I'm ready to be done with them." She didn't like how "Astrid and Andrei" seemed to fair unfavorably in the public eye compared to "Astrid and Jordan." The only thing the public seemed to like better was the alliteration of the names.

"It won't stop. You'll probably always have to deal with the comparisons."

Astrid took a deep breath. "Fine. But I want to get the public part of today over with."

"Then let's go."

This time she looked up to see him smiling down.

"Your groom is waiting."

She let him lead her slowly down the aisle until they reached the end. Jordan waited there with a big grin on his face. Soon her hand was tucked in his, then she faced him as they repeated the vows taken by millions before them.

Vows she'd taken once before.

No!

This wasn't the time or place for thoughts of the past.

Instead, she focused on the words she spoke and the ones Jordan said. She slid a ring on his finger and let him slip one on hers, next to the same ring that had appeared in the tabloids.

"Jordan, Duke of Bevingdale, you may kiss your bride."

Astrid looked up into Jordan's eyes. He cupped her cheek with his palm and kissed her gently. She rested her hands on his stomach and kissed him back, but found herself wishing they were supposed to wait until the balcony like some other royal couples, because she'd have a little more time to prepare.

But the kiss ended before she could think more.

"Your majesties, ladies and gentlemen, I present to you Their Royal Highnesses, Prince Jordan and Princess Astrid, Duke and Duchess of Bevingdale."

Polite applause filled the cathedral as Jordan helped her down the stairs. They stopped in front of her parents. Astrid curtsied while Jordan bowed, then they continued up the aisle.

Judging by the way Jordan covered her hand inside his elbow with his other hand, his smile wasn't nearly as pasted on as hers was. Fortunately, she was well-practiced at hiding her emotions or presenting favorable ones to the public.

Like at Andrei's fune...

No!

Astrid couldn't let herself go there. Not when she'd just married someone else. A great guy.

One she probably should have set free rather than trap into marriage when she still loved another man.

They reached the doors to the outside. Jordan helped her into the carriage waiting for them. As the attendants, Dare and Jacqueline Grace joined them, sitting in backwards facing seat.

"Congratulations!" Jacqueline Grace manage to squeal quietly. "You two did it!"

"Yes, we did." Jordan wrapped an arm around Astrid's shoulders and kissed her temple. "Can I call you Mrs. Haines sometimes?"

"Sure." She'd been Mrs. Barnes on occasion, generally just when the two of them were alone together.

Stop!

Astrid had to get a hold of herself. She couldn't keep comparing Andrei and Jordan. The two men weren't the same. Her relationship with Jordan wouldn't be the same as with Andrei. She'd fallen for Andrei fast and furious. Heat had boiled between them from the beginning.

Jordan would hate being told he was like a slow simmer. Eventually, they would get to the same place she'd been with Andrei. She had to believe that.

"Are you all right?" Jordan's voice couldn't be heard by the others. His warm breath on her ear told her how close he was as the carriage began to move.

"Fine." She waved to the crowd gathered along the side of the road, first one side then the other. Jordan, her sister, and Dare all did, too, though Dare commented that he didn't know why anyone would wave at him.

"Wave anyway," Jordan told him. "You'll be able to hold it over Bets forever."

Dare grinned. "That I'm in a royal carriage with two princesses and a prince, even if he's only been one for like four minutes? Oh, yeah. She'll never let me live this down."

"It's not always all it's cracked up to be." Astrid kept the smile plastered on her face, waving to the crowds on both sides of the street. "It doesn't stop life from being so painful you can barely breathe."

Dare's smile slipped.

She raised a brow and nodded at him. "And forced to smile while you're dying inside."

His smile came back, though not nearly as dynamic as it had been a moment earlier. "You were in our prayers, you know. We were all here for Jordan's surgery."

Was it her imagination or did Jordan stiffen next to her?

"While we waited for Jordan to be well enough to travel home, we prayed for him to recover fully and for your family. Specifically, we prayed for peace as you faced days unexpectedly alone." Dare's smile slipped. "We also prayed that you wouldn't grow old alone."

Astrid forced herself to smile up at Jordan. "That prayer has been answered in a most unexpected way, hasn't it?" She kept waving as the carriage finally neared the palace.

Jacqueline Grace caught her eye. Astrid had always been closer to Kensington given their proximity to each other in age, but Jacqueline Grace had been there for Astrid as she faced pregnancy and motherhood alone. It bonded them in a way they never had been before.

And her sister was questioning whether Astrid was really all right.

Astrid just smiled a little more brightly and waved a little bigger as the carriage drove through the open gates of the palace. It rolled to a stop under the portico. Dare climbed out first and helped Jacqueline Grace to the ground. Jordan followed, the smile on his face as genuine as any she'd seen from him. He reached for her hand to help her down.

But even inside, they didn't have a moment to themselves. Jade and Thomas were waiting for them, along with the palace event planner and photographer.

Her smile couldn't slip again, not even for a few seconds, not even with Jordan.

Not until she was alone.

The first hour of marriage to Astrid wasn't quite what Jordan expected.

He barely saw his wife as she was bustled around by assorted assistants. The photographer had his turn with her. Jordan couldn't wait to see the pictures, but what he'd really like was a private moment or two. Was it impolite to stare at your own wife? He twisted the new wedding band as he turned that thought over in his head.

"You look pensive for a man who just got married."

Jordan looked up to see his new father-in-law standing there. Did he dare be honest? "I'm a little worried about her. It's a lot for anyone, and..." He looked around to make sure he wouldn't be overheard. "...you and I both know she wasn't ready for this, no matter what the general public wants to believe."

"But it's too late now."

"Yes. It is. And I don't want out. I don't really think she does either. Just another year to get ready." Another glance around. "And even though I feel it's necessary, I feel guilty about that secret. It would be one thing if I discovered it now, but I knew weeks ago."

"I happen to be in agreement with you on that, so any guilt belongs to both of us." The king tilted his head toward his daughter. "What do you see when you look at her right now?"

Jordan sensed more behind the words. "I see a woman struggling to keep it together, putting a bright smile on so no one would guess she's probably dying inside at the thought of spending the rest of her life with anyone besides Andrei."

"You're her husband," the king reminded him, his words gentler than Jordan would have expected. "What are you going to do about it?"

Jordan shoved his hands deep in his pockets. "What *can* I do about it? I'm just the new guy who doesn't know what protocols he can break and which ones he can't."

"Implying that as the king, I know and can?"

He shrugged.

The king rested a hand on Jordan's shoulder. "Maybe. But I'm no longer the one charged with taking care of her."

With those words, the king walked off, leaving Jordan to think about what his father-in-law had said. Maybe taking care of Astrid was more important than what protocol he might be breaking. That had been his thought, but he didn't want to inadvertently do something to offend his new family.

After taking a deep breath to steel himself, Jordan walked to the other side of the Reception Room, where the photographer was taking pictures of Astrid. He waited for the photographer to finish the series he was taking, then stepped in.

"Excuse me, but I'd like a moment with my wife." Jordan took her hand and turned to the photographer. "We'll be back in a few minutes." *Maybe.*

Astrid gave him a puzzled look, but didn't say anything as he led her to the closest set of doors. He had no idea where they went. In fact, the room was barely lit when they walked in.

"You know this is the throne room, right?" Astrid asked as the door closed behind them.

"I don't really care." Jordan dropped her hand and turned to face her before linking the fingers of both hands with hers. "I care that you're okay, and I don't think you are."

The mask finally slipped, just a little. She lowered her chin so he couldn't see her eyes. "It's harder than I thought it would be."

"Marrying someone who's not the love of your life?" he asked gently, letting go of her hands and pulling her into his arms instead.

"I want you to be," she whispered.

"I know, but I'm not. Not yet. And you have to put on your happy face for the rest of the world. But I'm not the rest of the world, Astrid. I'm your husband. I'm supposed to be your safe place."

"I shouldn't need a safe place an hour after the wedding."

"But you do." He looked around. How were there no chairs in the throne room? He didn't think she'd sit on either throne at the far end of the hall. With no other options, he just held her for a few minutes, but then she pushed away.

"Thank you. I did need a few minutes to gather myself, but I'm fine, and we need to be back in there." She squared her shoulders and headed for the door back into the other room. Sweeping her train to the side, she looked at him. "Ready?"

"If you are." Jordan opened the door and held it for her as she walked through. Once back at her side, he slid his arm around her waist and whispered in her ear. "But I'm sticking a lot closer for now."

She just nodded.

The photographer decided it was time for the pictures of the two of them. Jordan liked being so close to Astrid, even kissing her repeatedly. They took pictures inside and out, with and without Sofia.

Then Jordan was asked to stand to the side while pictures were taken of Astrid and her daughter. The small entourage started back inside, but Jordan had other ideas.

"May I?" he asked the photographer, pointing to the camera. "I'm not sure what happened to my camera when I moved to the hotel suite."

The photographer seemed hesitant, but changed the SD card then handed it over. Astrid and Sofia didn't seem to notice. Jordan looked through the viewfinder and snapped a couple of pictures. It wasn't the same as his own candid shots, though. He'd have to find his camera, or invest in a better one, and take some of his own in the next few days. Wasn't that why he had an assistant?

Handing the camera back, he joined the photographer walking inside. "Do you think you could get with Thomas for me? I have a camera somewhere, but I haven't seen it in a few weeks. I'd been thinking about upgrading anyway. Could the two of you come up with something in the next day or two?"

The photographer asked a couple of questions then said he'd take care of it. "Actually..." He stopped just inside the doors. "If you want it right away, I have one that I think would be perfect. You're not a professional, but not quite a beginner either. But, it is used."

Jordan shrugged. "Fine by me, as long as it works."

"The battery needs charging, but as far as I know it does. I used it a few weeks ago. I haven't used it often, because it's my personal camera, and I don't take a lot of pictures in my off time."

Jordan protested, saying he didn't want to take the man's personal camera, but the other man insisted. Thanking him, Jordan made a mental note to tell Thomas to make sure the photographer was well compensated.

Once inside, the photographer had them get in the car and head to the beach for pictures. Now that he knew Jordan was an amateur photographer, apparently he had some other ideas. The two of them walked through the sand and the surf barefoot. Jordan shed his jacket and rolled up his pant legs. The photographer gave him an old camera to take a few pictures of Astrid with. Probably not a true antique, but definitely not from this century.

After a while, they went back to the palace. Adam took care of making sure Jordan's legs and clothes were sand free, something Jordan found more than a little odd. Martina did the same for Astrid.

He put his shoes back on as the event planner motioned to him. Right. Time for the dinner.

He turned around. Where was his wife?

11

Astrid stood in her dressing room in her stockinged feet and waited for Martina.

"Are you sure you want me, ma'am?" Martina asked as she closed the door behind her. "Wouldn't your husband be more appropriate?"

Astrid swept her hair to the side to allow Martina access to the back of the dress, but didn't reply. She could sense Martina's disapproval as the other woman undid the clasp.

"It's not the same, is it?" Martina asked softly. "You're not ready."

"No. It's not." Astrid stared at the floor in front of her. Martina had been nowhere to be seen the night Astrid married Andrei.

A few minutes later, Astrid was in her pajamas, and walking into the room she would now share with Jordan. He waited for her in there, hands in his pockets as he stared out the window, one that overlooked the water.

"I told you I made sure I had an ocean view."

Jordan turned. He still wore his tuxedo, but his tie and sash were gone. The top few buttons of his shirt were undone, and it had come untucked.

"It's over," he said, leaning against the wall.

"It is," she confirmed. For nearly two years, the room had belonged to her alone. She chose the bedding, the curtains, the other furnishings around the suite. Now, it would likely all change. Jordan wouldn't like the prints she'd chosen because she loved them, because her more feminine style wouldn't fit his. Even the ornate chairs, dating from the time of the San Majorian Revolution, would likely be replaced or recovered. At least the stone walls couldn't be painted.

"What now?" he asked.

"We leave tomorrow for a week in Eyjania."

"We do?"

Astrid sank into a chair. "Our honeymoon. We're supposed to try to spend some time with King Benjamin while we're there. Sofia is coming with us, along with several staff members. We will be mostly left alone."

Jordan walked over and sat in the chair next to her. "I know you're not ready for this, but are you okay with at least *sleeping* in the same bed with me?"

"Yes." Because she didn't want anyone to know she didn't sleep with her husband.

He looked at her for a minute then stood. "Okay then. Good. I'm going to change."

By the time he returned, Astrid had settled into the bed, on the opposite side from where she normally slept. "Do you mind that side?" she asked.

"Not at all."

Astrid felt the bed dip and the covers move as he got settled.

"Good night, Mrs. Haines."

She closed her eyes as his fingertips brushed against the hair at her temple.

"I'm glad you married me."

It took supreme effort, but she managed to speak normally. "I'm glad I did, too."

"Sleep well."

"You, too."

Only the length of the day and the strength of her exhaustion allowed Astrid to drift to sleep quickly.

Twenty-four hours later, they were in Eyjania. Breakfast with their families had gone well. The flight had been smooth.

But Sofia had not settled into the new house well. In fact, she was throwing a fit. Astrid didn't want Gretchen to deal with it. She wanted to be a mother to her daughter. It was her job to take care of her little girl.

She stared at the picture in the frame hanging from the wall. Her grandparents. Her grandfather had always known how to calm Astrid down. Would any of his tricks work on Sofia? Did Astrid remember any of his tricks or did she just love her grandfather enough to let him calm her? Or was she in awe of him? He'd been king from the time she was born until his death when she was three. She hadn't truly understood what it meant for her until a decade later, when a girl she thought was her friend told her she'd never find someone who would love *her*. She'd only ever find one who wanted the glamour and prestige of marrying the crown princess.

Then she began paying a little more attention. Many of her friends were really more acquaintances, ones she couldn't trust to get close. That changed when she met Andrei. He saw her, really saw her.

Most of the time.

Even as Andrei's daughter threw a fit on the floor of the Eyjanian nursery, Astrid could admit that he hadn't *always* seen her the way she wanted to be seen. He saw more than the crown she'd one day wear, but he occasionally had more rigid ideas about what the Second Couple of San Majoria should and shouldn't do.

Like affection in public. He was okay with that to a point, just like Astrid was, but...

Push to be able to wear clothing that stood out a bit more than your average piece of toast? Never. Too much attention. Too easy for a sniper. Too plebian. Too not becoming a crown princess.

Not even pointing out Queen Elizabeth's wardrobe, or the Duchess of Cambridge's, helped. Astrid had always worn a lot of tan, beige, off-white, and she'd hoped he'd support her in filling her wardrobe with clothes more exciting than chocolate, but he never had.

Sofia's fit throwing slowed down until she finally fell asleep on the floor. Astrid let herself slide to the side until her head rested on the pillow of the extra bed in the nursery.

Jordan probably waited for her in the bedroom they were supposed to share, but she didn't have the energy or willpower to move. Her eyes fluttered closed, and she felt herself drift to sleep.

Married almost forty-eight hours, and his wife already slept elsewhere.

Jordan wondered if he should get dressed before he went to look for her, but decided not to. This was his home for the moment. He did pull on a t-shirt, but his Canucks pajama pants would work.

He didn't open any of the doors off the hallway, just in case someone else was sleeping or getting dressed, but he did peek in a few that weren't completely closed.

In one, a few doors down from the room Thomas had shown him to, Jordan found Astrid and Sofia.

Sofia lay curled up on a rug that likely dated back a century or more with the blanket he'd discovered was her favorite. An ornate crib hadn't been slept in, but the twin bed, likely put there for a nanny, served as a sleeping place for the exhausted mom.

Astrid still wore her clothes from the day before. The last few weeks had taken so much out of her. She needed the rest.

He turned to leave, but Sofia began to stir. Her eyes blinked open, and she reached up for him.

Jordan lifted her into his arms and left the room, quietly closing the door behind him. Sofia rested her head on his shoulder.

He carried her down the hall and then to the first floor where he found Nanny Gretchen in the kitchen. "I think I found a hungry little girl."

Sofia nodded against his shoulder.

"Well, it's a good thing I've got breakfast just about ready then, isn't it?" Nanny Gretchen held out her hands for Sofia. "Why don't we get you washed up, little one?"

Jordan left the two of them to do their thing then went toward the other hall where he'd been told his office would be for the next week.

Why did he need an office on his honeymoon?

It seemed this would be a working vacation of sorts, though. Not that he knew what his new job as Prince of San Majoria and Duke of Bevingdale entailed.

Two desks were set up in the outer office with doors on either side. Thomas looked up from one of them, stood and bowed. "Can I help you, sir?"

"I'd like to arrange something for my wife." It sounded so weird to say it like that. "Can you help me with that?"

"Of course." Did the man sound indignant? How was Jordan supposed to know what landed outside Thomas's duties?

"I'd like to give her a spa day of some kind. I don't really know what the options are, but definitely a massage."

"Of course, sir. Would you like this for today?"

"If you can, that would be great. If not, as soon as you can arrange it."

"I will see what I can do. I was just informed that you have a meeting with the head of Princess Astrid's security team in five minutes." He pointed to the door behind him. "Your office is in here when you are in Eyjania."

Jordan managed not to glance down at his attire, though he was sure Thomas had already noted it. "I'll go change and be back in a few minutes."

"No need, sir." The new voice startled him.

Jordan turned to see Astrid's main security guard walk in.

"This will only take a few minutes."

Jordan went into the office, and the guard closed the door behind them.

The man held out a box. "Your updated electronic devices, sir."

"Pardon?"

"We took your phone and tablet last night, cloned them, updated the security, and reinstalled everything onto new devices."

Jordan took the box from him. "And I didn't even notice."

The man didn't comment.

"I know we've been introduced at least once, but I'm afraid I've forgotten your name."

"Don, sir."

Jordan held out his hand. "Pleasure to meet you, Don. I promise I'll try not to forget."

Don looked unsure, but shook Jordan's hand, the expression on his face remaining unchanged. "I'd rather you promise to follow security instructions and protocol at all times."

"I can promise I will always do my best to cooperate with whatever you and your men deem necessary. Thank you for everything you do to keep my new family safe."

"It has been my family's honor for five generations, sir."

"Thanks to your ancestors then, too."

Don's eyes shifted to the side and then back to the front. His stoic expression flickered just enough for Jordan to catch it, but not enough to determine what it was. He'd have to keep his eyes and ears open in conversations with Don. Something bothered the man, but Jordan didn't know him well enough to ask.

Jordan held up the box. "Thanks for this."

"My pleasure, sir."

Another thought occurred to Jordan. "You may not know the answer to this, but Astrid said I'll have access to some bank accounts." Ones with far more money than he'd ever hoped to see in his lifetime, combined. "If I wanted to buy something online and have it shipped here or San Majoria, is all that information already in here? Am I logged into the right accounts on Amazon or whatever?"

"You should be. However, it would be better for you to tell Thomas what you want, and he can take care of procuring it for you. He likely has better channels to do so than you have access to."

Jordan nodded. "Okay. If I wanted to order something from my own bank accounts, ones I already have, is that an issue?"

A slight crease appeared between Don's brows. "I wouldn't think so, as long as you use the devices we've approved."

"Thanks." If he wanted to buy a present for his wife or new daughter, he might want to do it with his own money. Nothing extravagant, but something. And it should be from *him*, at least for now. Maybe once he felt like he was part of the family, he would have less of an issue giving them a gift purchased with money he had access to only because he'd married Astrid.

He'd look later, but in the meantime, he needed to get to know his step-daughter better. He thanked Don again, and went back to the kitchen to eat breakfast with his favorite little girl.

12

Astrid didn't know what time she woke up, but she did know she'd slept for a long time. Something she hadn't done nearly enough of leading up to the wedding.

One part of her felt guilty. Married for less than two days, and she'd already slept apart from her husband. The rest of her didn't. She hadn't wanted to marry him anymore than he wanted to marry her. He wouldn't care that she slept apart.

When she went to the room she normally occupied, she found her things, as well as Jordan's, put away in the closet. She took off her clothes from the day before, pinned her hair up and took a quick shower, then dressed in something casual. The tan slacks and white shirt, paired with darker brown loafers, fit her mood.

Downstairs, she found Nanny Gretchen putting up the rest of breakfast.

"Did you sleep well, ma'am?" she asked.

"Well enough."

"Would you like me to make something for you?"

Astrid shook her head. "No, thank you." There were supposed to be bagels. She found them in a cabinet and tore off a bit. "Where's Sofia?"

"She's with the duke." Gretchen put the bagel box back.

The duke? Right. Jordan. "Do you know where?"

"I believe they're in the ballroom."

That puzzled her. As ballrooms went, the room wasn't that impressive, but she supposed her daughter might like it.

The door stood ajar so she slipped through it.

What she saw surprised her.

Jordan was on his knees next to Sofia. She held a meter stick with a small box taped to the end. And were those balled up socks?

He wrapped his arms around Sofia. "Okay, kiddo, let's hit the puck." With his help, the makeshift hockey stick swung back then forward until it came in contact with the socks. They spun across the floor. "Great job! We'll make a hockey player out of you yet!"

"Isn't she a little young?" Astrid asked, taking a sip of her coffee.

Jordan turned and gave her a dazzling smile. "If anything, she's getting a bit of a late start. I had my first mini-stick when I was ten-months-old, or so my mother tells me. There are pictures."

"And that's why you were on a team that took Bantam's the year you were grounded?" She hoped she got that right.

His slightly widened eyes and the increased size of his grin told her she had. "You remembered!" He sat on the floor and pulled Sofia into his lap. She snuggled down next to him. "Not to be too braggy, but I was one of the best forwards in my level. When I was twelve, we won Regionals. My Spring team took provincials then went to Regionals and won there. We didn't have a national championship, but several regionals. We were the best team in four provinces. We went back the next three years, but got silver or bronze. When I was in grade 12, our high school team won provincials."

Astrid was impressed. "And college?"

"I hurt my knee in the last seconds of provincials my 12th year. I can still do most anything I want, but sometimes I need to wrap it up. It was just bad enough that I didn't want to push it. I had no chance or dream of going Major Junior or getting drafted, so it wasn't worth the risk that I'd hurt it worse and not be able to do anything I love, like skiing or pick-up games or surf. I hadn't heard, officially, if I'd win a scholarship or not, but I probably would have." He shrugged. "I had a university savings account and wasn't too worried about it. I had a couple other bursaries that covered a lot of the expenses, but since I wasn't playing hockey, I went to school near home and lived with my folks."

"Bursary?" She wasn't familiar with the term.

"Money from different organizations to pay university expenses."

"Like scholarships?"

"Yeah."

And in a couple of minutes, she knew far more about her husband than she had when she married him. "What's your degree in?"

"Business. My dad wanted me to take over for him when he retires, but that was never in the cards. Dare probably will. Even before he was officially family, he was a better choice, and I'd hinted to Dad more than once that he should consider Dare instead. I think he would have, even if he'd married someone else. What about you?"

Astrid moved to one of the tables to side of the ballroom floor and sat down. "You didn't look it up?"

Jordan shook his head. "I haven't looked anything up or asked my sister. I want to get to know *you*, not what some media type thinks about you."

He would be the first. Even Andrei had used the Internet and media stories to impress her with his knowledge of her interests, at least when they first started dating.

"I have a degree in government and international relations. It seemed like the best option, given my future job title."

"If you could do anything else, what would it be?"

Astrid stared into the coffee swirls. "I don't know. I never really thought about it." That wasn't entirely accurate. Would he know?

"Right now. Deep inside, if you could be anything you wanted, what would it be?"

She looked at the two of them sitting on the ballroom floor. "A mum. If I could be anything in the world, I'd want to be Sofia's mother full-time." With a half-shrug, she went back to staring into her coffee. "I'm sure that's not very enlightened or noble of me, or whatever, but there you go."

"I don't think there's anything wrong with that, at all. My mom stayed home with us, and I promise, she worked hard. Being a good stay-at-home wife and mother isn't for slackers."

She hadn't said anything about wife or more kids. Had he noticed?

Her phone buzzed. "Apparently, I have an appointment in fifteen minutes. A massage?" When had that been scheduled?

"Enjoy it," Jordan told her with a smile. "Miss Sofia and I are gonna hang out for a bit."

Astrid stood. "I will. It's just what I need." She'd have to thank Jade, or more likely Martina, for making the arrangements.

And maybe, for a few minutes, she'd be able to relax enough to forget everything else shaking the world around her.

"Am I supposed to bow when I meet this guy?" Jordan shifted in the back seat of the limo. In a few minutes, he'd meet the second king of his life, though likely not the last.

"No, not really. A nod and a very slight bow at the waist for you. If you meet any of the other family members, they get just a nod."

"I can handle that."

"They're just people, Jordan." Astrid stared out the window as the car drove through the capital city. "Just like me and my family."

"I know. But it's still intimidating. You grew up knowing your family as your family. They're Mom and Dad, and your younger siblings, but for the rest of us, it's different. Like an actor or national politician. The Canadian Prime Minister or President of the United States. People like King Benjamin and his family are your peers. That's not so for the rest of us."

"I suppose."

Before the conversation could continue, the car pulled through the gates of the Eyjanian palace. A footman opened the door. Jordan climbed out first then turned to help Astrid exit the vehicle.

She tucked her hand inside his elbow as they walked up the stairs to the wide doors. Once in the giant foyer - there was probably a fancier name for the room filled with statues and assorted ancient looking knick-knacks, but Jordan had no idea what it was - they were greeted by King Benjamin.

"Welcome to Eyjania." His tone was polite, but not welcoming. Neither was his posture.

Astrid gave him a slight nod of her head. "Hello, Benjamin. I would like to present my husband, Prince Jordan, Duke of Bevingdale."

Jordan gave the small bow and nod like she'd told him to. "It's a pleasure to meet you, Your Majesty."

"Likewise."

Jordan didn't buy it for a minute. The king didn't want them there. He'd stake his provincial championship trophy on it.

King Benjamin turned and sort of motioned for them to follow. Pressure on his arm from Astrid's hand confirmed his suspicion.

They followed him down a wide hallway, then into a dining room. Jordan guessed the ornately carved dark wood table could seat at least forty, maybe more. Only four places were set at one end. A young woman stood near them. More paintings graced the walls here, along with vases and intricately carved designs in the wood paneling.

King Benjamin turned. "Princess Astrid, Duke Jordan, my sister, Princess Genevieve."

Jordan nodded to her.

A waiter walked into one end of the room. "Dinner is served."

King Benjamin held the single chair for his sister, leaving Jordan and Astrid with the seats together. Astrid subtly indicated she was to sit next to Benjamin. He was grateful she didn't just let him flounder.

He kept an eye on his wife, following her lead, and that of the king, when it came to which fork to use and which glass to drink from.

Genevieve gushed about the wedding, which she wished she'd been able to attend. "Your dress was gorgeous, Astrid. Benjamin said you planned the wedding in just a few weeks. How did you get such a gorgeous dress on short notice?"

Astrid glanced at Jordan. "I worked with the same designers from my wedding to Andrei. There were two dresses I loved almost the same back then. I wore the other one, but the designer made several changes that made me love this one even more than I had before. I don't know why she'd kept it, but she did. It worked in my favor."

Jordan didn't say anything, but took a bite of his salad. He didn't know how he felt about Astrid wearing a dress she'd first considered for her wedding to Andrei but needed to let it roll off his back. She'd married him. That was the important part. Given their time frame, that was probably the only way she'd have a dress she liked in time.

"You grew up in our latitude, didn't you, Jordan?" Genevieve asked him.

"Not quite this far north, but closer than San Majoria. New Brunswick, Canada."

"Did I read that you're a hockey fan?"

"And a player." Astrid commented before he could. "He was quite good while in school before an injury forced him to stop."

"Really?" Genevieve looked duly impressed.

"I could hold my own. Our teams did well, but I think a big part of that was because my best friend and I could read each other's minds. Most of us had played together for years and could anticipate what the others were going to do. Teamwork like that helps a lot."

"I would imagine so." Genevieve took a sip of her wine. "We never had the opportunity to play organized sports, though we've all done some horse riding and swimming. Alfred, our youngest brother, is doing competitive swim for the first time this year. He would love to play hockey." Her eyes twinkled. "He's far enough down the line of succession that I think Mother just might let him."

"How old is he?" Jordan figured he should probably know this, but he didn't. He wasn't even sure how many siblings were in the family.

"He's nine."

Jordan's confusion must have shown on his face. Benjamin and Astrid both looked intently at their food.

Genevieve just sort of shrugged. "Our mother was pregnant when Father died. There is almost fourteen years, and eight other children, between him and Benjamin."

"There are ten of you?" Jordan blurted out before he could stop. "I knew you had a large family, but I didn't realize it was that big."

Genevieve laughed. "We're used to it. I think we're the largest generation of royals in any country where monogamy is practiced."

"I would think so."

She grinned. "The public didn't see it much, but our parents were a total love match. They couldn't keep their hands off each other."

"Genevieve." King Benjamin's sharp rebuke made her glare at him.

"It's true. That's what I want when I get married. Not some arranged thing Isaiah forces on me." She pointed her fork at him. "He's been trying, and you know it."

Jordan had no idea who Isaiah was, but clearly things weren't as idyllic as they seemed in the Eyjanian royal family.

13

Astrid stared at her salad but tried to watch Benjamin and Genevieve out of the corner of her eye. At least she'd never had anyone try to arrange her marriage, not really. Yes, she'd been cornered into marrying Jordan, but at least she already knew she liked him.

"This isn't the time, Genevieve." Benjamin's low tone held an unmistakable warning.

"Why not? You won't talk to me any other time, and Mother just tells me not to worry. It's not like we have to worry about either one of them running to the press, so it seems like a perfect time to have this conversation."

"Uncle Isaiah just wants what's best for all of us. That's all." Benjamin's voice was more conciliatory this time.

"Well, what's best for me is *not* marrying one of his stuffy old friends."

Astrid finally looked up to see a sheen of tears in Genevieve's eyes. She tried to give her best sympathetic smile.

"He's not old."

"No. Isaiah's not old, but the guy he wanted me to marry was older than Father would be!" Genevieve glared at Benjamin. "I refused, but he made it clear it wasn't the end of it. You're the king. You can tell him to back off, and he'll have to."

"We'll discuss it later."

"As long as you promise we *will* discuss it." The princess appeared to be able to hold her own.

"We will."

Genevieve smiled sweetly at Astrid. "You heard him. If he won't talk to me this week, I'm calling you to come over and help me make him."

"I'm happy to assist in any way possible." Astrid wouldn't really get involved, but maybe the thought that she might would convince Benjamin to talk to his sister.

"How about another topic," Genevieve went on. "What are you doing while you're in Eyjania on your honeymoon?"

Astrid glanced at Jordan who was looking at her. "We don't have any specific plans. It's the wrong time of year for the really good skiing, and we have my daughter with us. We'd rather not leave her for an extended period of time, so probably just some site seeing here in Akushla."

"The zoo is fantastic," Genevieve told them. "I would imagine Sofia would enjoy it. I saw the pictures from the turtle farm a couple weeks ago. She looked ecstatic."

"The sanctuary is one of my favorite places," Astrid gently corrected. "Sofia loves turtles." She couldn't help but smile. "They're her favorites. Mine, too."

The small talk turned even more stilted after that, though Astrid had heard enough to give her father a report. Isaiah still had his hands on the reins in Eyjania, though she wasn't sure how much influence he exerted over the day-to-day running of things. He definitely wanted to interfere in the personal lives of Benjamin and his siblings. With that interference, he could certainly be more influential in other areas - especially if he convinced Benjamin to marry someone of Isaiah's choosing. Her father probably wanted more, but it's all Astrid would be able to give him.

After dinner ended, Astrid and Jordan left in the same car they'd arrived in.

"Are all dinners with other royal families that personal and awkward?" he asked as he settled into the seat on the other end of the bench from her.

"No. The Eyjanian family has a reputation for being a bit cold and not very personable. The Eyjanian people tend to be ambivalent about the royal family as a whole. They don't actively dislike them, but they don't like them a whole lot either."

"So, it's them not me?"

"Most likely." At his puzzled glance, she went on. "I mean, you may have felt uncomfortable because they're royalty and all that, but most of the weirdness was because they tend to be very reclusive. I'm not sure why that is. Genevieve seems like she would want to be out more and interact with the people more, but she must not be allowed. That's all I can figure."

"Why did we have dinner with them then?"

"My father wanted to see if I could get any sort of gut feeling about what's going on here."

"Isn't that espionage or something?"

"No. Father and King Alfred IV were good friends. Things were different back then, from what I understand anyway. Father's worried that Isaiah is running things somehow. Isaiah was always power hungry. Alfred and Isaiah have a sister named Louise. Because Louise is older than Isaiah, she was Benjamin's regent and ran everything on his behalf until he turned eighteen. Isaiah tried to push her out and run things himself, but couldn't. Father worries that his influence is part of why Benjamin isn't more well liked."

Jordan reached over and took her hand. "Well, I'm glad we met with them, and I survived." He slid his fingers between hers. "And with that done, we can enjoy the rest of our trip. How long are we here anyway?"

"Another five days." She needed to ask Jade to arrange another massage when they returned. The one the day before had been just what she needed.

"Any ideas for what we can do with Sofia while we're here? The zoo sounds great, but that's only one day, if that, since she'll need her nap in the afternoon."

Astrid slid her hand out of his and pulled out her phone. After a minute of tapping. "There's also an aquarium, a magic house, and a children's museum."

"What about an ice skating rink?"

She looked a little further. "Yes. There is."

He gave her the grin she'd fallen for that first day on the beach. "Then I definitely need to take you both there. Do you skate?"

"I've been a couple of times, but not well."

The grin widened. "Then I'll get to teach both of you."

Astrid felt color climb into her cheeks. She had a feeling it would involve being very close to him, and she wasn't quite sure how she felt about that.

She'd managed to fall asleep in the nursery again the night before, because she wasn't sure she could handle being that close to Jordan as they slept. Or any other time.

Ice skating could go very, very well.

Or it could get her heart even more involved before she was ready and then shatter it into a thousand pieces all over again.

It had cost a little bit of money, but Jordan was able to rent out the Akushla Ice Rink for just the three of them. He'd used the bank account he'd gained access to after the wedding, because he just didn't have enough in his personal account to justify it. Maybe someday it wouldn't feel so weird.

"Isn't Sofia too little to skate?" Astrid asked him as he put the toddler skates on the little girl.

Jordan looked up at her with a grin. "Nah. If she can walk, she can skate. Besides, today I won't let go of her hands. We'll just take a few laps around."

Astrid stood. "I'm going to find her a helmet."

Sofia wouldn't need one. He wouldn't let her hit her head, but it would make Astrid feel better.

He finished with the tiny skates. "I'll help you in a minute, okay?"

Sofia nodded.

Jordan put on the borrowed hockey skates, annoyed with himself that he hadn't thought to bring his own.

"Here, sweetheart." Astrid put the helmet on Sofia's head.

Jordan stood and reached for his step-daughter. "Come on, kiddo." Once on the ice, he set her down. "Hold my hands." Standing behind her, with his forefingers tightly in her grasp, he started forward.

Sofia squealed as her skates glided across the ice. They did one full lap then came to a stop. Carefully, he maneuvered until he was in front of her skating backward. "Ready to go again?"

"*'Gin*!" Her giggles filled the rink.

Jordan skated backwards, this time able to see the delight on her face. About two-thirds of the way around, he whispered, "Do you wanna go fast?"

She squealed louder.

Jordan picked her up and twirled around a couple of times to Sofia's laughter. He didn't go *fast*, but faster than the very slow pace he had set while she was on her feet.

One little arm clung to his neck as she squealed and laughed.

"Be careful!" Astrid called from the side of the rink.

"We're fine!" Jordan called back with a laugh. He took a spin around the center of the rink then went back to the opening where Astrid waited. Once there, he handed Sofia to her mother. "Your turn."

"I don't have any skates." She turned and went back to the bench.

"Taken care of."

She tried not to wrinkle her nose and only partially succeed. A pair of hockey skates waited next to the bench.

"Those are boy skates," she protested.

"They're hockey skates in your size. Hockey skates are much easier to learn on than figure skates."

"Really?" The arch of her eyebrow said she didn't believe him.

"Promise. They're more stable. They don't have a toe pick, which makes it easier to stop on a dime. When you're a beginner, you really don't want that." He knelt in front of her, put her foot on his thigh, and winked at her. "If you hang out with me long at all, you'll be in the figure skates before you know it."

Jordan unzipped her boot and slid it off her foot before putting the skate on. After pulling the laces tight all the way up and tying them off, he set her foot back on the ground. He shifted his weight then did the same with her other foot. "All set." He stood and held out his hands. "Come on."

She wobbled like a blindfolded newborn foal but made it to the ice. "I don't think I can do this."

"Look at me."

Astrid looked up, and he could see fear trying to take over.

"Right in my eyes." He held her gaze. "Good. Take a deep breath." She did, and he glided back a bit until he was almost as far as he could be and still hold her hands. "Push off with one foot."

She wobbled again and gripped his hands tighter. "I can't do this."

Shoot. "You're right. You can't. Not yet." He helped her back to the wall. "Hold on. I'll be right back."

He whispered with Nanny Gretchen for a moment. She went to the counter and returned with something for Astrid. Jordan took it and skated the few feet to his wife. "We need to put this on you."

This time she didn't even try to hide the wrinkled nose. "That looks gross."

"I know, but you need a helmet, and they only had hockey helmets. I promise it's been disinfected."

She managed to scrunch her nose up even further. "Why do I need it?"

"Because you're probably going to fall, and if you don't fall the right way, you'll get a concussion."

"Fall? You think my balance is that bad?"

"No. I think you're that inexperienced as a skater. All skaters fall. And you, sweetheart, are the Crown Princess of San Majoria. The entire country would never forgive me if I let you get a concussion." He buckled the helmet in place. "Or a broken wrist. The first thing I'm going to do is teach you how to fall."

Her nose finally unwrinkled. "There's a wrong way to fall?"

"Yes. You do not want to land on your wrists. You will get hurt. You can sprain or break your wrist or even break your clavicle." He demonstrated what he wanted her to do. "Bend your knees. Hands in the air so you don't land on them. Try to lean to the side and land more on your thigh and hip. If you do fall backward, do your best to keep your head forward so it doesn't hit hard."

"Fine. I'll do my best."

"Not good enough." He made her practice.

She complained about the cold.

He made her practice again.

Then he took her hand, spun around behind her, and settled his hands on her hips. "Here we go."

The cold seeped into Astrid's bones. She grew up in a climate far too tropical to enjoy ice skating.

But with Jordan's hands on her hips and him pushing her forward, it suddenly seemed much warmer.

With him so close, her concentration was basically shot, but she managed to push off first with one foot, then the other. They made a complete circuit of the rink.

"Good job. You're getting the hang of it."

"If you keep holding onto me like that, I won't have to worry about falling." The helmet didn't stink like she'd feared, but wasn't exactly comfortable either.

"Do you really think I'd let you fall today? I won't let go of you."

But he did just that, at least until his hand slid down her arm and grasped hers. He whirled in front of her and took her other hand, but stayed almost as far away as he could.

"You're not good enough for me to be closer," he told her, as though he'd read her mind. "Too easy for skates to get tangled and for both of us to fall." She envied his easy backward motion.

"How long until I'm good enough?"

"Depends on how often you practice. Is there a rink in Cabo Juan-Eduardo?"

"I think so. I've never had occasion to notice."

"If there is, we'll have to get out there sometimes."

She felt them slowing down, and he let her get closer before he spun around behind her again. With his hands on her waist, he pulled her back against his chest.

"I thought we couldn't be too close."

"I can keep my feet spread wider, and it's easier to keep track of where yours are without actually looking at them." He nuzzled her neck. "I like being this close to you."

Astrid liked it, too. More than she should for a woman still in love with another man. So much it distracted her. Her feet drifted outward, but before she could correct it, she found herself lifted off the ice.

With his arms tight around her waist, Jordan chuckled. "I guess I shouldn't distract you."

"No, you shouldn't."

She had no idea how he did it, but he held her in his arms, like a groom carrying his bride over the threshold, something he hadn't done on their wedding night.

Astrid wrapped an arm around his neck, his face only inches from hers. "I think skating like this is more my speed."

Before she could say anything else, his lips were on hers. She cradled the side of his face with her hand as she kissed him back, though she kept a tight rein on the emotions bubbling beneath the surface. They wanted to break free, to kiss him more fully, to tell him she wanted more.

But before she could, he pulled back.

Jordan stared into her eyes, but Astrid couldn't read what was written there. Finally, he closed them, released a deep breath, and pushed off with one foot propelling them across the ice again.

He set her down on the carpet and helped her walk back to the bench.

"Give me ten minutes?" he asked as she sat down.

All she could do was nod.

He picked up a hockey stick and a puck as he stepped back out onto the ice.

She'd seen the grace in his fluid movements as he skated with Sofia, but this was different. He was poetry in motion as he went faster than he had yet today. He did a lap around the entire rink before dropping the puck on the ice.

His hair fluttered in the breeze of his own making. Why wasn't he wearing a helmet? She'd have to ask him later. Astrid unbuckled hers and set it to the side as Jordan tapped the puck one way then another, nearly stopping, then starting, first one direction, then to the other side.

His movements didn't make any sense until she realized he was playing an imaginary foe, perhaps one of those championship games he'd told her about. After several trips up and down the ice, he finally pulled the stick back to about his waist and slapped the puck into the goal she hadn't even noticed earlier.

Jordan's hands went over his head as he glided across the ice, stick raised in victory. "And San Majoria takes the Olympic gold!"

Astrid couldn't help but laugh. "We don't have an Olympic hockey team!"

"You should! I could totally be on it." He turned his legs to the side and scraped a layer of ice off as he came to a stop near her.

"Actually, given the fact that you're not even sure there's an ice rink in Juan-Eduardo, I would probably *be* the team."

When he walked off the ice, his steps were sure. "There's probably not a skate sharpener in Juan-Eduardo either."

"If not, you can order one online."

He chuckled. "It's not a thing. It's a person. They keep meticulous notes on how each player who comes in likes their skates sharpened. I should probably get a second pair. That way I have one set in San Majoria but can send the other ones to Dare, so he can get them sharpened for me. Rotate them."

Maybe she'd talk to Dare or Betsy and find out what the very best kind of skates were and order him two brand new pairs.

Before he took his skates off, he knelt in front of her and gently loosened the laces of hers. His tenderness as he did something as simple as helping her off with skates and on with boots was almost too much. Before her eyes could fill with tears at the thought of life with this man and what could be between them, she stood. "I'm going to find Sofia so we can go as soon as you get your shoes on. It's almost her naptime."

Being close to him hurt too much.

He wasn't Andrei.

He never would be.

But somehow, in the comparisons of her mind, she wasn't sure Andrei was still the clear winner.

And she didn't know how she felt about that.

14

Jordan stared out the window of the plane as they headed back toward San Majoria.

As honeymoons go, the last week had been pathetic. One kiss, on the ice, with several spectators, though they were all kind enough not to mention it. A bride who slept in another room the entire time. A groom who wanted to find a way to earn her love and affection, but kept a huge secret from her. A toddler princess who glowed in the attention lavished on her by both of them.

As a vacation, it wasn't too bad.

His ears popped as they descended toward the island nation. Maybe being home would help. They could find their routine and maybe he'd have a chance to win his wife over.

But for the first few weeks, he barely saw her or Sofia. He spent his days, in what used to be the schoolroom for Astrid and her siblings, having prince lessons. Thomas and Adam were there for most of it, but Jordan's new brothers-in-law came by to help, too, as did the king.

He learned how to properly hold a seat for a woman, which fork or cup or plate to use when, the best way to give a speech while making certain each member of the audience thought you were talking directly to them, and on and on and on. Jordan's head spun with all the information. Names of the members of the royal families he'd be expected to interact with regularly. Geography. History. Names of important political leaders in San Majoria. Laws. Regulations. Charities to choose from.

At least one of those was easy. The San Majorian Children's Hockey League had hoped for a royal patron for a long time, but none of the other family members were interested enough to make it happen.

"Andrei considered it," Kensington told him. "But in the end, he just wasn't feeling the hockey."

Jordan really didn't want to consider anything about his dead rival, but needed to know. "What was his cause? The one thing he was most passionate about?"

"I don't know if it's what he was most passionate about, you'd have to ask Astrid about that, but he was a vocal supporter of organ donation. Astrid carried out his wishes when he died and donated his organs."

Jordan rubbed the center of his chest. "That's a cause I can get very vocally behind." At Kensington's puzzled glance, he sighed. "I had a heart transplant."

Kensington's expression changed. "Seriously?"

"A couple years ago, at Cabo Juan-Eduardo General Hospital actually." He had to be careful. No one else could know the truth until he finally told Astrid.

"So that's probably a charity you'll join with Astrid then. It's a little odd that her first husband donated and her second husband received an organ. Finding one of those would be a great thing for you to do together."

"I'll talk to her about it later." He needed to look up more information about the organization and let Astrid decide how involved she wanted him to be. Maybe in the future she'd be more open to it, when the wounds weren't quite so fresh.

Jordan and Kensington walked back to the family's portion of the palace. He went to his quarters, turning what Kensington had said over in his head. Would there be some way to honor Andrei's memory? An award or something maybe. And if so, did he really want it to be related to organ donation, a cause so near and dear to Jordan's...

He stopped the thought before it completed. It was too convoluted.

"We leave in five minutes." Astrid came out of her dressing room fastening an earring to one ear. "Did they just release you from your lessons?"

"A little while ago. I talked to your brother for a few minutes. I don't remember anything being on my schedule for tonight, though."

She sighed. "It wasn't. We were last minute replacements since my mother isn't feeling well. My parents were planning to attend, but asked us to instead."

Jordan bit back a sigh. "If I can find my suit, I'll be ready in ten minutes. I know we'll be late, but only a few minutes." He started for his dressing room on the other side of their bedroom, the one he'd shared with her only once.

"That's all right. Kensington was going with us. He's probably ready." She started for the door.

"I don't know about that. We were together right before I got here."

"His valet likely has his things laid out. It will only take him a few minutes." She didn't look at him, but picked up her clutch. "I'll see you later." She walked out the door without a backward glance.

Jordan texted Thomas and Adam, telling them he was going with her, and they needed to make sure the car didn't leave without him. He looked around his dressing room. Could there be a wrong suit? They all looked so similar. Astrid wore a tan dress that came to about her knees, so it couldn't be too formal.

He chose a navy suit, white shirt, and a tie in the San Majorian national colors. They couldn't fault him for that, right? Jordan didn't think he'd changed clothes so fast since he came home as a teen and wanted to get out on the ice. With his tie in his hand, he hustled out the door and to the portico where the car waited.

Inside, both Astrid and Kensington waited. Kensington focused on his phone and didn't seem to care about the short delay, but Astrid looked annoyed.

"You didn't have to get ready so fast. Your hair's not even combed."

Jordan flashed her a grin. "I have a comb and a reputation for stylishly messy hair."

"Your tie's not on."

"That'll just take a minute." The car began to pull out of the front gate as he measured the sides of the tie against each other.

By the time he finished tying it, and running a comb through his hair, they pulled up to one of the swankier hotels in town. Time for his first official event as a prince of San Majoria.

Astrid took Jordan's hand as he helped her out of the car. She didn't want to admit that he had managed to pull off a quick change. They were two minutes later than planned, not bad given how much warning he'd had. She'd wanted him to want to come, but wasn't sure she actually wanted him there.

The dichotomy troubled her, and she couldn't explain it even to herself.

With her brother trailing a couple steps behind, they waved to the small assembled crowd and went into the hotel lobby. Off to one side was the ballroom that looked just like every other ballroom she'd ever been in, though this was a semi-formal dinner, not a ball.

They weren't announced, but directed to the head table up on a stage. At least there wouldn't be any speeches or dancing this evening, just an appearance and mingling after dinner. Astrid was grateful - she wasn't sure how well she'd handle dancing with her husband.

She was seated near the middle of the head table. Jordan sat to her right. Kensington to the other side of him.

As expected, dinner was delicious. Afterward, with a glass of champagne in her hand, Astrid circulated among those gathered. She managed to answer question after question about the wedding, the honeymoon, and how much Sofia loved Jordan, and vice versa.

The smile plastered on her face would fool most people, but not all of them. Lady Haverford wasn't taken in.

"How are you, dear?" she asked when they were off to the side. "And don't give me that smile and fine routine."

Lady Haverford was a distant relative and Astrid's second or third cousin. She was friends with Astrid's mother, and Astrid knew she wouldn't get away with her usual pat answer. Finally, she went with a version of the truth. "It's hard seeing the comparisons."

"Of course it is. Both of your relationships have been in the public eye. You and Prince Andrei were more open with your affections, but given how your relationship with Prince Jordan became public, it's not surprising you've decided to be more circumspect in public."

"Exactly." It sounded good anyway.

"And the two men are sure to be compared, both favorably and unfavorably to each other, but you love them both. You don't want either one of them to come out looking poorly."

Astrid nodded as she took a sip of her champagne. It wasn't entirely the truth. On one level, she liked Jordan and didn't want anyone to think poorly of him, but she was more concerned about the public's memory of Andrei being tainted.

On another level, Jordan was going to be at her side for a very long time. It would be good if the people loved him like they thought she did.

"It will take some time to find your footing, with each other and with the public," Lady Haverford went on. "Every new relationship, with a spouse or a royal couple with the public, needs time to sort itself out."

"I know, and we are."

Lady Haverford reached out and squeezed Astrid's arm. "We're all rooting for the two of you to figure out who this new couple is. You're going to be fine."

Astrid gave a weak smile. "Thank you. We appreciate the support."

Lady Haverford smiled. "And here he is now."

A hand slid around Astrid's waist and pulled her close. Without looking, even without knowing anyone else would do such a thing, she knew it was Jordan.

"Good evening." Jordan nodded his head toward Lady Haverford.

Astrid introduced Jordan to the other woman, and the three of them made small talk for a few minutes before Kensington joined them. After another quarter hour with Jordan's arm around her waist, and inane discussions with people whose names she'd never remember, they finally made their way back to the car.

Astrid laid her head back against the seat and closed her eyes. Most of the time, she loved being among the people of San Majoria at events like that, but not this time. She didn't let herself delve too deeply into why that might be.

Jordan helped her out of the car when they returned to the palace. Jade waited for her near the door.

"Ma'am, Princess Sofia needs you."

Worry settled deep inside. "What is it?"

"Nanny Gretchen said Princess Sofia is not feeling well and is asking for you."

By the time Jade finished the statement, Astrid was halfway up the first staircase leading toward the family area of the palace. "How long has she had a fever? Is she throwing up? Messy diapers?"

"I'm afraid I don't have those answers, ma'am. Nanny

Gretchen called me about five minutes ago since she knew you'd be arriving home soon."

Astrid stifled a sigh and hurried to her daughter's room, right across the hall from the one she'd lived in since not long after Andrei's death. Nanny Gretchen sat in the rocking chair holding Sofia. "How is she?" Astrid whispered.

"I gave her some medicine to bring the temperature down," Nanny Gretchen said softly. "It's starting to help. She just fell asleep."

"How high was it?"

"About 102." She rested her cheek on Sofia's forehead. "She feels a bit cooler now. Would you like to take her?"

"For a few minutes, then I'll need to go change." Astrid gently took the sleeping little girl and rested Sofia's head on her shoulder before taking Nanny Gretchen's place in the rocker. Warmth from Sofia could be felt through Astrid's dress. "Any idea what it is?"

Nanny Gretchen shook her head. "Nothing specific. Just a bit of a bug, I think. Kids get them all the time."

"She doesn't. She's never really been sick before," Astrid reminded her.

"But she is a little girl, and this is what happens to little girls. They come into contact with a bug they've never encountered before and get sick. She's going to be fine, ma'am."

Astrid kissed Sofia's clammy forehead. "I know."

Nanny Gretchen moved quietly around the room, picking up toys, and straightening things. After about fifteen minutes, she came back to Astrid's side. "Let me take her, ma'am. Why don't you go change?"

They traded the toddler back, and Nanny Gretchen took the rocker as Astrid leaned over and kissed Sofia's head again. How quickly could she change and get back? She hurried out the door to find out.

15

Jordan tugged at the knot in his tie until it came loose in his hand. Astrid had hurried away with Jade as soon as they walked in the door. Kensington had answered his phone and taken off in a different direction.

And Jordan just wanted to find a kitchen where he could have a snack.

In a palace with several kitchens - he didn't know how many - he didn't know how to get to any of them.

He pulled out his phone, but he didn't know who he planned to call to ask. It wasn't like there was a map on it.

That would be useful though. Maybe someone had one he could use.

Up near the family quarters made the most sense. He did know how to get there.

The top floor of the residence wing held the monarch's quarters. He figured, eventually, he'd end up living there. Someday. He had married the future queen and all. The next-to-top floor had a bunch of suites off the wide hall that ran the length of the wing. The stone walls were broken only by the widely-separated doors and occasional tapestries. A carpet ran the center of the entire length of the hall, with about a two-foot-wide section of stone floor on either side. He always did his best to stay on it, though he wasn't sure which was actually more delicate.

The suite he was supposed to share with his wife was on the side facing the bay. Across from it, another two-bedroom suite and sitting room belonged to Sofia. A set of empty rooms served as a buffer between the Crown Princess's family and the rest of the siblings. It was oddly reminiscent of a very fancy college dorm. He wasn't sure which set of rooms belonged to which of his in-laws just yet.

But surely a kitchen hid behind at least one of the doors.

One of the other doors opened, and Queen Miriam walked out, closing it behind her.

"Jordan! How did the dinner go?"

He bowed slightly. "It went fine. At least as far as I know." He shrugged. "I've never been to anything like that before. How are you feeling?" Wasn't she under the weather? Wasn't that why he, Astrid, and Kensington had attended?

"I am feeling much better, thank you. I didn't sleep well last night, and it caught up with me. I'm not as young as I used to be, you know." She gave him a smile and a wink before sliding her hand through his elbow. "Would you be so kind as to escort me to my quarters?"

"It would be my honor, but I do have a favor to ask in return."

"Name it."

"Where's the kitchen?"

Laughter bubbled out of the regal queen. "Did no one give you a tour?"

He couldn't help but smile. "No, can't say that they did."

"Then I'll give you a brief one." She pointed to the door she left from. "Do you know who lives there?"

"I'd say one of your children, but I have no idea which one."

She gave him a very un-regal smirk. "You're correct." She ran a finger over the frame attached to the door. All of the rooms had them, bolted down so they wouldn't rattle when the door opened and closed. "Each picture is chosen by the resident of the room. This room belongs to Jacqueline Grace. She loves horses."

That explained the countryside scene with a family of horses in the foreground.

The queen pointed across the hall. "This room belongs to Harrison. He's a fan of knights, or he was when he chose the picture. He may have outgrown it by now."

They walked down the hall to the next set of doors. "Which one do you think belongs to who?" This time she was able to confine the smirk to her tone.

Jordan looked at the pictures. "I'm going to guess the unicorn, as wild as he looks, belongs to Princess Esther. Which would mean the door with the mountains is Prince Kensington."

"Very good. However, you do know you don't need to use their titles, don't you? I know you have spent a fair bit of time with my sons especially."

He felt his face color. "It's the way I was raised. Even after my aunt and uncle told me I could call them by their first names, I couldn't bring myself to. Prince, princess, queen, king, your royal highness, your majesty, all of that is pretty ingrained."

"Do you still call your wife Princess Astrid?" she asked gently. "Or use Sofia's title?"

"It's easier with Sofia," he admitted. "She's a toddler." They stopped in front of a door with a basket of fruit. "I'm going to guess this is a kitchen."

"You guess correctly."

Across the hall was a room with what seemed to be ancient Greeks reclining on sofas with strategically placed sheets. "And a common living area?"

"Right again." She let go of his arm and went into the kitchen. "But do you call your wife by her title? Or your royal highness?"

"Not usually." He hesitated then decided to go for it. "But the truth is, I've been so busy learning this prince thing that I haven't seen her much since we got back from Eyjania."

A frown marred the normally smooth skin of the queen's forehead. "I thought your lessons were confined to working hours. Have they extended to commandeer your evenings as well?"

"No, ma'am."

"Then you don't see your wife in the evening? For dinner? Conversations before bed? Pillow talk?"

She was surprisingly unembarrassed by her last statement. Jordan dared to be relaxed in the presence of the queen and leaned with his forearms propped on the stainless steel counter. "I rarely see her for more than a few minutes." He needed to confide in someone. From everything he knew about her, his mother-in-law seemed like a good choice. "She sleeps in Sofia's room. At least, I presume that's where she sleeps." He couldn't look his mother-in-law in the eye.

"Ah." There was far more understanding in her voice than he would have expected. "And you're afraid to force the issue, as it were, because you're afraid she'll run. Or you're afraid she'll get too close and discover your secret before you're ready to tell her."

His head jerked up. "He told you?"

"My husband and I seldom have secrets from each other, at least not any that aren't state secrets, and even then he keeps very little from me."

Jordan pinched the bridge of his nose. "And someday, I need to fill the role you do. I need to be the one she comes to, and she's going to need me to be that, but if this goes on much longer, we're going to be in this semi-affectionate, not-really-a-marriage thing and not know how to get out."

"Don't let her do that. She doesn't realize it, but she needs you to get into her world, into her personal space. Don't *force* anything, but turn on that easy Canadian charm and don't take no for an answer. Before you know it, she'll realize what a wonderful man you are and want to keep you around." She winked at him. "I don't think it will be all that difficult."

Jordan thanked her for the tour and advice, taking a snack out of the fridge and going back to his dressing room. Changing into his pajamas, he decided to leave his shirt off. He'd taken to wearing it in case Astrid showed up in their room, but this time he didn't care about making her more comfortable when she refused to really acknowledge their relationship. He stared out the window at the lights twinkling in the city and docks below.

The door to Astrid's dressing room opened, and he turned to see her walking out. "We need to talk."

"Can it wait?" She pulled her hair up into a ponytail. "Sofia's running a fever. She's never done that before, and I need to be there."

He steeled his resolve. "It won't take long, but there's something I need you to know."

"What's that?"

"I won't be friend-zoned, Astrid." As he talked to the queen, he'd realized that's what his wife was doing. "Whatever else is going on, I won't let that happen."

"What?" Astrid tried to look innocent of his accusation.

The Jordan who walked toward her was both familiar and not. The bare chest with its scars was the same on the beach paired with board shorts as it was in the bedroom with pajama pants covered in maple leaves.

The hard look in his eyes was new.

"I won't be friend-zoned. I'm your husband. I will take it as slowly as you need, but I will not be friend-zoned."

"I don't understand." She'd never heard the phrase, but understood its meaning nonetheless.

"You've kissed me once since the wedding, and that was when I kissed you out on the ice. You pat my shoulder. We occasionally do things together, but you won't hold my hand or take my arm unless we're in public. Then it's only because you don't want anyone to know what a sham this is. You smile a little too brightly, then make an excuse to sleep in your daughter's room. How long have we been married? And how many times have we shared a bed, regardless of the activities that would not be taking place in it?"

"Weeks," she whispered. "Once." Tears threatened again. Then only because she couldn't take the humiliation - for both of them - if it became known they didn't sleep in the same room on their wedding night.

His steady advance stopped when he reached her, her vision of his face blurred by tears. "I'm not your friend, Astrid. I'm your husband." His hand came to the side of her face cradling it as his fingers threaded into her hair. "You may not be ready for the physical intimacies that come with marriage, but if you deny me progress on the emotional side, there will be no more heirs, and I may as well go live in the cottage on the beach."

Before she could respond, protest that what he said wasn't true, though she knew it was, he kissed her.

But this kiss wasn't like any kiss before.

Hard. Demanding. Taking.

And yet, not.

Jordan would never take anything she didn't willingly give, be it a kiss or something more, and Astrid found herself responding to him in a way she never had before.

Not even with Andrei.

That last thought slipped in as coherence fled under the onslaught of Jordan's touch.

Astrid whimpered and wound her arms around his neck, lifting herself onto her toes as she kissed him more fully.

Just as quickly as it began, it ended, and Jordan was once more across the bedroom. One hand rested on his hip and the other ran through his hair then gripped the back of his neck as he stared out the window.

He turned. "I won't take from you, Astrid. I know society's made it a bigger deal for women than men, but I won't give to you what I've never given another woman. Not yet. Not until it's more than just physical. But don't forget who I am and whose name you said in front of God, church, and country."

"I won't." How could she when that kiss would replay in her mind for eternity?

His expression finally softened. "Go to Sofia. She needs you tonight."

Astrid felt her brows knit together. "But you said..."

"It's not about tonight. Tonight, she's running a fever and needs her mother. It's about all the other nights when you should sleep in your husband's bed, not your daughter's room."

His tone had changed so dramatically from a few minutes earlier that Astrid smiled at the thought.

"What?"

"That's not your bed," she pointed out. "Technically, it's not mine either. It's like three hundred years old. Meticulously maintained, of course, but dozens of other couples have likely slept in it before us."

He rolled his eyes. "And dozens of other couples have done far more than sleep. The point remains."

"I know." His words had struck where they were supposed to. "I promise I'll try to do better."

"Don't try. Do." He walked back toward her, his hand coming to cradle her face again. "One day at a time. One night at a time. Purpose in your heart to find a way to grow a little closer to me. We'll get there as long as we're both on the same path."

This time when he kissed her, it was the Jordan she'd known before the wedding. Tender, gentle, but underlying it all, bridled passion.

When he moved back, Jordan rested his forehead on hers. "Go take care of Sofia before I try to convince you to stay." With a kiss to her hairline, he let her go. "I'll see you in the morning."

Astrid watched him walk toward the bathroom and wondered.

What if she wanted to stay?

What if she wanted to be his wife in deed as well as by law?

Her phone buzzed in her pocket. Nanny Gretchen said Sofia was asking for her again.

One day soon, she'd join her husband in bed symbolically as well as physically, but that night wasn't this one.

Heart aching over what they'd both lost for the time being, Astrid turned and headed for her daughter's room across the hall.

For the first time since the second night of their marriage, she found herself wishing to fall asleep elsewhere.

16

"What is this thing we're going to? And why do I need board shorts? I thought members of the royal family didn't wear shorts in public." Jordan tugged his wetsuit shirt on as he walked back into the bedroom, the one he still hadn't shared with his wife. But, after two days, Sofia was on the mend, so soon. Things had been going better. Astrid had made a conscious effort to spend more time with him. In fact, they'd had dinner and breakfast together once and lunch twice, though only once alone.

"It's the annual carnival for sick and recovering children. Some have or had cancer. Some have chronic diseases, like diabetes or chromosomal disorders. Things like that."

"That doesn't explain the board shorts."

Astrid just smiled sweetly at him. "You'll see. There will be games and craft booths. Many of the children's families do fundraisers to help cover their expenses. You'll find booths with their t-shirts or artwork or other goods that they sell. We don't buy any, by the way. If we bought one, we'd have to buy them all. Instead, we make donations and raise funds other ways."

"Noted."

She looked at her phone. "We have four minutes to get to the garrison."

"Then we should go." He followed a half step behind, still not quite sure how to get to the garrison. He could get to the portico where they were often picked up and dropped off, but he'd only been to the garrison twice. He did know the word garrison, in modern terms, was a fancy name for garage. "Are we driving ourselves today?"

"We'll have security vehicles in front and behind, but yes, you're driving."

"I wonder if I should have my car sent down here," he wondered almost to himself.

"What kind of car do you have?"

"I have a truck, because winter, but I also have a 1931 Buick McLaughin Straight 8."

"I have no idea what that is."

"Well, for starters, it's a car from 1931."

Astrid rolled her eyes. "I figured that much."

"Eight-cylinder, starter pedal on the floor near the other pedals, three-speed, no radio, oak wheelhubs, ashtrays on the doors, pockets on the suicide doors in the back. The back seat has a fold-down metal footrest. The interior is dark green Cashmere upholstery and the outside is really dark navy and looks almost black. The seats are super comfortable. It has a really cool Flying 8 radiator cap hood ornament."

"Nice."

Jordan groaned. "Nice is an understatement, Princess. It's a very cool car. Trust me."

"If you say so. But today, you'll be driving one of the family cars. I do hope that's all right." The very dry sarcasm made Jordan smile.

"I'm sure I can manage."

Someone held the door open for them. A car waited, already running, in the garage.

Once they were both seated and buckled in, he grinned at her.

"One nice thing about a garrison with staff is that the car's already cooled down when you get in."

"Do you even need air conditioning in your cars in Canada?"

Jordan shifted into gear. "Where I'm from we do. It gets rather warm in the summer. I can just follow this other car, right?"

"Yes. Do not get separated."

He would do his best. He had a feeling the cars in front and behind wouldn't let him get too far away. It took twenty minutes to get to the park across the street from the hospital. The entire thing was filled with games and rides, and all the things you'd normally see at a carnival, though the children here had a different look about them.

"So where to first?" Jordan asked as they were ushered toward a back entrance.

"You'll see," she answered mysteriously.

He took her hand and slid his fingers between hers. It was only for a few minutes until they greeted the organizers of the event, along with a couple members of the children's medical staff, but he wanted the connection.

"Are you ready for your turn in the booth, sir?" one of them asked a minute later.

Jordan glanced at Astrid, who wore a Cheshire cat grin. "Um, sure."

"Then right this way."

When he realized where they were headed, Jordan glanced at Astrid and shook his head. She just smiled back, though it had become more demure.

"Really?" he asked.

"You weren't aware, sir?" He could hear the beginnings of panic in the man's voice.

"It's fine." Jordan rushed to reassure the man. "My wife is just having a little fun at my expense."

"We were most grateful that you were willing to step in. Prince Andrei manned the booth once, and it was a big hit."

"Well it's my pleasure. I've done it before, and it's not that hard."

The man grinned. "Not at all. Just interact with the kids when they come up and try not to get wet."

Jordan eyed the big tank in front of him. "Somehow that seems easier said than done." He let go of Astrid's hand.

"Have fun, *viejo*."

He turned to look at her and decided that smirk meant she needed to be kissed, no matter what the royal protocol on PDA was. Just a quick kiss, so he did.

But how he wished it could be more.

Another man, this one with a megaphone, walked over as Jordan let a still smirking Astrid go. "Ladies and gentlemen, boys and girls! Now's your chance! Prince Jordan, Duke of Bevingdale, is in the dunk tank!"

Before he could change his mind, Jordan pulled Astrid close and gave her a kiss. With a wink, he turned and climbed up onto the breakable seat. "Who's gonna be first?" he called, watching his wife. "Who thinks Princess Astrid should get the first shot?"

The gathered crowd cheered their approval. The glare she gave him was offset by the twitching corners of her just-kissed lips.

Oh, he was going down!

Okay, God. I know this is ridiculous, but if You could help me hit the target, I would really appreciate it. Astrid held the baseball in her right hand. Later, she'd read Jordan the riot act for putting her on the spot.

"Who thinks she can hit the target?" he called.

The crowd, growing larger by the second as word of their arrival spread, cheered.

Really, God. I could use Your help. Here went nothing. *At least make it so I don't throw like a girl.*

The first toss nicked the target, but not strongly enough to knock him in.

"Strike one!" he yelled, arms raised in the air. "Come on, Princess, you can do better than that!"

His wink nearly made her knees give out. Why exactly hadn't she spent more time close to him over the last few weeks? After a deep, steadying breath, she threw the second ball.

A direct hit!

Astrid clasped her hands together and laughed as Jordan fell in the water.

He swam around, making faces at the kids nearby. They loved it. A few seconds later, he'd climbed back up. "Okay, so the princess could do it! Who else wants to try?"

The kids lined up with calls of *me*!

Stepping to the side, Astrid watched as several kids managed to hit the target on the first or second try. Then came a bigger kid, maybe fifteen and bald.

"Watch out, your Dukeness!" the kid called. There was no malice in his words, just good-natured taunting.

"You think you can do it?" Jordan hollered back. "Let's see what you got."

The kid threw his hardest, but missed low.

"Aw! Is that all?" Jordan's grin made everyone laugh.

The kid tried again, but this time missed high.

"You can do it!" someone in the crowd yelled.

Jordan nodded toward the kid. "You hit the bullseye, and your family's lunch is on me and my wife."

And this time the ball hit the mark.

The crowd cheered as he went under the water.

Don, the head of Astrid's security team, motioned to her. She nodded. She'd need to have a word with Jordan about saying those sorts of things. Sometimes security was okay with them having lunch with random people and sometimes they weren't. Fortunately, this day it would be fine.

The head of the carnival asked for a moment of her time. Astrid stood off to the side, discussing another fundraiser in a few months, but watching Jordan while they did.

"He's great with the kids," the administrator told her.

"Yes, he is. Sofia loves him." And both of those things bothered her.

As she observed, he managed to convince a little girl, probably no more than four, that she could throw from about two feet away. Comparisons were inevitable, even in her own mind. Andrei had done this the year they were married, but despite the smile on his face the whole time, he'd abhorred every minute of it. The only reason Sofia even existed was because he knew she had to have an heir - and a spare. He'd barely been okay with having children because she was required to. If she'd been anyone else, there would have been no children. He had that little interest in them.

Astrid had told Andrei she would have been fine without children, except it was expected of her. Way deep down, in a place she never mentioned even to her first husband, she'd wondered, though.

Then Sofia was born.

From the moment she held the little girl, Astrid's main purpose in life became clear. Not to be queen, though she would do that to the best of her ability, but to be a mother.

She'd lain in the delivery room at the palace and snuggled her daughter, tears streaming down her face. Jacqueline Grace had been there with her and thought she knew where the tears came from, but she was wrong.

Astrid mourned the fact that Andrei and Sofia would never know each other. Even more she mourned that Sofia would never be an older sister, that Astrid would never have any more children.

So she doted on Sofia. Yes, Astrid hired a nanny. Like any mother, she needed help sometimes, and she could afford a live-in nanny.

Time and time again, she watched Jordan sink under the water. Did any of the kids miss? Every time, he came out of the water with a smile on his face and the right tone for the next kid. Some he taunted. Others he cajoled. Still others he encouraged. Sometimes all three. He had a knack for finding the right thing to say, and Astrid admired him for it.

After about two hours, he finally climbed out. Astrid walked toward him, but the gleam in his eye gave her pause. Before she could figure it out, he wrapped his arms around her.

"Ew!" She half-heartedly tried to push him away as they laughed together. "You're all wet!" This picture was sure to end up online. And the public would love it.

"And now you are, too. I find it interesting a princess never does the dunk tank." He let go of her and took the towel someone gave him.

"Of course not." She sniffed. "It would ruin our hair and make-up."

He leaned in close. "Sometime between now and the next carnival, we're going to make a bet. You're going to lose, and next year, you'll spend some time in the dunk tank, and I'll be first in line."

"Keep dreaming." The smoldering look in his eyes made her wish they were already home.

Abruptly, he moved back "I'm hungry. Where's the kid we're having lunch with?"

And the moment was over.

Don motioned to them. The young man and his family waited off to the side. Towel wrapped around his shoulders, Jordan shook the kid's hand then talked with both parents and a younger sister.

Pasting a smile on her face, too confused by the turmoil inside, Astrid joined them as they headed for the food area of the carnival. The day was too beautiful to let confusion reign. She pushed the thoughts to the side and did her best to be present.

But before she could, she realized something.

Crown Princess Astrid was falling in love with her husband.

17

"Do you think I can do it?" Jordan crouched down next to a girl, maybe four years old.

She nodded, her lip caught in her teeth.

"I think I might need some help. Can you help me?"

Another nod.

He hooked an arm around her waist and moved her in front of him. "Which fish bowl should we aim for?"

"The big one," she whispered.

That was one option. "Is that the fish you want? They're awfully little. If you could pick any of the fish, which one would it be?" He'd try as many times as it took, but these games were designed for the kids to win. Not too easily, but they weren't slanted heavily toward the house either.

The girl pointed at a blue and green betta fish.

"Well, let's get you that one." He handed her the ping pong ball. "Ready?"

It took three tosses, but they landed the ball in the right bowl.

The girl jumped up and down, flinging her arms around him. "Thank you, Prince Jordan!"

He chuckled and hugged her back. "That was all you, sweet girl."

After shaking hands with her parents and high-fiving her older brother, Jordan took Astrid's hand as they walked toward the next booth.

"That was sweet," she said quietly.

"I don't need to win a fish," he told her. "But she'll remember that for a long time. I know I'm not a big deal, but the kids seem to think so."

The next booth was basketball and a competition. Of the two people participating, whoever made the most baskets got the prize. The more baskets made, the bigger the prize.

"Duke's got next game!" one kid called.

It took Jordan a second to realize that meant him. It was one of the kids he'd interacted with at the dunk tank. Their good-natured ribbing had made the crowd laugh.

Someone passed him a basketball. Jordan pointed at the kid with it. "You up for a game?"

Swagger came natural to the kid. "Let's do it!"

Basketball wasn't really Jordan's sport, but he had a half-decent jump shot. At the sound of the buzzer, he took a deep breath and then his first shot. It bounced on the rim, but went in. Several balls rattled around in the return area, so he picked up the next one and shot again. It ricocheted off, a bit too short. Laser focused, he took shot after shot, but then the more practical side kicked in. He wanted to ignore the kid next to him, but this wasn't a game for him to win. If he won, fine, but it wasn't to feed his competitive streak.

The counter said the kid had one more basket than Jordan did. Good. But then he missed one allowing Jordan to pull even. "And it's a whole new ball game," he said loud enough to be heard.

Apparently, the kid was good at ignoring him. Jordan kept going, but in the end, lost by two baskets.

He and the kid shook hands and did the man hug thing. "Good job, kid."

They backed off. "Thanks. You're not too bad yourself."

"Next time, we'll try at the hockey rink. I'd take you there."

The kid shrugged. "No shock. I've never been ice skating."

Jordan clutched his chest. "Say it ain't so!"

"Nope. The rink didn't get built until I was seven, and no kids' hockey until a few years ago. They started with the younger kids so they could grow up into it."

Jordan needed to look into what he could do to help. He'd have Thomas research it - and into getting some time on the ice with this kid. "How about baseball? I can hold my own there, too."

"Some other time." Astrid took his arm. "Unfortunately, we have to take our leave. It was lovely spending time with all of you."

After saying their goodbyes, it took far longer to leave the carnival than Jordan expected. Every few feet someone stopped them, just for a minute each. He wondered if Astrid and the others planned for it. They must have because they didn't seem annoyed by it.

Eventually, they made it back to the car, and Jordan drove them back to the palace. He tapped a random beat on the steering wheel as they waited for the door to the garrison to open.

"What are you doing?" Astrid sounded annoyed, though he didn't know by what.

"What?"

"The tapping."

Jordan stilled his fingers. "Sorry. I didn't know it bothered you. I'll do my best not to do it anymore."

"It's not that."

He looked over at her, but she stared at her hands folded neatly in her lap. "Then what is it?"

The door in front of him opened, and he eased the car through.

"Nothing. Never mind."

A minute later, they were out of the car and went inside. Astrid muttered something about needing to get some work done and headed for her office. Jordan followed her, but went to his own office next door to hers. They had a connecting door, but he hadn't yet used it.

Thomas followed him in from the outer office. "How was your outing, sir?"

"It was good." Jordan glanced down and realized he'd never changed clothes after the dunk tank. "I do need something from you, though. Can you find out about the kids' hockey league here in town and see what I might be able to do to help? A scholarship fund maybe or funds for equipment for kids who can't afford it or..." He shrugged. "Whatever else there might be that I can help with? Maybe an annual clinic or something."

"I'll see what I can do, sir."

"You might look at the TimBits in my hometown. We had an NHL player come out of there in the 90s, and he's actively involved in doing stuff. Maybe something along those same lines here. I'm not NHL obviously, but it seems I've got star power, and I do know what I'm doing on the ice."

"Pardon me, sir, but what are TimBits?"

Jordan chuckled. "The kids' league in Canada. What Americans would call Little League for baseball."

Thomas nodded his understanding. "I will see what I can find."

"I think I'm going to take a shower. That's all from me for the day." He hadn't had anything for Thomas to do earlier either. He went upstairs, took a quick shower, but startled when he went into his dressing room wrapped in a towel.

His wife sat on the edge of the chair, biting her bottom lip.

"Hey. What are you doing in here?" She'd never ventured in there before.

Astrid stood and took a few steps toward him, stopping when they were inches apart.

"This," she whispered.

And then she kissed him.

Astrid curled up in her chair, sipped her coffee, and looked out over the bay. Acting on her attraction to Jordan after seeing him spend the day with all the children had surprised her more than him, though he'd been plenty surprised.

"Good morning." His gravelly voice didn't startle her.

"Good morning." She took another sip of her coffee.

She could hear the rustle of sheets as he climbed out of bed. A minute later, he sat in the other chair. "How are you this morning?"

Underlying the question was the one he had to be afraid to ask. *Do you regret last night?* "I'm good. Slept well."

She'd stopped in the kitchen and picked up some food on her way to his dressing room then locked out the world. The rest of the evening had been about just the two of them.

Jordan reached over and took her hand. "I'm glad. I know it couldn't have been easy for you to decide you were ready to move our relationship to that next level."

Astrid took her hand back and wrapped it around her mug. "I knew it was time. I've been attracted to you since you wouldn't leave my beach. I made my vows the same as you did. You're my husband. Those sorts of things belong in a marriage. And I just knew it was time." She didn't know how else to describe it.

"Do we have anything unavoidable on our schedules the next few days?"

"Not that I know of, but I'd have to ask Jade."

"What would you say if we took Sofia, and maybe Nanny Gretchen, and went to that other house for a few days? Just the three of us on the beach. Unless we want some kid-free time, in which case, Gretchen will be there."

The thought of being out of the city for a couple of days appealed to Astrid. "I like that plan. Let me see what we can work out. I do know the San Majorian Independence Ball is this weekend. We'll need to be back for that."

Jordan groaned. "I'm going to have to wear a monkey suit, aren't I?"

"With tails and a sash," she confirmed. He'd look amazing. Most of the men did, but Astrid found herself looking forward to dancing in Jordan's arms for the first time.

"Great." He reached out and rested his hand on the satin robe covering her shoulder. "As long as I'm with you, it'll be all good."

She pulled her phone out and checked the calendar. Nothing pressing. A quick text to Jade put the wheels in motion.

"Are you hungry?" Jordan stood. "I think I'm going to get something to eat."

"I'm fine. There's some of your favorite cereal in my dressing room and milk in the refrigerator in there."

He didn't leave their suite but returned with a bowl. While he ate, Astrid continued to sip her coffee in silence. A reply from Jade told her things would be ready to go in a couple of hours. Astrid and Sofia already had clothes and toiletries at the other house. A few of Jordan's things would need to be packed.

By lunchtime, her little family sat on the beach under the umbrella. A picnic lunch had been packed and kayaks waited for them to use during Sofia's nap time. After they finished eating, Jordan took Sofia to the edge of the water. They made a primitive sand castle using a cup from lunch. He carried her out into the water and let the waves splash her toes.

Sofia's giggles drifted back to Astrid. As much as Jordan clearly loved Sofia, what would he be like with their own child? Would he be any different? She wasn't sure he would. He doted on Sofia the same way she expected he would their own child. In fact, he'd probably adopt her in a heartbeat if he were allowed to. He'd never brought it up. Because he already knew he couldn't? Or because he didn't think she'd be okay with it? Or because he wasn't interested?

She'd have to ask him later. For now, he held Sofia's hand as they walked back up the beach.

"I think someone is about ready for her n-a-p. If you want to wait here, I'll run her up to the house."

Astrid nodded.

He swung Sofia up onto his back and made horsey noises as he galloped off. Her little girl's squeals brought a smile to Astrid's face. Ten minutes later, Jordan was back, stretching out next to her on the blanket.

Leaning so close she could feel his breath on her cheek, he rested a hand on her stomach. "If I kiss you while we're on the beach will it end up plastered on the front of another tabloid?"

She rolled her head to the side so she could look up at him. "I can't imagine why. We're an old married couple now. There's no scandal."

His grin and the sparkle in his eye told her what he planned before he kissed her. She noted a change in the kisses from the last time they were on this beach. They were more confident, more intimate, more purposeful.

But her husband moved away from her before things could get carried away. "Are you ready to kayak?"

The butterflies in her stomach began to settle down as he moved to stand. He held out a hand. "Come on."

They spent about an hour paddling around the cove. She could tell he held back, not even coming close to testing his abilities, but Astrid's movements were more deliberate.

"Your technique looks great." He paddled, literally, in a circle around her. "We'll have to build up your endurance and maybe next time there's a war to fight, we can kayak around the island to help stake the San Majorian claim."

Astrid laughed. "Next time we fight the war, we can kayak around the island." She pointed her paddle at him. "But, fair warning, my siblings love fighting the war as much as you did. It won't always be us that gets to go into battle."

He grasped her paddle and pulled her kayak to his then leaned over and kissed her. "Then we'll have to find something else to keep us busy that day."

18

Flirting with his wife while on vacation on a secluded beach had to be Jordan's new favorite thing to do. They kayaked the first day. Had dinner in the gazebo. Took a walk on the beach at sunset. The second day, Jordan surprised Astrid. Thomas had helped, but only because Jordan didn't know who to call. Once they walked Sofia back up to the house for her nap, Jordan made Astrid close her eyes as he led her back down the beach.

"Why exactly? What's changed in the last fifteen minutes."

"We're at the steps." He avoided her question. When they reached the water's edge, he stood next to her. "Open your eyes."

A boat sat a few feet out with a couple of people in it.

"What's all this?" she asked.

Jordan slid an arm around her waist. "We're going parasailing."

Her gasp told him it was the right move. "Really?"

"You said you love it but haven't gone for a long time. I thought we should change that." He wondered what had kept her from it, but wasn't about to push.

He barely had time to catch her as she flung her arms around his neck. "Thank you," she whispered.

It took about half an hour to get out of the cove and to the location where they would take to the air. They sat in the back of the boat, Jordan with his arm around Astrid's shoulders. He leaned close so she could hear him. "You're going solo first, then we can go tandem if you want."

"Why by myself?"

"Because I want you to have that experience all to yourself without me distracting you. In fact, if you don't want to go tandem, that's okay, too." This day was about her. If he didn't get a turn, that would be fine with him.

When he looked through the zoom lens of his camera and saw the delight on her face, he knew it had been the right move. Her smile made it all worth it.

The captain and one of the crew members worked together to let her float down and dip into the water before going back up.

"How far up?" he shout-asked the captain.

"About 1200 feet," the captain shouted back. "She looks like she's enjoying it."

"Yes, she does."

The captain glanced around as though to make sure he wasn't overheard. "It's been far too long since our princess smiled like that. We're all very glad you're making her smile again."

Jordan held the camera back up and peered through the viewfinder. "I like making her smile. It's a job I'm happy to take on."

After another few minutes, they brought Astrid back to the boat. Once out of the harness, she threw her arms around him again. "Thank you," she whispered.

He held her for several minutes. "I'm glad you enjoyed it." And he got some great pictures. He'd have to look at them more closely later.

"Go with me?"

"I would love to."

The crew got them situated in the tandem harness and in just a few minutes, they hovered high over the sea.

"It's beautiful up here." Astrid laced her fingers through his. "I'd forgotten just how much I loved it."

"Then I'm glad I could help you do this."

She squeezed his hand. "For everything else Andrei loved doing, he had an irrational fear of parasailing. I never knew why. I haven't gone in years out of respect for his wishes. After his death, I couldn't bring myself to."

Well that explained it.

"But this is perfect." She pulled him closer so she could kiss him. "Thank you."

"My pleasure."

"And thank you for arranging the massage on our honeymoon. I didn't know until yesterday that you were the one who'd done it."

Jordan shrugged. "I asked Thomas to. I didn't actually arrange it. I had no idea how. I still don't."

"But you made it happen." She kissed him again. "I don't think you knew how much I needed it that day."

They drifted downward until they dipped into the water and then the rope let back out, the breeze causing a chill over his wet skin.

Eventually they were back on their beach, Astrid's head resting on his shoulder as they lay on the blanket.

"Is there anything I need to know about San Majorian Independence so I don't make a fool of myself at the ball?" he asked, his thumb rubbing over her shoulder.

"You should have learned about it in your prince classes."

"I did, but that doesn't mean there's some obscure fact that everyone but me will know."

"Not that I can think of. It is one of my favorite nights of the year, though."

"Why is that?"

Her finger traced over the bottom couple inches of his heart scar, reminding him of the secret he still kept. He needed to tell her.

Soon.

"Because it's one of the few occasions where I get to wear something that's not boring and blah."

"Like tan or beige or brown?" He'd noticed the surprising lack of color in her wardrobe.

"Exactly."

"And you don't like dressing so blandly?"

"I hate it, but my grandmother insists we're not to draw attention to ourselves."

Then the present he'd bought her would be perfect. "You don't think it draws more attention when you don't match the rest of the people? San Majorians tend to dress fairly colorfully."

"I know this, and you know this..." Her voice trailed off.

Jordan didn't want to upset the royal applecart but maybe this was some small change he could affect. Give her the gift and let her use him as an excuse to wear it in public. Would she go for that?

Before he could decide, she kissed him. Kissed him in such a way that he decided the time had come to leave the beach and head back to their quarters.

Because the kinds of things he wanted to do with her were best done where there was no chance of cameras watching.

"I got something for you."

The blue organza skirt swirled around her legs as Astrid looked up from where she had been putting her lipstick into her clutch. A gift bag hung from Jordan's finger. "What's that?" It distracted her from how breathtaking he looked in his black tuxedo with the tails and the sash that matched her dress.

"Just something I saw that made me think of you."

She took it from him and pulled out the fabric, gasping at the sheer swirls of green and blue. "It's beautiful!" Setting the bag down, she laid the shirt out on the top of the dressing table. "I love it." The teal undershirt matched the ocean she loved, as did the swirls in the overshirt.

"Would you do something for me?"

That made her hesitate slightly, though he slipped his arms around her waist. "What's that?"

"Wear it when you go to that thing in the garden next week. If your grandmother says anything, tell her I gave it to you, and you didn't want to disappoint me."

Unexpected tears filled her eyes. "Jordan," she whispered. "Thank you." He was giving her a reason to wear the colors she loved.

"I have a feeling it's going to look fantastic with your eyes."

"I hope so." She moved away from him and put it on a hanger. "I will wear it next week."

"Good."

"But now it's time to go."

They didn't have to go far, just to the first floor and the main ballroom. With Jordan's hand in hers, they made their way to an ante room near the ballroom. Her siblings were already there. Kensington told her their parents were on their way as was Grandmother.

A few minutes after seven, Grandmother was introduced, followed by Astrid's siblings, then Astrid and Jordan. They walked through the crowd, standing and applauding politely as the royal family took their seats. A blast on trumpets preceded the introduction of her parents.

Dinner was delicious, delicacies from the waters surrounding San Majoria, fruit from their orchards, and dessert from somewhere else.

After dinner, her father gave a short speech detailing the fight for San Majorian independence from the Commonwealth of Belles Montagnes. A mostly political war, very little blood had been shed.

And then came dancing.

Her parents had the first dance. Astrid and her siblings joined them for the second one. Jordan held her far closer than any of the other couples on the dance floor, but they were newlyweds.

"I could get used to this," he murmured as they moved to the music.

"Me, too."

The way his arm around her waist held her close felt familiar and comforting, but also different and exhilarating at the same time.

His finger tapped against her waist in a familiar rhythm. She'd noticed it several times before, but this time it was too much.

"Could you not tap like that?" she asked quietly.

His finger stilled. "I'm sorry. I honestly don't realize I'm doing it."

"It's fine."

"Clearly not. It's the second time you've mentioned it."

"I don't want to talk about it right now." Right now she wanted to enjoy being in his arms.

"Promise you'll tell me later."

Astrid nodded, though she wasn't sure she could bring herself to. It was too painful. The song ended, and she passed her husband off to her mother while she danced with her father.

"How are you?" he asked. "The two of you seem to be doing a lot better."

"We are."

"That makes me happy for you both. If there's anything else your mother and I can do, be sure to let us know."

"I will. He took me parasailing the other day."

"And you loved it."

How well her father knew her. "I did."

"I never understood why you refused to go."

"Respect for Andrei's irrational fear." She shrugged. "He didn't go free climbing because I would prefer he didn't."

Her father chuckled. "Why do you think I don't skydive? My parents weren't crazy about the idea. They would have let me, but your mother is petrified."

"I never knew."

"It's part of being married. Sacrificing for each other, both to calm their fears and to make them happy."

"Should I have been okay with Andrei free climbing because it made him happy?"

"Not necessarily. Some fears are too real, and that's all right. Some you know are irrational and you have to trust the other person to know it's really okay."

"Like Jordan playing hockey?" She knew he still wanted to play whenever there was an adult game at the rink, but the chance of taking a hit to the chest scared her. He'd promised it was safe.

"Exactly."

One of her many conversations with Jordan over their days on the beach together had been about the implications of his heart transplant. He took several medicines a day to prevent rejection. He needed to not purposefully do certain high-risk activities with sudden pressure changes - like skydiving or SCUBA diving more than a certain depth. That had been a bigger deal in the early days, but he still didn't because it bothered his mother. He had to make sure he wore sunscreen as the long-term effects of the immunosuppressant drugs made skin cancer more likely. They also made him more susceptible to getting sick, though he said he hadn't had any issues with that so far.

Astrid danced with the head of Parliament then a duke visiting from Eyjania. For dance after dance, she made small talk and answered questions about how wonderful her husband was. From time to time, Jordan caught her eye and winked. Each time, she felt the color rise in her cheeks.

Maybe she would tell him the significance of the tapping of his fingers, though she didn't know how he could know to use the rhythm he did. Maybe he really didn't do it on purpose.

But mostly she was just looking forward to spending some more time alone with her husband.

Jordan hadn't danced with this many women in his whole life, combined. Fortunately, he'd picked up the basics quickly in his prince lessons. The older woman had known what she was doing, but her grumpy demeanor left a lot to be desired. Kensington said she was the one who had taught all of them.

The next woman reintroduced herself as Lady Kathleen. Jordan remembered her, but not her name, from the dinner the week before.

"It's nice to see you again." Even a vaguely familiar face was better than another complete stranger.

"And you, sir. You and the princess looked like you'd been dancing together for years."

"I'm glad to know it looks that way. We haven't had much time to practice."

"You didn't even have dancing at your wedding, did you?"

Jordan shook his head. "No. We had a dinner reception but no dancing. It's not something I've been doing long. At the wedding, I would have just embarrassed all of us."

"Then you've made wonderful progress." The music came to an end. "I believe the next dance is with your wife."

His grin widened. "I can't complain about that."

She chuckled as he moved back. "Good answer." Lady Kathleen walked off, and Jordan looked around for his wife. In just a minute, she was back in his arms.

"How much longer is this thing?"

Astrid's head tipped back so he could look into her eyes. "Why? Do you have somewhere to be?"

His gaze flickered down to her lips. Why couldn't he kiss her again? "I was thinking some time with my wife would be good."

"Your wife likes that idea."

He looked back up at her eyes and could see the desire smoldering in their ocean blue depths. "So how long before this shindig ends?"

She looked to the side. "We can leave now."

A second later, she was out of his arms, but her hand had been tucked securely in his elbow. This time, as they headed *home*, they weren't stopped by everyone and their cousin. Those near them smiled and nodded their heads, but that was it.

All eight members of the royal family were walking down the wide hall together. Astrid's grandmother didn't stay up as late as she used to and had left after just a couple of dances.

The walk was a little weird. They were having everyday discussions while all Jordan could think about was getting back to the room he shared with his wife and locking them all out.

Astrid let go of his elbow and lifted the skirt of her dress. Jordan rested his hand on her lower back for support as she climbed the stairs. The king and queen took a different route from the second story. Jordan didn't know the most direct route to the monarch's quarters. Maybe there was an elevator somewhere.

The rest of them reached the hallway with the doors to their rooms. Jordan and Astrid turned right while her siblings turned left. Jacqueline Grace and Esther went into Jacqueline Grace's door while both brothers went to their own quarters.

Jordan let Astrid take care of opening their door. He glanced down the hall to make sure they were alone.

"Hey," he whispered.

She turned back, one eyebrow raised in question.

Until he scooped her into his arms and carried her into their room. With a squeal, she grabbed his neck.

"What are you doing?"

Jordan kicked the door closed behind him. "Carrying you over the threshold. I haven't had the chance yet."

He walked through the sitting room and into their room, setting her on her feet near the bed, and kissed her.

Sometime later, they were curled together with the covers pulled to their waists. With Astrid's head on his shoulder, his fingers played with the hair at her temple. The sleeve of her pajama top whispered against the skin of his chest as her finger traced his scar.

"What was the weirdest thing about your transplant?"

"You know how they say sometimes recipients have changes in the foods they like or don't like and stuff?"

"I've heard that."

"One of the first things I really remember after surgery was *craving* chocolate covered strawberries."

"You didn't like them before?"

"I was allergic to strawberries as a kid. Not too bad. Just enough Mom didn't let me have any. The doctor told her I could outgrow it, but I never bothered to try. The reaction was a bit of a rash. I could handle that, so a few days later, I convinced Dare to get me some." He let his eyes roll back into his head a bit. "They were probably the best thing I'd ever eaten, ever, in my life, hands down. And no reaction either. So I binge on them sometimes."

Astrid's silence washed over Jordan, and he realized what he might have just done. Did Andrei love chocolate covered strawberries? Didn't a lot of people? It wouldn't be a dead giveaway would it?

She rolled onto her back and pulled the covers up under her arms. "Andrei loved chocolate covered strawberries. It makes me wonder about his recipient. Does he or she love them, too?"

Jordan didn't say anything, afraid whatever he said would be the wrong thing and give her the clues she needed.

Abruptly, Astrid sat straight up and turned to look at him. He could almost see the wheels turning in her head. "When was your transplant?"

He wouldn't lie to her and told her the date.

The second she knew, he saw the change.

"No," she whispered. "No." She scrambled out of bed. "It can't be."

Jordan didn't say anything, but pushed himself into a seated position.

"Everyone was told Andrei died more than twenty-four hours after the car accident, but that's not true. It was less than eighteen before I gave them permission to donate his organs." Tears streamed down her cheeks. "It's you, isn't it? You have Andrei's heart?"

Jordan ran his hand through his hair. This wouldn't go well.

Another realization came over her. "And you know it." Her voice grew louder. "You *know* you have Andrei's heart, don't you?" she screamed.

He nodded. "I figured it out a while ago, but I wasn't sure how to tell you."

"How did you figure it out?" She didn't scream, but her quiet tone scared him more.

"I was told the truth about his death before we got married." No point in implicating her parents just yet.

"How?" she demanded, swiping at her cheeks. "How *exactly* do you know *for sure* that you have Andrei's heart?"

Jordan sighed. No turning back now. "Your father and I put two and two together. Someone gave my family a private jet back to Canada. The only non-San Majorian recipient was a Canadian man who received Andrei's heart. Your father paid for his plane ride home. When I mentioned that, he knew."

Astrid clutched at her stomach. "All this time, you knew? I told you I could never be with someone who had a piece of Andrei, yet you married me knowing you did? You let me fall in love with you knowing this?"

Her words sank in. *You let me fall in love with you.* "I love you, Astrid," he told her. "We love each other. That's all that matters, isn't it?"

With all his heart - with all Andrei's heart - he hoped she believed that.

19

Astrid could barely see through the tears blurring her vision, but she heard his words loud and clear. "No, that's not all that matters!"

She wanted to throw him out of her room, but she couldn't think straight enough to form the words. Instead, she turned on her heel, grateful she was at least clothed for this fight. She bolted through the apartment, her bare feet hitting priceless rugs and bare stone floors before she emerged in the hallway. The door slammed behind her as she ran down the corridor to the stairs that would allow her access to her parents' quarters.

"Astrid!" Jordan's voice behind her didn't slow her down.

Neither did Kensington opening his door and asking what was going on.

The stone steps were cold under her feet, but she didn't care.

She pounded on the door to her parents' apartment with her fist. "Father! Open this door! Mother!"

"Astrid." Jordan's voice sounded behind her. "Can't we talk about this before you wake up the rest of the palace?"

"No." She pounded again. "Father!" Even if he couldn't hear

her, a member of the security team would have woken him. Nothing went unnoticed outside of their private quarters.

The door finally opened. "What's all this?" Her father stood there, looking very unkinglike.

Astrid did something she'd never done before.

She put both hands on her father's chest and pushed as hard as she could. "You knew!" she shouted as he stumbled backward. She pushed him again. "You knew about Jordan's heart, and you didn't tell me!"

A strong arm wrapped around her waist before she could push her father again. "That's enough, love."

Even angry at him, Jordan's voice seemed to have a calming effect on her. She hated that.

Then she realized her whole family was there. The slamming door, the flight down the hall, Jordan calling after her... all of it must have alerted her siblings.

She broke down, sobs shaking her body. Another arm came around her shoulders, pulling her back into Jordan's strong chest.

"No!" Astrid wrenched away from him. "Don't touch me. Don't ever touch me again."

She started to crumble again, but this time her parents were closest.

"Not you either," she ground out between clenched teeth. "Father, you don't keep secrets, which means Mother knew."

The rest of those in the room seemed to be communicating with their eyes and leaving her out. Before she could sort out what they were doing, Kensington was at her side, his arms wrapping around her as her knees gave out. He picked her up and carried her into the sitting room, the most comfortable one in the building, with the rest of the family trailing behind. He sat her in a chair, but didn't sit next to her. They had sat there together plenty of times before, so why? Because she wasn't about to land in a heap on the floor?

Because Kensington thought her husband, no matter his traitorous nature, should be the one with her?

"Someone want to tell us what's going on?" Jacqueline Grace asked.

Everyone looked at her. "Ask him." She nodded toward Jordan.

He sighed. "I have Andrei's heart. When Astrid agreed to the organ donation, I became the recipient of his heart. Your parents and I have known since before the wedding but were afraid of Astrid's reaction."

"Rightfully so, it seems," Harrison chimed in.

Astrid glared at him.

"One thing your father and I really didn't want was for her to call off the wedding because of the implications for her, Sofia, the line of succession, all of that."

"And you didn't think to tell her sooner?" Esther asked.

Jordan glared at her. "Without being too rude, the personal relationship between myself and Astrid is really none of your business. I'm not planning to comment further, even with just this group, as to the timing of the discussion at this point."

"He has a point." Her father stood. "The rest of you need to leave for now. If there's something you need to know, we'll make sure you do. But at this moment, it's mostly between Astrid and Jordan." He ushered them out of the room then returned, sinking to the couch just to the side of Astrid. "We did what we thought was best. The reasons you should marry Jordan didn't change because of who his donor was. You still would have been forced to renounce your claim to the throne and been exiled upon my death. Jordan was willing to accept the chance that you could hate him for the rest of your marriage to make sure that didn't happen."

Astrid didn't know what to think about that, but she did know she didn't want to be anywhere near any of them. Pushing herself out of her chair and to her feet, she glared at all of them. "I'm going to bed." With a pointed look at Jordan, she continued. "Alone."

Not willing to go back the way she came in case one or more of her siblings were keeping an eye out, she went to a tapestry hanging from the wall and slid behind it, not caring that Jordan knew where one of the secret passages could be accessed. She pressed against the right stone and the door swung silently inward.

Years of playing in the tunnels and her parents' insistence that she carry a mental map of them helped her back to the quarters she no longer shared with her husband. Even in the dark, her feet carried her the right way. After the narrow staircase, and counting the number of branches shooting off, she finally reached the narrow hall leading to her quarters.

When she stepped out from behind another tapestry, Astrid was in the sitting room of the quarters she'd left in such a hurry. Only an emergency light kept the room from being completely dark.

Unable, or was it unwilling, to spend the night alone in the bed, she curled up on the couch and tugged one of Sofia's blankets over her.

And cried herself to sleep.

Jordan cradled his head in his hands. He didn't want to impose on the king and queen any longer than he had to, but where was he supposed to go?

"It's going to be all right, son."

He looked up at the king's choice of word.

"I never called Andrei that. I don't know that I ever would have."

"Then why me?"

"Because I see something in you I never saw in Andrei."

"What's that?"

"My daughter's best interests at heart." He snorted. "Kind of ironic, but it's not your heart that makes you who you are, at least not your physical heart. Your metaphorical heart is a different story."

"And Andrei didn't?"

The king kind of winced and shook his head and shrugged all at the same time. "I wouldn't go that far. I think Andrei wanted what he thought was best for my daughter. I don't think what he thought and what really is best for her always aligned. You want what's best for Astrid, even if it's something that scares you or makes you uncomfortable. Andrei wasn't like that."

Jordan wasn't sure how he felt about being compared to a dead guy who had told his wife he wanted his organs donated. "I see." He wasn't sure he did.

His in-laws shared a look Jordan couldn't interpret. "There's more," his father-in-law said. "I won't get into it now. Just know that I know far more about you, or could with the snap of my fingers, than you can imagine. Even things you think are secret. Like the friend of your sister's you had a crush on as recently as a few weeks before you moved here."

Jordan had to think for a second. "Laura?"

"Yes."

"I had maybe half a crush on her a few years ago. I wouldn't describe my feelings for her, or lack of feelings, before our trip to Serenity Landing as a crush. Curiosity maybe. I thought about taking her to dinner while we were there, but crush is a bit strong." Maybe. He didn't want to delve that far back to figure it out.

"You see my point though."

"Yes, sir."

"You may assume the same was true for my last son-in-law."

Jordan thought that over. "So you know things about Andrei that Astrid doesn't. Things she wouldn't like."

The king just stared at him.

That was enough confirmation for Jordan. "What do I do about it? How do I get through to her?"

"Give her time and space," the queen answered. "Not too much. Don't disappear from her life, but don't force her to let you be around. Go to your office. Play with Sofia. Whatever you would normally do."

"I have a meeting with the kids' hockey league tomorrow. We were supposed to spend the rest of the day together." He sighed. "I'll find something else to do. Brush up on my San Majorian history. Somehow, independence didn't feature that prominently in my education the last few weeks. We skimmed over it."

The king leaned back in his chair and stared at Jordan until he grew uncomfortable.

"I've been debating something even before tonight. I believe I'm going to kick you three out."

Jordan blinked a couple times. "Pardon?"

"There's a palace on San Minoria, the second largest island in our country. I would like the three of you to move there. It's not far. You can take a boat over in about less than an hour - a helicopter in less - which will allow you to fulfill your obligations here and do things like be a patron of the children's ice hockey league. Andrei never even visited that palace. I think it will be good for the three of you to get away from here and stand on your own a bit."

"If you say so, sir."

"I'll break the news to my daughter in the morning. I'll give you a few days to wrap up things here."

They all stood and Jordan, once again, realized how underdressed he was to have a discussion with the king and queen. At least the last time he'd been wearing a shirt.

As they walked toward the main door, the king rested a hand on his shoulder. "I don't think I told you the great things I heard about the carnival. Everyone I've talked to had simply wonderful things to say. The pictures also said a thousand words. We both especially loved the one of you hugging Astrid while you were soaking wet."

"It was a pleasure, sir. The kids were easy to be around, and it wasn't my first dunk tank." He might have to print that picture just for the reminder that, somewhere deep down, she did love him.

"I know."

As they stood at the main door leading back into the palace, Jordan turned. "Where do I stay tonight? She's made it quite clear I'm not welcome in our quarters."

The king raised one brow. "Where did she sleep the first month of your marriage?"

He had a point.

Jordan just nodded. The normal sized staircase reaffirmed Jordan's suspicion that there was another way in and out of the monarch's quarters, something much more ornate. The painting of a child's room on the outside of the door to Sofia's quarters made Jordan stop and think. Wasn't it odd that they were across the giant hall from each other?

What if the little girl got up and wandered around overnight? Who knows where she would end up?

Jordan looked around the hall. He couldn't see them, but he suspected there were cameras keeping an eye on everything. Otherwise, how else would the king have known Astrid was banging on the door? He didn't know where their rooms were, but based on the little he'd seen, they weren't close.

He opened the door quietly. The first room was the play room. He texted Nanny Gretchen so she would know he was there then slid into Sofia's bedroom. At least his phone had been in the pocket of his pajama pants.

For several minutes, he watched his step-daughter sleeping in her crib. He wanted to reach out, to run a finger along the side of her soft cheek, but he didn't want to wake her.

Would he ever see Astrid holding his child? Would he ever rock his newborn to sleep?

Without any answers, he pulled the covers back on the twin bed in the corner, the one Astrid had slept in for several weeks. It seemed to take an eternity, but eventually, he drifted off to sleep.

20

"No!" Astrid hadn't raised her voice to her father in years until the night before and here she was doing it again.

"It wasn't a request, Astrid." His face gave away nothing. "You, your husband, and your daughter will be moving next week to Minorian Palace. You will remain active in the community here, but you will also become a member of that community. It's quite common for the heir to spend several years living on different islands. You know that."

He was right, but she didn't care. "You didn't make me and Andrei move away from everything I've ever known and loved."

"No. I didn't. Maybe I should have. I'd planned to wait until about now, actually. Give you a few years then move after your next birthday. Instead, you're going next week. End of discussion."

"Why should you have sent us there?"

His face hardened even as his shoulders seemed to slump. "Nothing. But it might have been good for you and Andrei to begin your lives outside the home where you grew up, where your whole family still lives."

She stood and glared at him. "And maybe we wouldn't have been in the car that night."

"You would have. You'll be back for any number of functions, and you would have attended that one."

"Andrei might not have," she protested.

"Maybe. Maybe not." She didn't think he believed that. "Regardless, you're moving next week. The press release will be sent in half an hour."

"Fine." She turned on her heel and started for the door. "But don't think I'm going to like it."

"You don't have to like it. You just have to do it."

And she would. She would loathe every minute of it, but she'd do it.

In her outer office, she noticed the door to Jordan's office open. He sat in his chair, tie flipped over his shoulder and feet propped up on the desk. Did he have any idea how old that desk was? She had half a mind to tell him, but that would mean talking to him, and she didn't plan to do that in the foreseeable future.

Instead, she asked Jade to join her in her office, instructing her assistant to close the door behind her. "Have you seen the press release?"

"Just a moment ago, ma'am."

"Do you have an issue with relocating?"

"No, ma'am. I've already spoken with Martina. She doesn't either. Thomas, Adam, and Nanny Gretchen will be moving as well."

"Good. Thank you for taking care of that."

"My pleasure."

For the next hour, they went through her schedule, noting which events would need to be canceled or rescheduled so she could fit a number of events in during a one day trip to Cabo Juan-Eduardo rather than going back and forth more often. "I would like to find out what organizations I could be involved in once we get there."

"Any idea what kind of organizations, ma'am?"

"Women and children. Expectant mothers. That sort of thing I suppose. Perhaps an organization for children in foster care. I would like my focus to be on the younger members of society and helping them, at least for the time being."

"I will see what I can find out."

"Thank you."

Jade left the office, and Astrid turned to some communications she needed to address. Emails, letters, even a phone call or two.

She didn't let her mind wander to where her husband might have spent the night. All she knew for sure was that he hadn't spent it in their quarters.

At lunchtime, she went to Sofia's playroom to eat with her daughter.

"Are you feeling all right, ma'am?" Nanny Gretchen asked her.

"Of course." Astrid sat next to her daughter.

"The prince texted me that he was sleeping in here last night. I thought perhaps he was trying to let you sleep since you weren't feeling well." The way Gretchen stared Astrid right in the eyes told Astrid what she needed to know. The nanny wanted her to know that she knew things were amiss.

At least she knew where he was.

Not like the times where...

No! She wouldn't let her thoughts go there.

She wouldn't sully Andrei's memory with her uncertainties.

For the next half hour, her attention focused solely on her daughter. By the time she rocked Sofia and read her a book before laying her in her crib, Astrid felt more at peace than she had been since the wave of realization washed over her the night before.

Why couldn't she spend the afternoon with her daughter curled against her?

Right. Because she was the Crown Princess and certain things were expected of her, like an appearance at a tea one of the local battered women's shelters held every fall to raise money.

Martina already waited in Astrid's dressing room. More boring colors, though at least this outfit was chocolate for fall instead of some variation on tan or beige.

At the tea, Astrid sat with Lady Kathleen, the third time she'd seen the distant cousin in a week or so. Had she seen her that much in the last year.

"I heard about your move, Your Royal Highness." Lady Kathleen broached the subject between sips of tea. "I think it's fantastic that you'll have the chance to be a family on your own without quite as much pressure."

Astrid nodded as though she completely agreed, but the woman's statement did make sense. The media wouldn't be nearly as intense outside of the capitol city. That was a good thing.

She plastered on a smile and made small talk with the other women at the table, but the one thing they all kept coming back to...

Was Prince Jordan as wonderful as he'd seemed? The reports all said he was wonderful with the children. Was he really like that or was it all for show?

At least she didn't have to lie. It wasn't like she could actually say, *Oh, no. He can't stand kids, but didn't he do a great job acting like he likes them? Even the kids didn't notice!*

Unfortunately, that thought had crossed her mind about Andrei more than once when she was in a snarky mood.

Jordan?

She didn't even have to pretend to lie.

And she didn't know how she felt about that.

Jordan wore a helmet this time, not because he really needed to, but because the kids were around. He was a role model, and he had to act like one.

He held up the hockey stick. "Who knows what this is?"

"A hockey stick!" All twenty voices sounded in unison.

"And this?"

"A puck!" they called.

He let out an exaggerated sigh of relief. "Good. You've got the basics down."

They all laughed, as did their parents in the bleachers.

For the next two hours, he spent time doing what he'd done best for so many years. He helped some of the kids with their slap shots, others with their goal tending, and still others with their footwork.

By the time he left, he knew he'd be a little sore the next day. He hadn't been slacking with his workouts, but these were a different set of muscles.

The announcement had been made right before the clinic that he was the new royal patron of the San Majorian Mini Majorians Hockey League. Maybe before Astrid became queen, they'd have that Olympic hockey team. He wouldn't play, but maybe he could help coach. Some of these kids showed raw talent.

Back at the palace, he didn't know where else to go, so he went to the suite he wasn't supposed to be in, took a shower, dressed in his dressing room - after refusing to let Adam help him - and reemerged to find Astrid walking in.

"I'll be out of your hair in just a minute," he told her, wishing he could run his fingers through the coppery strands.

"Thank you."

He sat on a chair and leaned over to tie his shoe. "I take you've heard about our big plans."

"My father exiling us to San Minoria? Yes, he called me into his office first thing this morning."

"I've never been there. Is the palace close to the beach?" Maybe he could get back out in the water.

"Nothing in San Majoria is far from the beach."

"You know what I mean."

"Yes. It has a stretch of private beach."

"Good." It also meant she'd have her quarters overlooking the water, just like she loved. "Do you know when we actually leave?"

"Tomorrow after church. My father moved up the timeline

about an hour ago. Apparently, there's some *thing* going on he wants us to attend so we may as well be there in time for it."

She still hadn't looked directly at him since she realized he was in the room. He finished tying his other shoe.

"I will see you in the morning then. I presume we're going to church together?" He hoped so. She'd at least have to sit by him.

"We'll see how I'm feeling in the morning." She started for the bedroom, then stopped. "The suite next door has been freshened up for you."

Ah. Her way of telling him he didn't have to sleep in the nursery. "Okay." He thought he managed to keep the disappointment out of his voice.

She disappeared into the bedroom and shut the door behind her. Jordan went back to his office and did some more research on organizations on San Minoria.

As soon as he saw it, he knew.

#StillKickin

The "about" page on the website told the story. A young man, an active soccer player and killed in a tragic boating accident, had told his parents he wanted to be an organ donor. They honored his wishes and now raised money and awareness for organ donation. Each year, a bursary was awarded to a student attending college in a health field, and they did registration drives, encouraging others to make their wishes known. They also sponsored a youth soccer team.

Jordan couldn't help but want to be involved. He forwarded the information to Thomas and told him to make it happen. He didn't want to step on any toes, but it was something near and dear to his metaphorical heart. He wanted to meet with the family of the young woman who inspired the organization and thank them for their selfless act.

He continued researching. Another youth organization or two would be good. Maybe an adult men's fitness adventure group. He stumbled across one that helped members achieve both weight and life goals, including things Jordan loved - like SCUBA diving or ziplining, that they might have been too heavy, or at least too out of shape, to do before. The website mentioned they were looking into starting a marathon training program.

When combined with what he'd just seen on the #StillKickin site, it was a perfect match. Their annual marathon, half marathon, 5K, and 1K fun run was in the spring. That was great timing for the other group to work toward whichever goal the individual wanted to. He sent that information to Thomas as well, with instructions to look into joining the two ventures. He wanted to do the marathon. It would be a challenge, but doable. And if he could get others to do it with him, all while raising awareness for organ donation, even better.

When dinner time came, he ate in his office. He probably could have joined some of his in-laws for a meal, but he didn't want to deal with the awkward looks and stilted questions.

Instead, he worked on formulating his thoughts about how he might be able to help some different groups. He called Dare and talked to him for a while, though he managed to keep his best friend from knowing about the trials he was currently going through. Eventually, it was late enough he could go to his temporary quarters without worrying about running into anyone.

Once there, he pulled out his tablet and decided to read a book. Nothing too deep or heavy, just a nice legal thriller without much romance. Surely that existed. It took a few minutes of digging, but he found one that looked good and started reading. He'd made it about halfway through before the call of nature sent him to the bathroom.

What he saw on the counter made him think. Someone - either Adam or Astrid - had made sure his medications had been moved to this room. He'd never had much of a discussion about it with Adam, and none of his clothes appeared to have been moved, so that left his wife as the likely culprit.

Maybe she cared more than she wanted to let on.

But it made him wonder. Did she care because of him - Jordan? Or because she didn't want Andrei's heart to get ruined somehow?

And did she know, or even suspect, whatever it was her father knew about his former son-in-law? Was Andrei deserving of the pedestal Astrid kept him on? After the king's statements the night before, Jordan was inclined to think not, but what did Astrid think? Would the king ever tell either one of them his suspicions?

He decided not to think too deeply on it. Instead, he took the medication, and decided to read in bed. When the book was about three-quarters done, Jordan figured out who the bad guy was. Maybe the author would surprise him, but he didn't expect him to. The whole book had been decent if predictable.

Setting his tablet on the side table, Jordan slid under the covers and wished his wife was with him.

21

"It's a great view."

Astrid turned to see Jordan leaning against the door frame to the suite he was supposed to be sharing with her. "It is." She turned back to stare out over the blues and greens of the ocean.

The waves didn't pound against the base of the palace itself, except in the most extreme weather. The cove was too sheltered, almost like the one where they'd met. From this angle, it looked more like the palace met the sea.

"Sofia will love it."

"Yes, she will." Astrid hesitated, then said something she'd meant to days earlier. "Thank you for helping her be so comfortable in the water."

His chuckle washed over her. "It was literally no trouble at all. You know I love being in the water, and she took to it quite naturally."

The scar, and all its implications, came back to her. "When are you planning to tell people about the transplant? I saw the stories after the turtle sanctuary wondering about that scar and what happened to make you need whatever surgery it was."

"They wondered about all the other scars, too. The PR people just said they didn't discuss my medical history with anyone. I'm kind of surprised it hasn't come out yet, though."

"Me, too."

"There's an organization here I want to get involved with." His soft tone surprised her. "But I won't without your blessing."

"What is it?"

"It's called #StillKickin. A young man, in his early 20s, donated his organs a few years ago. He was a soccer player and had joked with his parents that organ donation meant he'd be 'still kickin' after he was gone. I want to get involved as their royal patron, though that still sounds kind of pretentious to me, and then work with another group that gets people moving and into shape for marathons and such in time to run the #StillKickin marathon next spring. It gives me time to get in shape too."

"You're going to run a marathon?" Astrid didn't know how she felt about that. Short bursts of energy for things like surfing were one thing, but a whole marathon? Wouldn't that put a huge strain on his heart?

She might be mad at him, plan to live the rest of their marriage as roommates, but she didn't want anything bad to happen to him.

"As long as I train right, it'll be fine. I'm not just going to go out and try to do the whole thing tomorrow."

Astrid's phone buzzed on the table next to where she was standing. She picked it up and, after reading the text, closed her eyes and let her head fall forward.

"Everything okay?"

"Just some work to take care of. I'd hoped to have a few days off before getting into the mire."

"Is it anything I can help you with?"

Astrid shook her head, giving the ocean one more glance before turning around. "No, but thank you."

"Anytime."

He didn't move from the doorway, and she had to get uncomfortably close to leave the room. As she brushed past him, he stopped her with an arm around her waist. "I'm always here if you need anything." He kissed the side of her head. "I'm not going anywhere."

She didn't reply, but his words stayed with her long after she made it downstairs to her new office. It also had a fantastic view of the ocean. Unfortunately for Jordan, that meant his office did not, but only one of them could have the one with the best view.

A small inner voice protested. Her parents often worked out of the same room. Her office had plenty of room for both of them at the conference table or for a second desk when they didn't both need to be on the phone at the same time.

But not now. Maybe not ever.

Astrid logged into her computer and dealt with the email Jade had warned her about. The fundraiser, the one she and Andrei had attended that fateful night, had been pushed back to October this year. They'd been asking for weeks if she and Jordan would be in attendance. The email from her father told her she had no choice. She finally emailed them that her schedule was clear, and they would be there.

She dreaded the thought.

Not even being there with Jordan, but being there at all. She'd need a new dress, as different from the sea foam chiffon as possible. Maybe something sleek and form fitting rather than the flirty skirt from two years earlier. And not green. Maybe blue. Or orange or whatever she could find that was as far from green as possible.

She logged onto the website of one of her favorite designers to see what was in the new line that she could purchase or have modified. Maybe she'd call him up and see if he would have something he could get her quickly.

That was a better idea. Normally, she didn't bother with custom pieces, except for extra special occasions, but this needed something more than a dress modified by her seamstress.

She sent Jade a message asking her to make the call while she browsed the site.

Ten minutes later, she was on the phone with him, discussing the dress she'd found and fallen almost completely in love with. Yes, he could make the modifications she wanted. The back was really a bit too low for her taste - or her father's. And he would make it in a different color than was offered on the website. The slit up the side would also be toned down, just a bit. She didn't need that much thigh showing when she walked.

With that taken care of, she thanked him. There were already new messages, new requests for support for one cause or another. She wanted to give all of them everything they needed, but the reality was she couldn't. Despite the large amount of funds at her disposal, she simply couldn't give it away to everyone. Some of the charities were questionable. Some were worthy, but outside the scope of her mission. When she could she also chose to give some to them, but those within her passions came first. For now, those passions involved women's and children's issues.

Maybe someday she'd get back to some of the things she used to be more passionate about.

But not just yet.

Jordan sat across from the founder of #StillKickin at a local cafe.

"It's an honor to meet with you, Your Royal Highness." She looked nervous. "But I'm not sure what the purpose of this meeting is."

He stifled a sigh. Thomas hadn't told her? "I want to support your organization."

She blinked. "Okay. We're happy to have the support. May I ask why? Is someone you know still with you as a result of an organ donation?"

"You are aware this meeting is confidential, correct?"

She nodded.

After a quick glance around to make sure the only other people within earshot were his security team, Jordan leaned a bit closer. "I am a heart transplant recipient. For reasons of our own, we have chosen not to make this public just yet. We will soon." He outlined his plan to approach the other group and work together to get ready for the #StillKickin run. She was on board with that if they were. She mentioned approaching the board and offering a discounted entry fee for anyone in the other program. Being healthy both decreased the likelihood of needing a transplant for preventable reasons while also making someone a better candidate as an organ donor in the future, though a sedentary lifestyle wasn't automatically a disqualifier.

After they shook hands and parted, Jordan waited for his second meeting of the day, this one with the running group. By the time that meeting concluded, he was set to be involved with both groups, though he wasn't sure he'd officially be a royal patron for either. If he was, it was more likely to be #StillKickin.

He returned to the palace to find Astrid walking into the outer portion of their shared office. She didn't look at him, but did ask how his meetings went. After about half an hour in the office responding to emails Thomas marked for him, Jordan went upstairs to find Sofia playing with her blocks. After a few words with Gretchen, he went and changed then headed out the back door of the palace and onto the beach.

He put a life jacket on Sofia, then set her on the paddleboard. He wouldn't go out far - the waves were very mild in the cove and barely deserved the name - but she'd love it. When they were about fifteen meters out, he turned back to look. The imposing structure gave new meaning to ocean front property. On either end, the beach was blocked off by walls, partially constructed by seaside cliffs, and topped by manmade towers. About twenty meters of sand separated the base of the palace from the ocean. The bottom ten meters of the palace were windowless. The first entry point was well above where any but the largest storm surge - or possibly a tsunami - would be expected to make landfall. He imagined they could secure all of the windows and doors on this side of the palace though. Several balconies would have doors that would need to be secured, besides the one that led to the stairs down to the beach.

Sitting down on the paddleboard, he pulled Sofia back into him. The waves pushed them closer to shore until Jordan could hop off in water up to his mid-thigh. They played in the water for a bit longer before Jordan carried her onto the sand. Once on the blanket someone had thoughtfully provided, he read her a book about turtles then another about farm animals.

They went back inside and found a kitchen near the beach exit. They'd lived there for three days, but this palace wasn't as big or confusing as the one in Juan-Eduardo, and Jordan was learning his way around. Sofia sat on her knees at the bar and munched on a chocolate chip cookie. Jordan sat next to her with a couple cookies of his own.

Once done, they went back up to her new playroom. Jordan laid on the floor to play with her and her farm playset. They made the same noises they had with the book on the beach. A few minutes later, he felt like they were being watched. He looked up to see Astrid standing in the door way.

He leaned over. "Hey, Sofia. Mama's here."

Sofia's eyes lit up, and she pushed herself into a standing position, running in her toddler way to Astrid. "Mama!"

Astrid's smile was as big as her little girl's. "Hi, sweetheart. Did you go swimming?"

Sofia nodded. "My *s'im* Papa."

Jordan blinked as Astrid did a double take.

"What?" Astrid asked.

"My *s'im* Papa." Sofia pointed at Jordan.

"I'm glad you got to swim." Astrid set her back down. "Can you play with your toys for a minute?"

Jordan hopped to his feet, knowing Astrid struggled far more than he did with the honorific. "I never called myself that," he told Astrid quietly.

He could see her fighting back the tears. "I believe you. I knew she would call you that, or Daddy, or something, eventually, but I wasn't ready for it."

After a brief internal debate, Jordan wrapped his arms around his wife. "I know."

She relaxed against him for a few seconds then pushed back. "I'm fine. It just caught me off-guard."

"I still won't refer to myself as her father until you're ready for me to."

"Thank you."

Inside, he felt far differently than he tried to portray on the outside. It thrilled him that Sofia had begun to see him as her father. Another thought occurred to him. "You know, your father told me I wouldn't be allowed to adopt her as long as she retains her position in the line of succession. I would have told you I wanted to even before our wedding if I didn't already know it couldn't happen."

"Thank you for telling me that."

He wanted to kiss her but settled for taking her hand and giving it a slight squeeze. "I'm going to go for a run. If I can find the gym in this place, I'll use the treadmill. If not, do you mind me doing laps in the private portion? I wouldn't do it where there might be meetings or lots of staff members or anything."

She shook her head. "No. Go right ahead. Run wherever you like."

"Thanks." It took all his willpower to walk away, but he did.

Because in not pushing her, hopefully she'd come back to him soon.

22

Astrid stared at her reflection in the mirror. She had five minutes before she had to leave to take the boat over to the other island for the garden tea. The blue and green shirt Jordan had given her was perfect. She loved absolutely everything about it. His guess had been right, too. It did look great on her.

"Are you going to wear it?" Martina's face seemed purposely shuttered.

"What do you think?" Astrid twisted one way then the other. "What will Grandmother think?"

"Do you really care what your grandmother thinks?" Martina asked softly. "Or do you care far more about being able to break out of the confining mold you've been put in? Do you care far more about what your husband thinks, since he's the one who bought it for you?"

Mind made up, she turned and picked up the light wrap she'd need on the crossing. "I'm going to wear it."

"Good for you." The twinkle returned to Martina's eyes. "I'm sure the duke will appreciate that."

Astrid didn't respond to that comment. Martina knew things

were strained between Astrid and Jordan, that they no longer slept in the same room, though for now they shared a suite. They hadn't run into each other in it more than a couple of times so far, though.

With the wrap around her shoulders, she left the dressing room and headed for the stairs to the beach. There wasn't a pier, but a smaller boat would come right up to the sand and take her to the larger one for the journey between the islands. Once situated in the first boat, she pulled the wrap over her hair to keep it from getting blown about too badly. She would freshen up in the cabin of the second boat before they arrived.

In fact, she did that first thing. Martina had joined her for just that reason. While Astrid was at the event, Martina would take the opportunity to see her grandchildren.

Martina clipped Astrid's hair back in place. "There you go." She stared into Astrid's eyes in the mirror. "You know, if you wanted to get really bold sometime, you could get some of that fake colored hair. This outfit would look *fabulous* with matching streaks of blue or green in your hair."

Astrid laughed. "My family would have a fit, and you know it." She tilted her head and thought it over. "You're not wrong, though."

Her aide held up a bag. "Good thing I brought this then!"

Astrid gasped. "You didn't."

"Just try them. If you don't like it or your mother flips out, we can take them out before your big entrance."

Astrid bit her bottom lip and wondered if she dared. Finally, she nodded.

"Okay. We're going to do two, one on each side. They won't be stand out like if we put it on the top of your head." Martina spun Astrid's chair. "No peeking."

Astrid tipped her head to the side while Martina found the right place to clip the first strand in. It started blue and faded into green, all in one piece. She could tell the other strand didn't go exactly opposite, but close. Martina moved around to the front and fluffed and fussed over the exact placement of Astrid's hair, something she did regularly anyway.

Finally, Martina stepped back. "Okay. You can look."

Astrid turned, afraid she'd like it too much and still feel she should take them out. Instead, she gasped. "I love it, Martina! And it goes so well with the shirt!"

"Almost like they were made for each other."

That settled it. "I'm going to at least wear them to meet Mother. If she asks, I'll take them out."

The sound of the motor changed, and Astrid knew they were almost there. A car waited for her when she disembarked. The drive to the palace didn't take long. Astrid walked through the halls toward her mother's office where they were to meet. She took a deep breath and walked in, waving to her mother's assistant who just nodded and smiled.

"Good afternoon, Mother."

Her mother looked up. "Astrid! I didn't know you'd arrived yet."

Because Astrid had asked them not to inform her mother. She took off her wrap and set it on the chair. "How long until we're expected in the garden?" No sense in drawing attention to the changes. Let her mother notice them herself.

"We have about fifteen minutes." Mother pushed back from the desk. "But don't think I haven't noticed this blue and green thing you've got going on. I don't recognize the shirt. Where did you get it?"

"Jordan bought it for me. He gave it to me the night of the ball and asked me if I'd wear it today."

Her mother held out her hands, and Astrid took them. "I think you look truly lovely. Those are your colors." She leaned a little closer and squeezed Astrid's hands. "I like the hair, too."

Astrid finally smiled. "I'm so glad. I kind of love it." She let go of her mother's hands and separated her hair. "But it's temporary. It just clips in. Martina found them when she saw the shirt." Her smile faltered. "What will Grandmother say?"

Mother linked arms with Astrid. "I'm guessing she'll say her granddaughter hasn't looked quite this happy in a very long time." They started for the door. "That is the most important thing, as long as you're wearing actual clothing and not what passes for clothes in some circles." Her mother gave a delicate shudder. "You're fine."

They reached the drawing room nearest the garden a few minutes later. Grandmother waited for them.

Astrid held her breath as she underwent the visual inspection. Doing nothing but looking her up and down with only her eyes moving, Grandmother managed to intimidate. Astrid supposed it came from being queen. Her mother could do it as well, though she wasn't quite as good. Given a couple more decades, it was likely she would be.

"I like it," Grandmother pronounced. "It's about time you wore something besides those boring earth tones. No, you really just wear dirt tones. All those shades of brown. You're far too young to dress like that." She waved a hand toward Astrid's head. "And the hair is fabulous." With a pat on her own head, she continued. "You don't suppose I could pull off hair matching my outfit, do you?"

Astrid and her mother laughed. "You could pull off whatever you want, Grandmother." After giving the former queen a gentle hug, Astrid sat next to her. "But I thought that's what you wanted me to wear, all of us girls, really. You do mostly blacks and grays," she pointed out. "And Mother wears mostly muted tones."

Her genteel grandmother snorted. "I'm an old widow, and your mother looks best in muted tones. I never said any such thing. And you didn't always. It wasn't until your tenth year of schooling or so that you started wearing such bland colors."

Her tenth year? What had happened then that would change the way she dressed?

Then it hit her.

She met Andrei.

Leaning against the door frame to his wife's dressing room, Jordan shamelessly spied on her. He'd even make sure she knew he was there if she started to undress.

Instead, she was plowing through her clothes, taking hanger after hanger off the rod and tossing them into a pile.

"What did those clothes do to you?" he finally asked.

Astrid jumped, one hand clutching her chest, gripping the shirt he'd bought her. "You scared me."

"I didn't mean to." That was coincidence. "But what did all of those clothes do to you?"

"They're boring and blah. I'm done wearing boring and blah."

"I thought your grandmother insisted." Something had changed while she was gone for those few hours.

"Apparently not. She loved my entire ensemble today. Told me she didn't know where I got that idea from."

Jordan had seen a few pictures already, but up close, the color really did work well on her. "I really love your *ensemble*, too. The blue and green really looks great with your eyes." He just barely leaned into the room. "And I love the hair color."

A blush crept up her cheeks. "I kind of do, too. Martina order these hair clip things to go with the shirt. She said she'll order more once she knows what colors will go with my new clothes. I won't wear them all the time, of course, but sometimes, for fun things, I will."

"That's great."

She finally looked him in the eyes. "Thank you for the shirt, Jordan. I wouldn't have had the guts to get something like it and wear it on my own."

He bowed at the waist. "It was truly my pleasure, Princess." The title didn't seem to annoy her like it sometimes did, but he wasn't being snarky either.

"I really do love it. Did it come in any other colors? Because I just might buy up every option they have. Where'd you get it anyway?" She went back to pulling most of the hangers off the rods.

He named a boutique a few blocks from the palace on the other island. "To be perfectly honest, I sent Adam for it. I saw it when my car stopped at a light next to the store, but I didn't want to draw too much attention to what I was doing. Adam has daughters and a wife. He could have been shopping for one of them. Plus, I had no idea what size you wear. I told him which one, but he took care of the rest. I don't know if they had other colors. That was the only one on display in the window, though."

Astrid stared at him for a long minute. "Well, you did good. It was a great choice."

"Thanks."

She turned and looked at the growing pile of clothes. "I'm going to need to go shopping."

He pointed to another pile on the other side of the room. "Those aren't bland."

Once back to pulling hangers off, she spoke again. "But those are gowns I wore to events with Andrei. I'm not opposed to rewearing clothes, but I don't want to wear those again."

Because they would remind her too much of what she'd lost and of Jordan's perceived betrayal.

"I understand your logic," she went on, oblivious to his thoughts. "I don't agree with it. I think you and my parents should have told me and let me make an informed decision, but I do understand why you didn't. I'm not just going to be able to forget that and move on."

Jordan noted the way she worded it. She didn't imply she would be able to eventually move on. No, she implied she wasn't going to be able to move on at all. He didn't have to accept that. "What are you going to wear to the Women in Medicine dinner in a few weeks then?"

"My favorite designer is already working on it. The dress will actually be similar in color to this shirt."

"I'm glad to hear that." He needed to find out more about it, and decided to do so before he forgot. "I'll leave you to your closet clean out. I did want to remind you that the mayor and his wife are coming for dinner this evening. It'll just be the four of us, and fairly informal."

She nodded and pulled a dark brown outfit out, looking it up and down before putting it back. "I did know that, but it had escaped me. Thank you for the reminder."

"I'll see you in a bit then." At least she wouldn't change into pajamas or shorts and a t-shirt for dinner. Even with the relaxed standards on colors, that would mortify her.

He went back to his office and talked to Thomas about finding information on the fundraiser.

Thomas shifted in his seat. "I'm not sure what you want to know, sir, but that's the event the princess and Prince Andrei were on their way home from when the accident occurred. She didn't attend last year, but is attending under pressure from her parents. It was always one of her favorite organizations. She's still their royal patron, but she hasn't actively been involved with them since. No one really knows why, though the assumption is that it's because of the accident."

Jordan thanked him then went into his office and called his mother-in-law. If anyone would know and could help him piece it together, she could. Twenty minutes later, he had some of the answers he needed and a plan in place, with the queen's approval, to help make it a special night for Astrid. To take her mind off what she lost and hopefully, bring back her passion for the organization.

Whistling, he headed for the drawing room next to the small formal dining room. Though an informal dinner, the only informal dining areas were in the kitchen or the private quarters. The mayor and his wife weren't friendly enough to be on that level just yet, and probably wouldn't ever be.

Thomas motioned for him to go on in, though Astrid hadn't arrived yet. Jordan shook hands with first the mayor, then his wife, and invited them to have a seat while they waited for Astrid, who would be along shortly.

Though nearly petrified he'd say or do the wrong thing and offend the mayor of his hometown for the foreseeable future, Jordan found himself quite enjoying the conversation. At least he wasn't screwing this up.

23

The sounds of laughter reached Astrid as she approached the drawing room. Thomas waited outside.

"The duke is in there already, ma'am."

"I figured that's what the laughter was from." She didn't really like the man. There wasn't anything wrong with her husband's assistant per se, but Astrid was glad she didn't have to work closely with him. Or maybe she was just grumpy. She put on her best smile and entered the room. "Good evening, everyone."

All three of them stood. Jordan greeted her with a kiss on the cheek before introducing her to the other couple. The four of them sat down and small talk commenced. Nothing too deep or serious before dinner, but there were definite undertones Astrid wasn't quite used to. This was her father's area of expertise. She needed more practice. Maybe that was why her father insisted on the move.

After about fifteen minutes, an announcement was made. The four of them moved through the large door and into the dining room. The table had been made smaller, more intimate, with enough room for six or eight, but only four places set, one on each side. She preferred this to the way King Benjamin had them seated for that dinner, though she knew it wasn't always possible.

The lively conversation kept up throughout the meal. Astrid found she liked the mayor and his wife both, but once dinner ended, she and the mayor had some business to discuss. They all went out onto the balcony overlooking the ocean, but while Jordan and the mayor's wife went to the railing to look out and make more small talk, Astrid and the mayor took seats near the wall.

"What is it you would like to discuss?" she asked him, taking a sip of her wine.

"Exactly what your plans are while you live here, ma'am. We're most happy to have you, but we'd like to coordinate activities wherever possible."

She wasn't exactly certain what that meant. What kind of coordination? "I'm still making my plans as far as what kind of events I'd like to be involved in." Did he not want her attending certain charity or other functions because her attendance would overshadow his own? "If you would have your office discuss any concerns with my assistant, we will see what we can work out." She wouldn't skip a function just because it irritated him, not if it was something important to her.

He continued to press, though quite politely, but she held firm. When she invited him to join their spouses, he shook his head.

"I do believe we must be going. We have young children at home, and we both prefer to be there to tuck them in. We don't have a full-time nanny, of course, so we do have more limitations on our late-night hours."

The barbs tried to wound, but Astrid didn't let them. "I will keep that in mind next time we need to talk. Perhaps an intimate dinner setting isn't most appropriate. I'm certain you and I can conduct our business over the phone during regular office hours." So much for liking them. "Jordan, darling," she called, using the sweetest voice she had. "I'm afraid our guests need to leave."

Jordan motioned politely for the other woman to precede him. Astrid needed to talk to him about that. Sometimes it was appropriate. Other times, he needed to remember he was a Prince of San Majoria and some people would take his politeness as a sign of weakness. He didn't necessarily need to stop doing it, but he did need to be aware.

Thomas appeared out of nowhere to escort the mayor and his wife to their vehicle.

"Darling?" Jordan whispered in her ear once they were gone. "You've never called me that."

"He was being annoying. Insinuated we don't love Sofia as much as they love their children because we have a full-time nanny and must not make a concerted effort to tuck her in every night."

"He doesn't know what he's talking about." They started for their suite, with its third bedroom, turned playroom/nursery for Sofia.

"I know this, and you know this. He was quite rude. Subtle, but rude. So I made sure they would have the opportunity to tuck their own children in. In the process, I also made sure I'll be able to tuck my daughter in."

She looked in the nursery, but no Sofia. "Do you know where she is?" she asked Jordan.

"Taking a bath, maybe? I'm not sure."

Astrid headed for the bathroom, aware that Jordan didn't follow her. The door to the other room opened as she neared it. Gretchen came out with a freshly bathed and pajamad Sofia.

"Mama!" Sofia leaned away from Gretchen straight into Astrid's arms.

"You look so clean, sweet girl" She hugged the little girl close and nodded to Gretchen.

"My *baf*."

"You took a bath." Astrid swung her in a circle, making the little girl squeal. "That would explain it. Would you like to read a book?"

"Boo'!"

Astrid settled into the rocking chair. Once Sofia was snuggled against her, she picked up one of the books from the basket on the floor. Together they made animal sounds, then read about a llama and his pajamas, followed by saying goodnight to the moon and stars.

Sofia's head had grown heavy before the last book ended. Astrid carried her over to her crib and laid her down. Kissing her fingers, she placed them on Sofia's still damp hair. After making sure there was nothing in the crib except her blanket and stuffed turtle, Astrid left the room, pulling the door mostly closed behind her. Gretchen had likely already left the other direction.

Jordan's door was closed. For a minute, she thought about knocking and seeing if he wanted dessert. They were supposed to have had it after the conversation on the balcony, but that hadn't happened.

In the end, she decided to go straight to her room and get ready for bed.

In the morning, Jordan closed the door to his office and opened his photo editing software. He couldn't believe Astrid hadn't noticed him taking pictures of her with Sofia the evening before.

He'd manage to capture her spirit and laughter in the pictures where she spun Sofia around the room. Her tender side showed through as they rocked and read books. She loved her little girl more than anything. The mayor was crazy to insinuate she didn't.

He spoke with the king and outlined his plan for the fundraiser. The king approved and told him he would need to talk to the head of the organization. He edited the next picture while he waited for Thomas to get the foundation president on the line.

"Good morning," he said when the phone rang.

"Good morning, Your Royal Highness." There was unexplained amusement in the woman's voice. "It's very good to talk to you again."

Jordan wasn't sure what to make of that. "I'm sorry. I haven't caught your name."

"Dr. Catherine Lyttelton."

His jaw dropped, and he was glad no one was around to see it. "Dr. Lyttelton? I had no idea."

"I will admit to being a little surprised I hadn't heard from my favorite Canadian in a while."

Jordan chuckled. "I'm not Canadian anymore." Or was he? He hadn't renounced his citizenship or become a naturalized citizen of San Majoria yet either. He should probably discuss that with his wife, though it couldn't be a very big deal if no one had mentioned it yet.

"Imagine our surprise when we saw the news stories."

"You're not the only one, believe me."

"Does your wife know when your transplant was?"

"We've had discussions about my heart." Surely his doctor knew who the donor had been, but he didn't want to confirm it.

"I see."

So, they were going to dance around it. Fine by him. "It will be good to see you at the fundraiser."

"Agreed. But now that you're here in San Majoria, I expect to see you at least once a year. Preferably not more than once at the office though."

"Yes, ma'am."

"Now, to what do I owe the pleasure of this call?"

Jordan outlined his plan again.

"And you have the blessing of the palace?" she clarified.

"Yes."

"In that case, we would be honored to work out the details with you. Have your people get in touch with my secretary. We'll set up a time where we can all meet, either in person or via video conference if you can't be here, and go from there."

"Thanks, Dr. Lyttelton."

As they hung up, Jordan glanced at his watch. He had an hour. By the time he needed to leave for lunch with one of the city aldermen, he'd edited several pictures. He just needed to figure out how to make it all work.

Lunch went better than dinner the night before had. The Board of Aldermen seemed thrilled to have royals in residence in their city again. They hadn't on a permanent basis since the king took the throne.

Jordan wasn't sure what kind of decisions he was allowed to make as a royal, so he took notes and told the man he'd be discussing everything with his wife and get back to them to make actual arrangements. It seemed the board, in their enthusiasm, wanted Jordan and Astrid involved in absolutely everything. That seemed a bit much.

After leaving the luncheon, he headed to the park where he was to meet with the head of the local amateur photographers' club. He hadn't realized "Chris" was a woman, and made extra sure they stayed in full view of the playground and parking lot at all times. He didn't need anyone insinuating he was cheating on his wife. Jordan didn't want to be involved in leadership or anything like that, but he did want to be involved. They met once a month for a class from a professional photographer then practiced the technique they'd just learned. They met one other time a month just to take pictures. He doubted he'd make all the meetings, even the classes, but he would make an effort.

Their next meeting was in a couple of days. They would be at the park shooting wildlife, something Jordan wasn't particularly interested in - at least not the kind of wildlife they were likely to encounter at a park on San Minoria. It would be a good way to practice, though. He told Chris he would try to make it but needed to check his calendar.

Back at the palace, he found a package he'd been waiting for. With a grin, he went up to their suite and found Sofia. He settled on the floor in front of her. "I've got a present for you."

"Wha' da'?" She pointed at the box he'd brought with him.

"This is for me and you." He tugged at one flap until the tape broke, then the other. Finally, he pulled the package out. "This is for us to play hockey."

"Yockey?"

"Yep." He handed her one stick. "This pink sparkly mini-stick is yours." His step-daughter loved pink and sparkles. "The blue one is mine." He pulled the net out and turned sideways to assemble it. "We try to get the puck in here." He picked up the foam ball. "This." Standing to situate the net a few feet away and kicking the packaging off to the side, Jordan then knelt behind her. "Here we go."

He helped her hold it and turn sideways to hit the ball into the net. "Good job!" He let go of her, so she could go get it.

"My do!" She wrenched away from him.

Jordan chuckled. "Okay. You do it."

He leaned backward to avoid getting hit in the face with the stick. They'd work on technique later. It took several tries, but eventually she connected, and the ball sailed into the net.

"My win!" Sofia turned to hug him.

"You did it! You're a natural! The next Hayley Wickenheiser!"

"My do 'gin!"

Jordan moved back a bit and watched her hit the ball into the net over and over.

He could get used to this.

24

Astrid watched from the doorway as Jordan and Sofia played hockey in the playroom. They didn't notice her, so she left, not wanting to interrupt their time together.

She went back to her office, a bit unsure what to do with herself, since she'd blocked out the time to spend with her daughter. Before she could decide what to do, her door opened, and her mother breezed in.

"Good afternoon, darling."

Astrid stood. "Mother. What are you doing here?"

"I popped over to visit a friend and couldn't leave without stopping to see you."

"I'm glad you're here." She gave her mother a big hug then closed the door, certain her mother wouldn't want this conversation, whatever it would be, overheard by Jade or anyone else.

"What makes you think that was necessary?"

Astrid simply raised an eyebrow as she took a seat on the same side of the desk as her mother.

"Fine. When I told your father I was stopping by, we agreed I would discuss your marriage with you. How are you and Jordan doing?"

Astrid shrugged. How had she forgotten how mad she was at her parents? More her father, but a minute ago she'd been so grateful to see her mother, that it escaped her that she was still supposed to be mad. Of course, she'd been too caught up in the new shirt and the hair when she'd seen her the last time to remember then either. Maybe falling into the regular routine was easier with someone she didn't see often?

Or someone she didn't feel as betrayed by?

"It's a new normal," she finally said.

"And does that new normal include a real relationship with your husband? Or are you roommates?" Her mother held up a hand. "I'm not asking about intimate details, but are you working toward fixing things or just leaving them be?"

With a sigh, Astrid stood and walked to the window overlooking their mini-cove. "There's more to it than all that, Mother."

"More to it than Jordan not telling you who his heart donor was?"

"Yes."

"Are you ready to talk about it?"

Astrid thought that over then decided that, no, she wasn't. She shook her head.

"When you are, we're here for you. You know that."

Something in her mother's voice made Astrid turn. Did they know more than they were letting on?

"Your father and I are debating attending the Women in Medicine banquet this year," her mother went on, as though no turmoil existed internally for Astrid. "We wouldn't want to take away from you as the patron, but make it clear we're there to support the cause more informally. What do you think?"

Images from that night, both before and after the accident, ran through Astrid's mind. "I think I'd rather not go at all."

"I'm afraid that's not an option." Her mother's gentle tone reiterated what Astrid already knew. "You will be there, head held high, and smile."

"At least portray that I'm enjoying myself. I know." Which was why her father's words to her in the hallway the night Andrei died had stunned her so.

"You never know. You might end up having a decent time. Now, before I go find my granddaughter, something was mentioned to me in passing the other day, though I know far more was meant by it."

Astrid turned, her shoulders slumping further. "What? How I'm supposed to have another baby sometime soon?"

Her mother's delicately arched eyebrow told her all she needed to know.

"Who said something?"

"The prime minister."

Shocking. "If he mentions it again, would you kindly tell him my reproductive plans are none of his business?"

"I will not, because, to an extent, it is his business. Though the law requiring you to have at least two children is no longer technically in force, the law that replaced it strongly implies that you must."

"I'm aware of that. But what if I end up with secondary infertility?" She crossed her arms over her chest. "Then what?"

"That is an exception, and you know it."

She did. "Regardless of how well my relationship with Jordan is or is not going, I'm not ready for another child."

"I know that, but it has been mentioned to you nonetheless." She stood. "You are in the main living quarters, correct?"

"Yes." Astrid followed her mother out of the office and upstairs. When they reached the playroom, Jordan and Sofia were laying on their stomachs looking at a book.

Sofia pushed herself up and picked up the book. "Mama! Papa *boo'*!"

Astrid didn't look to see her mother's reaction to Jordan's honorific. "You got a new book?"

"Papa *boo'*!" Sofia held it up in one hand, her arms extended for Astrid to pick her up. "*Yockey.*"

Astrid looked at the book. "A hockey book?" They made such

things in board books? He'd probably had Dare ship it to him. It seemed like a Canadian thing anyway. "That sounds fun."

Before she could respond, Sofia noticed her grandmother and squealed again as she pulled away from Astrid. Her mother took the toddler and sat in a chair in the sitting room, reading the book to her.

Jordan came to stand next to her, his presence filling her senses.

"I saw you playing hockey earlier," she told him. "Sofia seemed to be having fun."

He laughed. "She was. Her form needs some work, but she'll get there."

"Does that mean my daughter will be on the future women's hockey team from San Majoria?"

"You never know."

"She loves you." Astrid leaned her head back against the wall. "I knew she was missing out on having a father, but I don't think I really understood how much she needs that father figure in her life."

"I'm not just a father figure, Astrid. For as long as she'll remember, I'm her father."

"I know, but you know what I mean."

Before he could say anything else, Sofia called to her, and Astrid was spared whatever else the conversation might bring. She just wasn't ready for it.

With a growl of frustration, Jordan pushed back from the desk.

It wasn't working.

He picked up his phone and flipped through the contacts until he found the right one. There was no answer, so he sent a text instead.

At least he had full access to the good photo manipulation software these days. Too bad he didn't know how to use it.

Rolling his chair back to the desk, he opened one of the other programs - the one he'd been using for years that he'd found for under a hundred dollars online.

With it, he could sort of do what he wanted.

His phone buzzed. Swiping across it, he breathed a sigh of relief. "Hey. Thanks for calling me back. I could use some help if you have time."

After half an hour on the phone, it still wasn't working.

"Would you mind coming by?" he finally asked. "Whenever is convenient for you. It's probably something simple that I just can't figure out."

Chris laughed. "Most likely. Seems like it usually is. Don't worry. We'll get it figured out in time for Christmas."

"Thanks."

They made arrangements for the photographer to stop by a couple of days later when Astrid wasn't supposed to be home. Jordan didn't want to hide anything from his wife, but he also didn't want her to know what he was doing. That would kind of ruin the surprise.

As he suspected, Chris was able to fix what was wrong in three clicks by setting a menu, one Jordan didn't know existed, to viewable.

"I knew it was something simple." He leaned back in his chair, movement outside his open office door catching his attention. Jade was already back. Astrid might not be far behind.

Chris spent several minutes explaining how to do what he wanted, walking him through doing it with two different pictures.

"I think part of my problem is I don't understand the one setting on my camera." He pulled it over from where it sat on the side of the desk. "How does this even work?"

She took the camera from him. "Is there a balcony or something we can use? I can show you."

Jordan pushed back from the desk and stood. "I'm sure we do."

For the next hour, Chris walked him through some of the camera settings, taking pictures of inanimate objects, then ones of

Chris to get practice with a real person. Those would get deleted as soon as he knew what he was doing. He wouldn't want Astrid to find them and get the wrong idea.

"Papa!"

Jordan let the camera hang from the strap around his neck. "Hey, kiddo. What are you doing down here?" He picked up Sofia. "Did you have a good nap?"

"No nap!" She fiddled with his collar.

Gretchen laughed. "She took a nap."

Jordan kissed Sofia's forehead. "She just hates them. I understand." He set her on the sofa. Was there a different name for one so fancy? "Can I take your picture, Sofia?" She was a little ham. She'd love it.

Sofia grabbed the back of the sofa and jumped. "Yay!"

He laughed and pulled the camera back up to his eye. Click after click, he took pictures of his step-daughter, the one he'd adopt in a heartbeat if he could.

Chris helped get Sofia situated in several different locations around the room, then out on the balcony, though far away from the railing. He wanted to get some pictures in her playroom, but he wasn't comfortable taking Chris up there. He'd have to practice elsewhere.

Jordan held Sofia in his left arm as he shook hands with Chris as she left. With his camera still around his neck, they went to Sofia's room. When he set her down, she went straight to her mini-stick and began practicing her swing.

He sat on the floor, his elbow propped on a knee to steady his camera and began taking more pictures.

If he could just keep the project a secret for a couple more months, he'd be able to surprise Astrid at Christmas.

25

Visions of Jordan with another woman danced in Astrid's head as she stared out the window of her office and willed the tears to stay put. She'd returned an hour earlier than expected to find them huddled around the computer in his office, though they hadn't noticed her.

When she'd worked up the courage to go find him, introduce herself because surely it was an innocent thing and no reason for her to suspect the worst, she'd found him taking pictures of her in the Green Reception Room.

All of it combined to be more than she could handle. Returning to her office, door locked behind her, she felt safer. Away from what could hurt her. It took nearly half an hour to get herself under control, to convince herself there was another explanation, though she wouldn't be able to bring herself to ask Jordan about it. Not yet. Maybe someday.

When she left her office, he was back in his, with Sofia in tow. The little girl toddled around, her little hockey stick in hand, and hit the ball all over before deciding to lay on the floor to color.

"Hey!" Jordan stood as soon as he saw her. "When did you get back?"

Astrid shrugged, but accepted his light kiss. "A little while ago."

"How'd the tea go?"

"Fine. Same as always." She sighed. "They're all about the same sometimes. Different food, different faces, same person on display."

He slid his arms around her and pulled her close. She didn't want to, not until she understood what had been going on, but she still relaxed against him. Her hands clasped together at the small of his back.

"I don't like that you feel like you're on display." He kissed the side of her head.

"It is what it is. People see what they want to see, and a member of the royal family at an event is on display."

"Still doesn't mean I like it." His hand rubbed up and down her back. "I wish everyone could just see the real you and not the princess they want to see."

Astrid wasn't going to hold her breath. No one had ever really seen the real her, except maybe Jordan those days on the beach, before he knew who she really was.

Not even Andrei.

Struggling to hold in a sigh, she moved back from the comfort of his embrace. She still wasn't ready to go there with him, even before seeing him take pictures of another woman.

"It's the way things are."

Sofia finally noticed her. "Mama!" She ran over for Astrid to pick her up. "My miss you."

"I missed you, too."

Sofia laid her head on Astrid's shoulder. Astrid closed her eyes and soaked up her daughter. Sofia saw only her mother. She didn't know anything about what made them different from everyone else.

At least there was one.

"I have to go back to work." Astrid hugged her daughter a bit tighter. "I'll see you for dinner, okay?"

Sofia squeezed then wiggled down and went back to her coloring.

Jordan turned off his monitor. "I think we're going to go upstairs." He gave her another quick kiss. "We'll see you in a bit." He held out a hand. "Come on, munchkin."

Astrid went into her office and stared out the window again. The little cove looked so much like the one where she met Jordan. With supreme effort, she went to her desk.

By the time she left her office, Jade and Thomas were both long gone. She stood in the door to Jordan's office, staring at his computer. What could he have been talking to the strange woman about?

Shoving her conscience to one side, she went and sat in his chair, turning his monitor back on.

No password was required. Astrid frowned. She'd need to have someone talk to him about that, but what she saw surprised her.

The folder held picture after picture. Tons of pictures of Sofia from earlier in the day came first. Then a few of that other woman, but they seemed... different somehow. Soulless almost.

And then...

Photo after photo of Astrid herself.

Some were of her with Sofia, rocking and reading a book or playing on the floor. A couple of her with her daughter at their wedding. Even a few on the beach in her wedding dress.

But then... more pictures of just her. Some had clearly been taken on his phone, but something about them...

Astrid perched on her heels talking to a little girl who held a bouquet of flowers.

Astrid on the phone in her office.

Astrid laughing at something unseen.

Astrid in her pajamas reading over some paperwork in the big chair in their sitting room.

Astrid on the beach the day they met, though she had no idea how he managed to take the picture without her knowledge.

Picture after picture as Astrid had never seen herself before.

As no one had ever seen her before.

As she scrolled back to the top, a picture of her with Sofia caught her eye. They were laying on the twin bed in Sofia's room. Astrid held a book over their heads. Sofia pointed at something, and they were laughing. She remembered the moment a couple of weeks earlier. She didn't remember what was so funny, but she remembered having a hard time controlling her laughter.

This.

She'd wanted this for so long.

What she'd spent her life wanting.

Someone to see her.

Really see her.

Whether she was in her pajamas or with her daughter or meeting the public or conducting business, Jordan really saw her.

Maybe the time had come to trust him with the truth.

After paddling close enough to shore, Jordan climbed out of his kayak. Astrid had come to the beach, sitting on a blanket, but not wearing the swimsuit he would have expected. Pulling the kayak far enough up the beach that it wouldn't wash away, he left it and went to sit next to her.

He didn't say anything, and Astrid didn't seem to be inclined to either. In fact, ten minutes passed before she did.

"We met on a beach a lot like this."

Where was she going with it? Had he forgotten some anniversary or something? "Yes, it was. The imposing palace was a bit further away."

"You wouldn't have come into the cove if you'd seen a palace."

He thought about that. "I might have. I was pretty worn out by then."

"When you said something about knowing you couldn't go any farther, you meant your heart, didn't you?"

It had to come back to that somehow. "Yes and no. I was in good shape. I'm in better shape now, though I'm not ready to run that marathon yet or anything. But sometimes, occasionally, I get tired more quickly than I'd normally expect, things like that. I've learned to listen to my body and know when I can push through and when I can't. I'm much more likely to listen now than I was before the transplant. Some of that is probably just getting a bit older and not being quite as stupid as I used to be. Some of it is probably the transplant."

"I see." She wrapped her arms around her legs. "There are a couple things we need to talk about."

"Okay."

"First, my parents had planned to attend a wedding in Ravenzario but have asked us to attend instead. Queen Christiana is getting married in a few days. We won't be there long. Just long enough to attend and leave that evening. We'll be gone less than thirty-six hours most likely."

"Okay." How old was this queen anyway? Surely not that old.

"We'll probably be seated with the Eyjanian representatives. My father will want us to pick up any bits of information we can. He's still worried about Benjamin's uncle having too much influence."

"I think you'll need to explain all that to me again later, so I know what I'm supposed to be looking for." He couldn't keep the politics of all of it straight.

"I will on the way."

"The second thing is a bit more difficult to talk about."

Jordan leaned his weight back on his elbows. "I can wait."

The silence lasted a few minutes. "The prime minister has mentioned to my mother that we are expected to produce another heir soon."

"And it's his business because why exactly?" It infuriated Jordan that others were so interested in their plans to have more kids or not.

Astrid launched into an explanation of ancient laws not fully repealed and their implications on the heir presumptive, which seemed to be a gender-neutral term for Crown Prince or Princess.

"So basically, they all think it's their business when we have a kid," he interrupted.

"Basically."

"And they got your mother to do the dirty work."

She nodded.

Jordan pushed back up to a seated position, and wrapped his arm around her shoulders, pulling her closer. "Don't worry about them, Astrid. It'll happen when it's supposed to happen and not before."

His wife surprised him by relaxing against him. "I know."

"Besides, isn't it still possible there already is another heir on the way?" The thought had occurred to him several times, but he hadn't found the opportunity to ask.

"Possible, but I don't think it's likely. I think I would have some clue by now."

That both relieved and saddened Jordan, but he could do nothing to change it.

"Andrei was cheating on me."

Her blurted admission caused Jordan's heart to stop in his chest.

Andrei's heart.

He'd never know how he managed to control his reaction, but he did and waited for her to go on.

"I think he was. If he wasn't, he would have been in before long."

"What makes you say that?"

"I saw him several times talking to one of the maids. When I asked him who she was, he shrugged it off like he was asking her for something innocuous. I asked her separately, and she said they'd dated once upon a time. The look on her face was too much, though. I knew there was more to it than a couple of old friends who dated catching up. They were standing too close together, glancing around too much, and too much guilt on her face when I asked her how they knew each other. That wasn't the last time either. I don't know for sure they were sleeping together, but it seems unlikely they wouldn't have at some point." She blew out a breath. "I was already pregnant with Sofia by then. I hoped a baby would put a stop to it."

He kissed the top of her head where it rested against his shoulder. "I'm so sorry, honey."

"You know how you crave strawberries sometimes?"

Where was she going with this? "Yes."

"What if it's more than just food cravings or aversions? What if the way his heart wasn't solely mine also means your heart isn't solely mine?"

Tears began to fall onto his bare chest. "Oh, Astrid. There's a big difference between a food craving and cheating on my wife."

"I know."

"But that's part of why you could never be with the man who had Andrei's heart, right?" So much made sense.

She nodded.

Jordan shifted until he could cradle her face in his hands and look her in the eyes. "This heart, my heart, is yours. Now and forever." Not waiting to see if she'd push him away, he leaned down and kissed her softly. "You are the only one for me, the only one I'll ever kiss, the only one I'll ever love."

Her tear-filled eyes stared into his as he brushed the moisture off her cheeks. "You mean that?"

"I do. I love you, Astrid."

"Oh, Jordan," she whispered. "I love you, too."

26

When she went to the beach, Astrid hadn't decided if she was going to tell Jordan about Andrei or bare her soul like that, but she was grateful to find herself in her husband's arms again, even if they didn't do more than share a few tender kisses before falling asleep together several hours later.

Well, Jordan had fallen asleep. She still stared out the window into the night.

The trip to Ravenzario could be good for them. They would have thirty-six hours more or less alone. A few of the hours would be spent at the wedding and reception, but most of it wouldn't be. They would fly overnight, freshen up at the consulate, attend the ceremony, mingle while waiting for the reception to start, mingle some more during the reception, then fly home.

She'd never actually met Christiana or the other young royalty from the Commonwealth of Belles Montagnes. It made her far more nervous than meeting with Benjamin had. Of course, she probably wouldn't do more than say hello to most of them, if that.

Eventually, she dozed off.

A couple of days later, they boarded the plane. Prior to take off, a text came in, something Astrid had completely forgotten about. She smiled, texted back, and slid her phone into her pocket.

"What's that grin for?" Jordan sat next to her on the couch.

Astrid leaned her head against his shoulder. "Nothing you need to worry about. A girl's got to have some secrets."

He muttered something she didn't catch, then spoke up. "I saw an article this morning."

"What about?"

"You and your sudden change in fashion. They quite love it. I know my sister does. They're all wondering what brought about the change, though."

"They can keep wondering, but I've had several comments about it myself." She yawned. "As soon as we take off, I think I'm going back to the bedroom to go to sleep."

"I'll probably join you before long."

The plane started to taxi and soon she'd fallen asleep in the bedroom. She woke to the news they were about an hour from landing. They didn't need to be ready for the wedding, but did need to be ready to be seen.

She emerged from the bedroom to see Martina looking a bit anxious. "What is it?" she asked.

"There's been a change of plans we weren't informed of. Your mother's assistant thought we'd been CCd on the emails, but we hadn't. We'll be landing on Biansola Island where the wedding is taking place. They've asked we not deplane for a while, but we won't be going to the consulate."

"Do you have everything we need to get ready on board or was some of it waiting for us there?"

"I think we have everything, just in case we were delayed for some reason."

"Good. Then there's nothing to worry about. Unless there's not enough coffee."

Martina finally relaxed. "We have plenty."

"Good."

Astrid sat on the couch and buckled in. "What else do we need to do?"

"Nothing really."

She dismissed Martina with a nod and turned on her phone. Two more texts confirmed the plans she'd put in motion several weeks earlier. Jordan would be in for quite a surprise when they returned home.

He wandered out of the bedroom, looking adorably mussed. Like he'd pointed out before, his hair did the messy thing quite well.

"I just heard from Dare," he told her with a yawn. "They're not going to be coming this weekend after all."

"That's too bad."

"I knew we wouldn't get to see them today like we'd talked about, but at least we'd get to see them Sunday." He buckled his seatbelt then leaned his head back. "We were going to celebrate Canadian Thanksgiving, too. I'm bummed."

"I know. You miss him and your family. I get it." She filled him in on the change of plans.

"Where exactly is this Biansola Island?"

"It's situated between the two main islands that make up Ravenzario, not too far south of the northern island actually. It has a private landing strip on the Baicampo property. That's a property owned by an American family, but holds the chapel where every Ravenzarian monarch in forever has gotten married."

"And who's she marrying?"

Astrid shrugged. "No one knows. It's a very closely guarded secret. Father even said he doesn't know."

"Then this could be an interesting wedding."

"It sure could."

"Were any of these royal people we're supposed to rub elbows with at our wedding?"

"No. It was short notice, and a relatively small ceremony. We invited Benjamin and the families from Islas del Sargasso and

Auverignon and a couple of others, but none were able to make it."

"Will Prince Richard be there?"

"I would imagine so. Christiana lived with his family for some time after the death of her parents when she was a child."

Jordan winced. "That's awful."

"And not the worst of it. Her little brother, who was the heir presumptive, and their nanny were also in the car when they went over the cliff. Her uncle took over as her regent but retained considerable power even after she turned eighteen. It's only been eighteen months or so since he was arrested. That's a big part of the reason why Father wants more information on Isaiah in Eyjania. He and King Alfred were close. Technically, we're related, if you trace the lines back far enough, though it's been centuries since there's been a marriage between our families. He's afraid Isaiah is much the same as Henry."

"And Isaiah was Benjamin's regent."

Astrid shook her head. "No. Isaiah is the youngest of three children. Benjamin's father was the oldest and king at the time of his death. The second child, their sister Princess Louise took over as Regent. From what I've gathered, she did her job. Prepared Benjamin to take over then let him, but Isaiah still seems to have undue influence. That's what we're supposed to be on the lookout for. Anything that can help Father understand the inner workings of the Eyjanian palace."

"Got it. I'll see what I can do."

The plane landed smoothly and taxied to its parking spot. When it was time, stairs would be rolled to the door for them to exit. They had an hour until Martina needed to start doing her hair.

Astrid decided to spend that time talking to her husband, and wished they'd had more time when it was over.

Jordan forced himself to keep his fingers away from his ascot. Otherwise he'd tug it loose, and one thing he didn't want to do was embarrass Astrid. This was his first real, official function on an international stage as her husband. He even wore a vest and learned what an ascot was.

But... did he flip the tails up like some guy sitting at a piano when he sat down? Or did he sit on them?

Why hadn't he thought to ask - or Adam to tell him? He'd try to observe some of the other men and see what they did.

"Jordan?"

He turned, keeping Astrid's arm tucked in his elbow. A grin crossed his face when he realized who was walking toward him, then he bowed. "Princess Ellie."

"Didn't I tell you not to call me that?" She smacked his arm. "But you do clean up nicely." The princess leaned closer and whispered. "Almost as nice as my husband."

Jordan looked around. "Is he here?" Maybe he could ask Rick.

Ellie scanned the side room where it seemed all of the royalty had been sequestered. "I don't see him. I'm sure he'll be here shortly."

A slight squeeze on the inside of his arm, brought him back to the present. "Ellie, this is my wife, Crown Princess Astrid of San Majoria." He'd probably screwed up who to introduce to who and how.

The two women shook hands, though Ellie did nod slightly, probably deference to Astrid's higher position in the line of succession than the one Ellie married into.

"It's a pleasure," Ellie said. "I have to admit, we were all shocked to hear the news so quickly after we met in Serenity Landing."

Jordan let Astrid take the lead. "We met not long after his sister's wedding. When something is right, it's right. It was a bit of a whirlwind."

Ellie wrinkled her nose. "We would have loved to see you again, but Rick reminded me that you had far more important things to worry about than inviting some random people you met for a few days a month earlier. I'm glad to have run into you, though. How are Dare and Betsy?"

Jordan gave her a brief update, but wondered why they hadn't been invited. Astrid said she'd never met them before. But weren't pretty much all royalty - at least Western-ish royalty - friendly? He'd have to ask Astrid later.

"Jordan! It's good to see you, my friend." Rick appeared and shook Jordan's hand, giving him a guy hug. "How are you?"

Ellie took care of introductions before he could answer. Rick also bowed his head a bit. Being gentlemanly? Or a hierarchy thing?

"Hey, Rick. I've got a question for you." Jordan glanced around to make sure no one else would hear.

"Where's the best place to ski in Ravenzario?" Rick asked with a grin.

"Not this trip," Jordan answered, looking around again. "What do you do with these tails when you sit down?"

Rick laughed. Ellie smirked. Astrid hid annoyance. What was that about? Who else was he supposed to ask at this shindig? Rick knew his background.

"Don't sit on them. You'll be uncomfortable. Move them to the side or flip them sort of back so they hang over the back of your chair."

"Good to know. Thanks."

"Hey, if you've never worn tails, how would you know? Better to ask than be uncomfortable for an hour because you don't want to draw attention to yourself by maneuvering. Ask women how hard it can be to make sure you sit down right."

Jordan looked at Astrid, who didn't look back. She looked gorgeous, though he didn't expect any less. It just looked like a nice dress, though. Nothing overly formal, but he was changing for the reception later. Maybe she was too. This was, technically, a morning coat. Later, he'd wear an actual tailcoat, complete with white bow tie and royal sash.

He'd gotten a glimpse of her dress while on board.

Shimmery pink, so light it was almost white except it wasn't.

He'd been surprised when she hadn't worn it.

She would look amazing, and he'd look like a guy who just pulled an extra fancy monkey suit out of his gear bag, trying to fit in with the rich kids.

"Your Majesties, Your Royal Highnesses, and honored guests," a woman with a clipboard said forcefully. "You will be entering momentarily. When I call your name, please come forward and line up here." She motioned in front of her.

Royalty lined up?

Apparently so.

Jordan and Astrid were near the front of the line. Probably based on some obscure ranking system he knew nothing about - age, proximity to relevant throne, home country's relationship with Ravenzario, and who knew what else. He noticed that King Benjamin and his sister, one of the twins - but not the same one they'd had dinner with, were a few people behind them. The uncle wasn't present.

"Oh, he's got to be mad," Astrid breathed.

"Who?"

Before she could answer, the doors opened, and the couples filed in. An usher directed them to the right when they reached a row near the front. A program sat on the seat. He picked it up before sitting down. He noticed Astrid looking at hers, so he did as well, though he didn't recognize any of the names, save Queen Christiana's.

The wedding wasn't that much different from most weddings, though there was no call to kiss the bride. Instead, the newly designated Prince Alexander, Duke of Testudines pressed a kiss to Queen Christiana's forehead. When Jordan asked Astrid why, she said the first kiss was on the balcony of the palace.

Once the wedding party and family left, the rest of those in attendance were dismissed by row. They followed the crowd toward a building a short distance away.

"Apparently, the chapel has water damage and couldn't be used today," Astrid told him. "The barn, which hasn't ever been used as an actual barn, was the replacement. We'll be mingling for a while in the smaller ballroom. Those of us staying for the reception will have made arrangements to change for the more formal dinner."

"And we're doing that back on the plane?"

"No. We have the use of a cottage on the property. All of our things should have been moved by now."

For the next hour, they ate appetizers and mingled with those who hadn't already made their way to the larger island.

Eventually, they went back to the plane where they had an hour or so to change. Astrid apparently had to get her hair completely redone too. Wouldn't do to have the same hairdo at both events, unless you were the bride. The queen would look the same, apparently.

And he would wear more clothes he barely knew the names of, but he'd have the most beautiful woman on his arm, so it was all worth it.

27

"Who were you talking about earlier?" Jordan asked.

Astrid winced as Martina tugged on her hair. "When?"

"Right before we walked into the ceremony. You said he'd be mad."

She'd heard murmurs from a couple of others, though no one said anything outright. "Isaiah, from Eyjania. He's wasn't even in the room with us. I heard he's present, which means the powers that be in Ravenzario have decided he's too far down the line of succession to 'count.'"

"How far down is he? He's a prince. Brother to the late king, right?" Jordan lay on the couch in the sitting room of the cottage, wearing shorts and a t-shirt. He needed much less time to prepare.

She winced again as Martina pulled a little too hard. Her hair better look fantastic. "I'm not certain, but he's at least eleventh. Benjamin has nine siblings, then Isaiah's older sister Louise, then any of her children and even grandchildren. I'm not sure if she has any at all, much less how many there might be. So, he comes after them. Another option might be that only official representatives from countries they're not as close to were included."

"There were a bunch of Montevarians in there. And the other country." He laced his fingers behind his head and crossed his ankles.

"True. But they are all part of the Commonwealth of Belles Montagnes. The last generation of kings, including the current king of Mevendia and the former king of Montevaro who retired just over a year ago, were all quite close. Christiana spent several years in Montevaro growing up. I believe she spent some time in Mevendia as well, though I'm less certain of that."

"Isn't San Majoria a former Commonwealth protectorate? Wouldn't that give you a closer relationship with them than some of the others?"

Astrid sighed. "Was there ever anyone in your life where that person was more important to you than you were to him or her? A girl you had a crush on maybe?"

Jordan nodded. "Yeah. I guess."

"It's like that. San Majoria fought for our freedom from the Commonwealth, though it was much more a political battle than a bloody one. They're important to our history. We are a footnote in theirs."

"I see." His foot tapped against the cushion of the couch. "I remember learning about that, but didn't understand the modern implications."

"Honestly, I'm surprised Isaiah was invited at all. In fact, if the muttering I heard from a couple of people is accurate, he wasn't, but they didn't want a scene."

"And this is why he wasn't at our wedding?"

She would have nodded if Martina hadn't tugged her head another direction. "He wasn't invited. Benjamin didn't come either, though. In fact, the only members of any royal family there was my family."

"I didn't think I'd met any there."

"You didn't." She heaved a sigh. "Are we almost done, Martina?"

"I'll be done when I'm done," her stylist muttered around the bobby pins in her mouth.

Jordan raised his eyebrows. "It looks fantastic."

His sarcasm made Astrid roll her eyes. "It will. Martina always makes it look great. You should probably go get dressed, though. Once she's done, it'll only take me a couple of minutes to change clothes."

He went into the bedroom and closed the door behind him. A few minutes later, Martina finished her hair. With no one else in the cottage except Jordan, Astrid changed out of her shorts and button-down shirt, letting Martina help her slide the dress over her head.

The sliver heels shimmered as she slid her feet in as Jordan walked through the door.

"Does this look ri..."

She looked up to see why he'd stopped mid-sentence, only to see his wide eyes and hear his whistle. Not a wolf whistle, but an appreciative one.

"You look fantastic, Astrid." He came closer, his eyes sweeping up and down her body then fastening on hers. "I'm pretty sure no one's going to notice if I've got this tie wrong."

Astrid finally let herself check her husband out. He looked nice. Very nice. "Very handsome," she told him, taking a step his way. With an ease borne of years of practice helping her brothers, she straightened his tie.

"Thank you."

After a long, slow kiss, she stepped back, and gave him a mock glare. "It's a good thing I didn't put my lipstick on yet." She did just that, slipped it into her clutch and turned. "Ready?"

They went back to the barn which had been transformed for dinner and dancing. On the walk over, Jordan had admitted to being scared he'd screw something up, but he did wonderfully. Christiana and Alexander both looked radiant. Christiana's gorgeous dress with the Ravenzarian blue accents was simply fabulous. Astrid didn't get to say more than hello to them, though.

As the night wound down, she danced in her husband's arm, and the tapping began again.

"You're doing it," she whispered.

His fingers stilled. "I honestly don't notice I am. I'll try to be more aware."

Astrid sighed and took his hand. They went outside to a private spot a short distance away from the barn. "It's not that. Andrei did it. As did I occasionally. It was our little way of saying something to each other." She rested her hand on his arm. One tap. Four taps. Three taps.

"I love you," he said before she could.

"Exactly." She felt her face color as the other code they'd used flashed through her mind.

"What is it?"

One tap. Four taps. Two. Four. Five taps.

"I have no idea what that one is."

She couldn't look at him. "I wish we were alone."

But Jordan pulled her close, a maddening grin on his face. "I could get on board with that."

That helped Astrid relax. "Unfortunately, we will be on board the plane with several other people, so we won't be alone until tomorrow night." And not then either, though he didn't know that.

Just like he didn't know she really had remembered what special occasion it was.

He kissed her. Another long kiss, but not as slow. Deeper, more meaningful.

Cheers sounded in the distance, and he moved back.

"It appears the bride and groom are headed out." His husky voice sent chills up her spine.

"Then it's time for us to head home," she whispered. If the next day went as planned, then, just maybe, they'd get their alone time the next evening after all.

Jordan felt better than he expected after two nights on a plane. Of course, it helped he hadn't flown coach. The bed hadn't hurt either.

The flight landed in Cabo Juan-Eduardo. They'd reunite with Sofia, have breakfast with Astrid's family, attend church, then take a boat to San Minoria.

Sofia was excited to see them. Astrid and her father carried on a hushed conversation on one end of the table while everyone ate. Likely about Isaiah and what they had learned about the prince, which wasn't much. She'd explained even more on the way home, and he understood better why the king was uneasy about the whole thing. Henry Eit, Christiana's uncle, had siphoned money, neglected the infrastructure, and indirectly caused the deaths of numerous people when a medicane hit the southern island. Princess Anastasia and her husband, the pediatrician, both of whom had been at Dare and Betsy's wedding reception, nearly died in that storm - or at least were trapped and waded through waist deep water at times. They, along with the orphaned girl they'd eventually adopted, survived, but it seemed like it had been a close thing at times.

King Edward wanted to make sure there was nothing along the same lines going on in Eyjania.

Jordan, with the little he knew, thought it would be harder for Prince Isaiah. Isaiah hadn't been the regent. Benjamin's mother was still alive, along with his many siblings. And King Benjamin seemed to have a much better support system than Queen Christiana did.

He talked with the rest of the family while keeping his ears open for any nugget of information he could overhear from Astrid and her father - and for any comment about the other importance of the day.

Nothing.

They went to church, then Astrid asked him to take her to the boutique where he'd found her shirt. They went, Sofia in tow.

"What about this one?" Astrid asked, holding up a light green shirt. "I want to try it on, but I like it."

"This way, Your Royal Highness." The man, who had introduced himself as one of the owners, practically tripped over himself to open the dressing room door. "We were so honored to see our shirt on you." He lowered his voice. "It sold out online in a matter of days."

Astrid gave what Jordan called her princess smile. The polite one that didn't reach her eyes. "My pleasure. But you can thank my husband. He's the one who saw it and procured it for me." She went into the changing room and emerged a moment later in the same shirt she'd been wearing. "I'll take this one."

She walked around and chose a couple of others, but didn't try them on. They checked out, then took the boat to San Minoria.

Something was off about his wife, though. Jordan couldn't put his finger on it, but she became more preoccupied with her phone the closer they got. Normally, they would walk up the beach and the stairs together, but she hurried ahead, leaving him to deal with Sofia.

He didn't mind, but it was odd.

By the time he and Sofia, who insisted on walking up the stairs herself, made it to the doorway, Astrid was long gone. Inside, Thomas waited.

"Your presence has been requested in the White Drawing Room, sir."

Jordan didn't reply but headed that way. Something seemed very off.

Before he could put his finger on it, he reached the White Drawing Room and walked in. It seemed deserted.

The puzzle pieces were there, but he wasn't assembling them fast enough. And then...

"Surprise!"

Jordan took a step back and clutched Sofia's hand a bit tighter, ready to scoop her up and run.

But then the faces and the laughter registered.

Dare. Betsy. His parents. His in-laws.

His laughing wife.

"We got you!" Dare called from his spot near a sofa.

Jordan's heart began to resume a more normal beat. "Yes, you did. Not necessarily the best idea for a guy with a borrowed heart."

Astrid's face fell.

"I'm fine," he rushed to reassure her. "It's a Dare thing. I give him a hard time whenever he does something that startles me." He glared at his best friend. "Like tells me he wants to marry my sister."

"Really?" Astrid stepped to his side, and he slid his free arm around her waist.

"Really. There's nothing to worry about." He kissed her. "Was all this your idea?"

She nodded. "Happy birthday."

He kissed her again. "And here I thought everyone forgot." Releasing Astrid and Sofia, he greeted his family, giving them all big hugs. His in-laws all got a hug as well. He turned to his wife. "This is why you wanted to go shopping. To give everyone time to get over here."

Astrid shrugged. "You got me. But I do love shopping, too."

Lunch was served in the same dining room where they'd had lunch with the mayor, but the table was much larger with room to seat all thirteen of them. Astrid and the king even gave him the seat of honor. Dare told him not to get used to it.

Loud and boisterous, two words he never thought would describe lunch with the royal family, but perfect for a meal with his, though the addition of eight extra people made it more like when he had hockey friends over. His mom would make all the food, and they'd plow through it like nobody's business.

When lunch ended, they went back to the drawing room. Gretchen started to take Sofia to put her down for a nap, but Dare stopped her. Presents had appeared while they were eating.

"We brought a present for Miss Sofia," Dare explained, handing her a box.

Jordan sat on the floor and helped her open it.

Sofia squealed and pulled a plush moose out of the box. "*Moo'*!" About two feet tall, the Mountie Moose looked quite snuggly, and Sofia hugged it tightly.

"She needs something Canadian," Dare told him with a shrug.

They all laughed and sent Sofia with Gretchen and Mountie Moose to take a nap, before turning to the rest of the presents.

"This one's from us," Dare told him handing him a box.

"I don't get a present from each of you now?" Jordan asked sliding a finger under the paper.

"Deal with it." Dare grinned as Betsy rolled her eyes.

The box was nondescript but as soon as Jordan opened it, he knew what was inside. "My skates!" The ones he'd spent years getting just right. "And you got them sharpened."

"Of course. I doubt you have a good skate sharpener down here."

"The one at the rink's supposed to be decent, but nothing like Bob. He's the best."

Jacqueline Grace handed him another box. "This is from me and Esther."

Jordan knew what it was as soon as he removed the paper enough to see the exterior of the box. "New skates. That's great!" How did he tell them he really did appreciate the thought?

Both sisters just smiled at him.

The next one was from his brothers-in-law and as soon as he saw the package, he knew it was another new pair of skates. They seemed unperturbed by the duplicate gift.

Something else was up. When would he be let in on the big secret?

Instead of dwelling on it, Jordan went to the next present, letting his subconscious try to figure it out.

28

Nerves swirled around in Astrid's belly. The presents both families had brought for Jordan were nice, but the truth was she could outdo them all.

Or it could all flop horribly.

Finally, he'd opened all of them.

But she still hadn't decided which one to give him first.

Astrid stood. "My gift isn't here. Neither of them are. Well, there's kind of three," she amended. "You're all going to have to follow me." Most of the rest of the families knew about one or two, but few knew about both, and her siblings were as in the dark as Jordan. She held up a scarf. "But you're going to have to be blindfolded."

Dare hooted, and Jordan glared at him, but took the scarf and tied it around his eyes.

She took his hand and led him a roundabout way to the garrison. Once they were all inside, her brothers stifled their gasps.

"Seems like whatever it is will be good," Jordan said.

"It is," Kensington told him.

Astrid reached up and loosened the scarf, letting it slip down.

"Yes!" Jordan turned and picked her up, swinging her around.

"You brought my car!"

She laughed and held on tight. "And your truck, but yes, we had your car shipped down here."

He set her down but took her hand and led her over to it. "Check it out."

Astrid thought it looked like a cool old car, but the way Jordan ran his hand over the hood she knew it meant more to him.

"This is the Flying 8 radiator cap hood ornament I told you about." He pointed to it. "And check out the wheels."

She looked and hoped she sounded properly impressed.

"Feel the seats."

Jordan opened the door, and motioned for her to sit down. He'd been right. "It's very comfortable." She climbed out and let her father and brothers gawk. She went to stand by the women. Even Dare and Chris were at the car.

"The three of them rebuilt it," Betsy explained. "Dad and Jordan did most of it, but Dare helped when he was around."

"It looks cool."

Betsy laughed. "You have no idea. I wouldn't either if I hadn't been thoroughly indoctrinated over the last few years. He'll love having it here even if he doesn't get to take it out often."

It took nearly twenty minutes for them to finish their inspection of the vehicle. Jordan came back and gave her another big hug. "Thank you, Astrid." He kissed her right in front of both families. Nothing too intense, but enough to let her know he would like her plan for later.

"One more," she told him. "If you're ready to leave your car."

"Lead on, Princess." He kissed her again and reached for the scarf. "Do I need this?"

She shook her head. "Not this time."

Everyone followed her to a door in the basement. Both of Astrid's hands pressed against her stomach in an attempt to calm it down. "I hope you like it."

He pried one of her hands loose. "Hey. Whatever it is, I'm sure I'll love it."

"It's a compromise," she admitted. "Not what I'd really wanted to get you, or what you'd really want, but what I could get that would work as best it could."

Jordan shot her a puzzled look. "Okay. Where is it?"

"Open the door." The light should already be on.

He twisted the knob and tugged, peeking through the crack. "Is that what I think it is?" he asked before throwing the door open. "Ice!" He picked her up again. "You got me an ice rink?"

She held on and waited for him to put her down. "It's synthetic. A real ice rink would be too costly and difficult to maintain."

Jordan rested his hands on the door frame and leaned inside. "Still. This is fantastic!" He turned back around. "Is this why I have three pairs of skates now?"

Astrid nodded. "It was Dare's idea. He brought you yours, freshly sharpened for when you go to the actual rink. The other two pairs are for you to use here. I know the synthetic ice is a lot harder on the blades, so when one pair needs sharpening, you send it to Dare and use the others. Then trade. That way you shouldn't ever be without a pair."

He hugged her again, this time just holding her close. "I don't know what to say," he whispered. "Thank you. I can't begin to know how I can match this for your birthday."

"You don't even try. You find something you think I'll love. It has nothing to do with money or anything else. Just the thought behind it."

With one hand, he cupped her cheek then kissed her, more thoroughly than he had earlier. Somewhere her other senses heard her brothers and Dare acting like teenagers, but then someone ushered them all away.

"You really like it?" she whispered when the kiss ended. "I know it's not as good as real ice..."

"Real ice is beyond impractical," he reassured her. "That room is good sized. It's not hockey rink sized, but almost half. I'll be able to do plenty of skating in there."

"Sofia and I both have two pairs of skates now too," she told him.

"Perfect. We'll bring her down here soon, and I'll work with both of you. You'll be skating circles around me before you know it."

Fingers laced together, they went back to the White Drawing Room to hang out with the rest of the family. She wouldn't begrudge Jordan his time with his. They wouldn't be able to stay long. Originally, the surprise party had been planned for Friday before her parents left for Ravenzario so they could be there. Jordan's family would stay through the weekend. Instead, they'd come Friday anyway, spent time with the rest of her family, then traveled to San Minoria while the rest of them were at church.

She sat next to Jordan, her head on his shoulder while conversation flowed around them. Finally, she felt truly at peace.

Jordan stood on the balcony, his forearms propped on the railing.

"You finally told her." Dare stood next to him, leaning against the rail with his back to the sea.

"A couple weeks ago. It didn't go well, but not for reasons either of us would have imagined. And that's all I'm going to say about it." He wouldn't violate his wife's confidence.

"I understand, but I'm glad you got it out in the open."

"It's been rough, but she finally confided in me the other day. Everything makes a lot more sense. I think we're back on the right track." He glanced over at his friend. "I half-expected you two to tell me I'm going to be an uncle."

Dare shook his head. "Not in the plans anytime soon. You?"

Jordan stared over the water. "We haven't really talked about it, though there are those that expect it sooner rather than later."

"I see."

Jordan wasn't sure Dare did, but decided not to elaborate further. "I wish you guys could stay longer."

"We do, too, and not just because Bets is excited about staying at a palace. We'll come back sometime soon, or you could come home. The flight's not that long."

"I will. Probably not for a while, but eventually."

"Need to feel established here before you go home?"

It never failed to amaze Jordan how well Dare knew him, could almost read his mind. "Something like that."

"I'm glad things are going well, though. I saw the pictures of Astrid at the garden thing in the blue-green shirt with the hair. Betsy made sure to show them to me. She said you had to have gotten her the shirt or encouraged her to wear it anyway."

"I did. When I gave it to her I said I hoped she'd wear it that day, but it was ultimately her decision. The hair was all Martina."

Dare turned around, his posture mimicking Jordan's. "You've been good for her."

"I hope so."

"I think she's been good for you, too."

"Probably. Isn't that how a marriage is supposed to work?"

Movement below caught Jordan's eye. Someone had been setting up blankets and umbrellas so they could enjoy a barbecue on the beach instead of a more traditional Thanksgiving dinner, but this was different. He leaned forward as the shadow reappeared. "Is that Sofia?" he asked Dare.

Dare leaned over, too. "Looks like a little kid."

"Where's Gretchen? Or Astrid?" He didn't see anyone else out there. Leaning further out he could almost, but not quite, see the base of the palace. Someone could be standing up there, and he'd never know it. "Sofia!" he yelled.

She stopped and looked up.

And waved.

Then headed for the water again.

"Something's not right." He looked again for an adult, then back at the piece of his heart wandering closer to the water.

Jordan didn't wait to see if there really was someone else out there. He pushed off the rail and bolted for the door, Dare hot on his heels. Inside, the rest of the family stood around, right in his way.

"Move!" He didn't wait for them to and probably knocked the king over in his hurry, but didn't look to see if the other man was okay. More than one employee was knocked into a wall or pushed out of the way as he went down corridors and staircases until he reached the door to the beach.

The door propped open by a rock.

He couldn't see where Sofia had been from here. Umbrellas blocked his view of that stretch of shoreline.

God, please!

The clatter of footsteps down the stairs behind him told him it was no longer just him and Dare, but they were likely the best prepared.

His dress shoes dug into the soft sand, Dare passing him then going to the left while Jordan went right.

There.

His heart fell when he saw her little body, still and face down with waves washing over her.

"Sofia!" Jordan was at her side in seconds, but he feared they were already too late. He scooped her up, not caring the sea water would likely ruin his expensive shoes and that the bottom of his pants were now wet and would soon be coated with sand. He ran back toward the building. He needed a hard surface, not the sand. "Get her out of here!" he yelled to the king whose arms were around Astrid's heaving shoulders. "We need room."

He laid Sofia down on the sidewalk thing near the stairs. Dare knelt across from him as Jordan leaned down to see if his little girl still breathed.

"She's got a pulse," Dare told him. "You count."

Jordan realized tears were streaming down his cheeks as Dare leaned over to try to breathe life into the little girl. He didn't know what he was supposed to be counting, though. They weren't doing chest compressions. Dare would breathe until she coughed, or he needed someone to take over.

"EMS is on their way."

He looked up to see the king standing there behind Dare, though everyone else had moved back. Before he could say anything, movement on the ground caught his attention.

Sofia coughed.

Jordan helped Dare roll her onto her side as water gushed then trickled out of her mouth. The thump of chopper blades grew closer until an emergency services helicopter landed up the beach.

Emergency personnel emerged, running toward them backboard in hand. By the time they reached the patio, Jordan cradled a crying Sofia to his chest. In a few words, he explained what happened. The EMS personnel laid her back down, talking softly and reassuring her.

"We're going to take her to Children's Hospital on San Majoria," one of them told Jordan. "One of you can accompany us. The rest will have to meet her there."

"Two will," the king said. "A member of security will go with you as well."

The man nodded.

Jordan ran a hand through his hair as he paced near them. He glanced at the water to see the boat used to ferry them back and forth already approaching the shore. "Astrid!" he called. "You need to go."

She nodded and moved away from Kensington who had been holding her back. Before she started across the sand she stopped, gave Jordan a quick hug, and whispered, "Thank you for getting to her."

Before Jordan could reply she was gone, walking across the sand with one of the other EMS men supporting her. Two others strapped Sofia in.

She still cried, heart-wrenching sobs.

Jordan could only pray he'd reached her before any permanent damage had been done.

29

Astrid had been in a conference room at Children's Hospital alone for at least ten minutes before the doors burst open, and her family poured in.

"How is she?" more than one of them asked.

She shook her head. "They took her as soon as we got here. I haven't seen her since."

Her mother was first to her side, wrapping her arms around Astrid. "She's going to be fine."

"You don't know that." Tears began to fall again. "None of you do."

Her father pulled them into his embrace. "We're praying. Whatever happens, God will give you the strength you need."

"Didn't you tell me that before?"

"A few times."

None of which were in her top ten memories.

She pushed away from her parents and looked around. "What happened? How was she on the beach unattended?" Was it her fault? "Where's Gretchen?" Wasn't the nanny supposed to be watching Sofia?

"Gretchen said she was in the sitting room the whole time," her father told her. He'd likely been getting updates non-stop. "She's with security now, looking at the video to see if they can figure it out."

"The door was propped open with a rock," Jordan told them. "I thought it wasn't supposed to be left like that, ever, for security reasons."

"It's not." Father crossed his arms over his chest. "They're reviewing the tapes from that area, too. Someone is about to lose their job, at best. At worst, they'll be charged."

"Charged?" Astrid couldn't imagine this being anything but a horrible accident.

"Neglect, most likely. Dereliction of duty is possible." Her father rested his hands on her shoulders. "There's going to be a police investigation, sweetheart. They're going to have to ask all of us a whole bunch of questions. We're going to have to make official, legally binding statements, and we're going to have to hold at least one press conference before it's over."

She tried to soak that in. "They're going to say it's because we were neglecting her, aren't they? That she was unsupervised, and we're horrible parents. We're going to be arrested and charged with neglect, too, won't we?"

"No!" Her father's stern tone made her head snap up. "Whatever happened, it was a tragic accident that could have been so much worse. Jordan and Dare were on their way to the beach before she made it to the water." He touched his eye which she could see swelling shut. "How many other people can say they gave the king a black eye with no consequences whatsoever?"

"Sorry about that, sir." Jordan didn't sound sorry in the slightest.

"Nonsense. If you'd waited for me to get out of the way, I would have asked for an explanation, and it would have taken far longer to get down there. As long as Sofia is okay, we'll be laughing about the time you knocked your father-in-law, the king, on his butt for years."

Betsy stood next to Jordan, her arms around her brother. Astrid wondered why he hung back, why he wasn't at her side? Did he blame her? She already did, even without knowing what happened. What kind of mother didn't know where her child was? What kind of mother allowed her child to wander unsupervised around a palace, then slip unnoticed down that huge staircase leading to a beach? It would have taken her at least five minutes to get down the staircase on her own. Were there cameras out there, too?

"Whoever propped the door open, why would they?" Dare asked the question.

"I'm guessing it was to get the beach ready for us to be out there later. We were supposed to have a barbecue for Jordan's birthday and Canadian Thanksgiving."

"Then why was that person inside so long that he or she didn't see a toddler on the way up or down? That had to have taken half of forever," Betsy chimed in.

"We're looking into it." Her father's hand cupped her shoulder. "We'll find out exactly what happened, but whatever it was, it was *not* your fault. I want to make sure you know that."

"And if the police decide otherwise?"

"They won't."

He couldn't guarantee that. One thing she knew for certain - her father wouldn't interfere with an investigation or its results.

The door opened again, this time letting a doctor in. "Astrid Cordova?"

Astrid took a step forward. "That's me."

The doctor looked up, her eyes widening as she looked around the room. "Oh, my." She curtsied to the room as a whole. "I had no idea."

That had to be good news. She wouldn't be talking about not knowing who they were if Sofia was critical. "How's my daughter?" Astrid asked, trying to get back on track.

"Well, I had no idea who she was, but that wouldn't have changed our course of action. A member of security has been with her the entire time, but..." She shrugged and looked at her clipboard. "She's going to be fine. Probably sore and tired for a few days, but otherwise we don't see any immediate signs of long-term issues. We'll keep her here for a day or two and run some more tests to be sure, but I don't see anything that indicates any long term damage. Whoever got to her, got to her quickly." She tilted her head as she looked near Astrid, but not at her. "Has anyone looked at your eye, sir? I know we treat kids, but I'm certain we can make sure you're not looking at something serious."

"My physician will later," her father told the doc. "It's annoying, but not unbearable."

"Still, make sure you get it checked out and there's not damage to the eye socket."

"I will."

The doctor turned back to Astrid. "Princess Astrid, would you like to see her?"

Astrid started for the door. "Of course." She expected Jordan to follow her, but he hung back. Why? Because he wasn't Sofia's father?

"Jordan, why don't you go with her?" Her father took charge of the situation. He was good at that. Would she be when it was her turn to be monarch? If this was her grandchild?

"If we both can, and Astrid wouldn't rather one of you go with her." Did he not want to see Sofia?

"You both can," the doctor answered.

Astrid looked at him, pleading with her eyes that he come. She needed him.

By the time she exited the room, he was on her heels, then held her hand as they followed the doctor.

The little voice in the back of her head had been buzzing since she first saw Jordan and Dare fly through the room. As soon as she'd seen them, she'd known something was seriously wrong, but it finally registered what the buzz had been.

She'd been praying.

Without realizing it, without ceasing, she'd been praying for her little girl.

Now to see if the prayers had been answered.

Jordan hung back as they reached the room where Sofia was being watched over. Astrid should be the one here, not him. He wasn't her father, not really. What right did he have to be there?

But his heart broke just the same when he saw her laying there, so little in the big hospital bed, reaching for Astrid.

"Can I?" she asked the nurse, who nodded. Astrid picked Sofia up, then sat on the bed, maneuvering around the oxygen tubes and IV until she laid with her daughter snuggled close.

He took a seat in the chair near the wall, his mind a jumble of thoughts he couldn't sort out. The nurse left, and the three of them sat there in silence.

"Thank you," Astrid finally whispered.

He didn't deserve it. "For what? I didn't know where she was until it was too late."

"But you got to her."

He didn't reply. The feeling that he'd let them both down settled over him like a thick blanket on a warm day.

The door opened, and a man walked in, the emblem on his collared shirt and badge on his belt identifying him as a member of the San Minorian Police Department.

"We know why you're here," Astrid said before he could even introduce himself. "We'll cooperate fully."

"I know you will, ma'am. I've already spoken briefly with your father, who assured me the whole family would." He turned to Jordan. "Sir, if you could step outside, there's another officer here to speak with you."

Jordan nodded and fought his instinct to kiss his wife and daughter. He stepped outside where an investigator stood, along with another member of palace security. He followed them to an office.

The investigator set a recorder on the table and turned it on. "This is Inspector Stewart with Prince Jordan, Duke of Bevingdale discussing the incident at the San Minorian Palace earlier this afternoon. Sir, if you could acknowledge that you are aware this conversation is being recorded?"

Jordan stifled a sigh. It was necessary. "My name is Jordan Haines, well, formerly Jordan Haines. I'm now Prince Jordan, Duke of Bevingdale. I'm not sure what my legal last name is. Probably still Haines, though no one uses it anymore." *That* was relevant. "I am aware this conversation is being recorded."

"In your own words, sir, could you tell me what happened this afternoon?"

"It's my birthday. My family and my in-laws threw a surprise party for me at the palace on San Minoria. We had lunch. When it was time to open presents, Gretchen - our nanny - took Sofia to put her down for a nap. An hour or so later, I was on the balcony outside the Red Drawing Room talking to Dare - my best friend and brother-in-law, Darren Weaver. I saw Sofia on the beach. I yelled at her and hoped she'd turn around. She waved and kept going toward the water. I couldn't see any adults out there, so I turned and ran. Dare followed me. I think I gave the king a black eye when I knocked him over because he didn't get out of my way fast enough. By the time we got to the beach, she was unconscious. I carried her up near the palace onto solid ground and checked her vital signs. She had a heartbeat but wasn't breathing. Dare did rescue breathing until she coughed up the water. The helicopter landed a few seconds later."

"Where was Princess Astrid during all of this?"

"We were together with the rest of our families until Dare and I went out to the balcony to talk. They were all in the Red Drawing Room. I saw her in there as we went back through to get downstairs."

The man scribbled some notes. "How did Princess Sofia get outside?"

"I have no idea how she got out of her crib or downstairs without being seen, but someone propped the door open with a rock. It's not supposed to be left open or unlocked for security reasons. I'm told it's a water tight door, too, in case of some sort of huge storm surge, though I can't imagine one that high, but maybe hurricane winds and rains too, I suppose. It's a heavy door."

"Who else would have been near the nursery who could have let her out of her crib?"

"I haven't spoken with her, but I've been told Gretchen was in the sitting room the whole time. She would have seen anyone else entering or leaving. There's another entrance to the nursery room, but it's locked from the inside. You can't get into it without being given access."

"It's a palace. Are there any secret passages? Or is that all a fictional construct?"

How was Jordan supposed to know? "I have no idea. If there are, I haven't been told about them. As for others who *could* have gone up there without anyone really thinking twice about it... probably any member of the royal family or security. I don't think my family could have, just because they're not known to the rest of the staff yet. But, if Gretchen was in the sitting room, she still would have noticed one of them entering the room."

Jordan hated that Astrid was going through the same thing in another room, with her daughter in her arms.

"Do you know anyone who would wish to harm Princess Sofia? Who might have helped her down to the beach in the hopes that something would happen to her?"

"She's a member of the royal family," Jordan reminded the man. "I'm sure they have at least some enemies or some crazies out to get them. But I've only been a part of the family for a couple of months. No one's mentioned any specific threats to me. I don't know if that's because there aren't any, because they're not relevant to me personally or because it's not standard operating procedure for me personally, to be notified if the threat isn't an immediate danger."

"I see." The man made some more notes.

Was this almost over? What else could he want to know?

"What about you? What's your relationship like with your step-daughter?"

30

"I would never hurt my daughter." Astrid forced herself not to yell, not while Sofia slept against her chest. "I would never knowingly leave her somewhere she could get hurt."

"Then how do you explain her wandering unattended around a palace full of people and no one noticing? If someone carried or led her to the door, wouldn't that have been far less noticeable than a toddler princess on her own?"

"Anything is possible. All I know is that I had nothing to do with it. I don't believe my husband, our nanny, or either of our families had anything to do with it either."

"How long have you lived at this location?"

"A couple of weeks." What was the relevance? That Sofia couldn't have known how to get to the beach access door?

"Do you personally know all of the staff members?"

"No, but I doubt my father personally knows each staff member either. All of them have been vetted by the Palace Personnel Office. Every member of the staff at all of the residences have been."

"What about your husband?"

"What about him?"

"Princess Sofia isn't his daughter."

She bristled at the implication. "He adores her, and she adores him. He knocked my father over and gave him a black eye - *on accident* - while trying to get to Sofia. She calls Jordan 'Papa', he's teaching her to ice skate and play hockey. If it were legal for him to do so, we would have started adoption procedures the minute he'd met whatever other legal qualifications there are."

"Why can't he?"

Astrid managed not to roll her eyes. "Because of Sofia's spot in the line of succession. The way the law is currently written, it assumes the heir presumptive is male. Therefore, if the heir presumptive dies, there is a widow who could remarry. Her new husband, the stepfather of the new heir presumptive, cannot adopt the child. The law makes no concession if the father wasn't the member of the royal family. A direct descendant within a certain number of spots of the throne - I think it's twenty or twenty-five - cannot be adopted by a step-father without giving up their place in the line of succession."

"I see." He made a few notes. "And you don't think he'd prefer his own child take the throne someday?"

She closed her eyes and took a deep breath in through her nose and out through her mouth. Then another one. She looked him straight in the eye. "I know you're just doing your job, but that accusation is completely baseless. I'm not sure if you can be brought up on grounds of slander of the royal family during an interview as part of your investigation, but you can bet I'll be finding out."

"And how is your marriage?"

"Our marriage is fine. All marriages have a few snags, and we've had a few minor disagreements." Sure, that's what it was, but in the grander scheme of life, her statement held. "But we're fine. I love my husband, and he loves me." At least they'd patched things up before this happened. Though she didn't doubt for a second he would have reacted the exact same way, at least she could honestly say they were in a good place.

The rest of his questions were as invasive and annoying. She managed to remain civil, but reiterated that she'd be looking into the slander charges, after he implied pretty much everyone in her family could have some motive. From Kensington hoping to become the heir to Esther's alleged jealousy and who knew what else.

But he didn't threaten to take Sofia away from her. She took that as a good sign.

Finally, he left, though a member of the local police stayed outside with palace security. Jordan came in a minute later.

"How are you?" he asked. "How is she?"

"She slept through the whole interrogation. I would imagine you've been given the same instruction I was, though, and that's not to discuss the interview with anyone."

"Basically." Jordan sat in the same chair he had earlier, but this time he pulled it closer to the bed. He reached out and rested a hand on Sofia's back. "Have the doctors been back in yet?"

"No, but none of the monitors have gone off."

"She's going to be fine," he told her with conviction Astrid wished she shared.

A knock on the wall drew their attention. They both turned to see her parents walk in.

"They said we could come two at a time." Her mother came immediately to her side. "How is she?"

"Sleeping. She slept through the whole thing."

"They've already talked to us," her father told them. "They've got at least four investigators here. They want this to be closed as quickly as possible, too."

"Any word on what the video showed?" Astrid needed to know how to prevent something like this from happening again.

Her father shook his head. "They're not allowed to talk to me about it for the time being, unless there's a serious security breach I need to be aware of. If, like we suspect, it's a tragic combination of little factors, there's no reason for them to discuss it with me at this point. If someone managed to sneak inside unobserved and removed her from her crib, that kind of thing, it would be different." He rested a hand on Astrid's calf. "But once one of your siblings is done with their interview, we need one of them to come in here with her, because the four of us need to have a frank discussion about how this is going to play out."

Her mother's fingers gently stroked the top of Astrid's head. "Why don't I stay with her and the three of you talk? I'm fairly certain I know how that conversation will go, and you can fill me in later concerning anything else."

With a nod from her father, Astrid knew her mother's plan was going to happen. Jordan took Sofia from her so she could stand up, then handed the little girl back over once Astrid's mother was situated.

Astrid leaned over and kissed her daughter's head. "Have them come get us if anything changes."

"I will."

She turned and followed her father and Jordan as they left the room.

How on earth was she going to survive this without having a complete meltdown?

The hospital administrator's office had been given to the family to use for anything they needed. Jordan sat on the couch and brushed sand from his slacks. Once most of it was gone, he sat with his arm around Astrid, and she leaned into him.

"It's already being picked up, isn't it?" she asked.

Her father sat in a chair at a right angle from them. "That something medical happened at the San Minorian Palace, but that's it. They don't know what, though speculation is that something happened to Sofia since we're here. There are pictures of the rest of us getting here by car and walking inside. The sand on Jordan and Dare has drawn attention as well."

"It's going to be bad." Astrid wasn't asking a question.

"The police are going to make a statement. As a courtesy, I've already seen the text." He glanced at his phone. "They're going live now." The king picked up the television remote and turned the TV on. The man who'd interviewed Astrid stood in front of a bank of microphones.

"Thank you for coming. I will read a short statement. I will not be taking questions at this time." He looked at the podium in front of him. "At approximately 1400 hours, an emergency call was made from the San Minorian Palace. A female minor, aged twenty months, had been found unresponsive in the water on the private beach. A medical helicopter was dispatched along with a number of police officers. By the time the medical team arrived, the female minor was breathing on her own and was conscious. She, along with her mother and a member of the palace security team, were flown to Children's Hospital on San Majoria. As would be done in any similar case, an investigation is underway to determine exactly how the child came to be where she was. The royal family, along with the family of Prince Jordan, were at the San Minorian palace at the time of the incident. They are cooperating fully with the investigation. That is all we have to say at this time."

He turned and walked off, ignoring the shouted questions.

"Well, it's clear it's Sofia." Astrid sighed. "What other twenty-month-old would it be? And why would palace security go if it wasn't her, but a staff member's child or something?"

"That's a reasonable presumption." Her father rested his forearms on his knees. "The reality is that there will always be questions. It would be worse if the outcome was had been different, but it will be bad enough for a while. Almost anywhere you go, someone will ask questions, blame you both. To a lesser extent, the rest of us will get it as well, since we were there. Just ignore them. Once Sofia is home, and has been for a few days, continue with your lives as normal. Talk to the people who come to see you without giving those who criticize and accuse your attention. Be polite, but don't get drawn into the debates."

Jordan wasn't sure he'd be able to do that, but he kept his

thoughts to himself. If someone accused Astrid of trying to hurt Sofia, would he be able to walk away?

"With permission from both of you, I think we should start referring to Jordan as her father. We've not really said anything one way or the other, or referred to him as more than 'future step-father' perhaps in the lead up to the wedding. If anyone questions it, ignore the question or respond that Jordan would have already legally adopted her if he could."

"I would have," Jordan confirmed.

"At some point, we will probably need to sit down and do an interview or two about it all, but not for a while."

Two quick raps sounded on the door before it opened. The head of her father's security team poked his head in. "They're asking for you in the princess's room, ma'am."

Astrid jumped to her feet before Jordan could offer to help her. They hurried to Sofia's room. The doctor waited there. Jordan could almost feel the waves of panic flowing off Astrid. A now-wide awake Sofia reached for her mother immediately.

"Everything's fine," the doctor rushed to reassure them. "We're moving her to a private room for observation. We're going to watch her overnight, and then, if all goes well, look at sending her home tomorrow."

"Thank you," Astrid said for all of them.

"She'll need some follow-up tests done later, and the neurologist will come see you tomorrow before you leave. Someone will be here in a few minutes to move her."

They all thanked the doctor again. Astrid sat on the bed with Sofia in her lap.

"Are you both staying here tonight?" the king asked them.

Jordan shook his head. "I would love to, but I need to get back to the palace before bedtime. My medication is there."

His father-in-law chuckled. "You do know we can have it brought here, right?"

Jordan glanced at Astrid, who didn't seem to be paying any attention and lowered his voice. "I know, but honestly, I know my limits. After two nights sleeping on a plane, even a very comfortable one, and the adrenaline rush and everything today, I need a good night's sleep. Knowing that she's going to be okay, I think it would be better for me to sleep back home then come over tomorrow. I'll be fresher, and it'll let Astrid rest more tomorrow."

"In that case, I think it's a good plan. Just make sure she understands why, but that there's no real potential impact to your health."

"Something I haven't told her yet, and I know we're not supposed to talk about the interviews, but he asked if I was on medications. I had to tell the truth. We hadn't planned on telling anyone about my transplant until the Women in Medicine thing coming up. I told him I was on medication, that it had no bearing on the case, and I would be happy to tell him off the record. If, later, they felt it relevant, they could talk to me again. I told him after the interview concluded, and he agreed he didn't think it needed to be part of the official record. My fear is that, if the fact I told him off the record comes out soon, rumor will spread that it's something awful that we just don't want disclosed because it's embarrassing. That might push up the time frame to tell everyone else."

The king nodded thoughtfully. "I'll discuss it with the chief."

"I'll talk to her after we get to the room and get settled." He realized he didn't have any form of transportation. "Unless you need me to go before then so the boat can get back here."

The conversation was interrupted by the arrival of someone to transport Sofia. After hugs, the king and queen left. He told Jordan the boat would be at his disposal, and that Jordan's family was still in the hospital talking to investigators.

A few minutes later, they were upstairs in a room, just the three of them, waiting on a nurse to come back in and get everything situated.

Astrid laid on the bed next to Sofia. Jordan reached out and brushed her hair back where it had fallen in her face. "Hey. I don't want to leave, but I'm going to have to. As soon as I talk to my folks, Betsy, and Dare, I need to get back." He explained why, emphasizing that he would be fine, just needed sleep, and then he could take over for her tomorrow.

She gave him a tired smile. "One of us should get a good night's sleep. Go on. We'll be fine."

"Have someone call me immediately if something changes." He leaned down and kissed her softly. "I love you both."

"We love you, too." Her smile turned to a bit of a smirk. "Happy birthday."

"Thanks. I may try out those skates when I get back. Just for a few minutes."

Her smile vanished. "I wanted to be there."

"Then I'll wait." He kissed her again. "I'm going to go find my family and see you in the morning."

She pulled him back down for another, more searing kiss. "And one day soon, I'll give you your other birthday present."

31

Two days later, the words of the neurologist didn't want to sink into her brain. "What's the bottom line?" Astrid interrupted.

"She has an excellent chance of no long term neurological issues. She was pulled from the water quickly, never lost her pulse, was given CPR immediately, and started to breathe on her own quickly. That's all part of a good prognosis, but there's a chance she may have some learning delays or difficulties that may not be evident until she's in school. However," the doctor gave a reassuring smile, "I wouldn't expect them to be the kinds of significant ones that are probably running through your mind right now. There tends to be two kinds of results from drowning. Those with severe, significant issues, and those who have none to slight. There is every expectation that Princess Sofia will fall into the latter category."

Some of the stress seemed to bleed away. "How did you know?"

The doctor chuckled. "You're not the first set of parents I've talked with."

Astrid shared a look of relief with Jordan. "Thank you."

"All that said, I'm certain you'll have the very best care for her whenever she needs it. I'd be happy to take a look at her every so often or pass my notes on to a neurologist of your choosing." She stood. "It was very nice to meet both of you. I'm glad the circumstances weren't any worse, though I wish they could have been better."

"Agreed." Astrid shook her hand. "Thank you for all your help. We appreciate it."

"My pleasure." The doctor shook hands with Jordan then left the room.

"That's got to be a huge relief." Jordan sat back in the rocking chair.

Astrid wasn't sure she agreed.

"Don't go there." The warning tone in his voice caused her to look up. "I know what you're thinking. That she's going to have severe mental damage and all of that. It's just not true. Listen to what the doctor said, not what the freaking out part of you heard."

"I know. It's hard."

"And like she said, we'll have the best specialists in the country, or Canada, or the States, or Europe, or wherever we need to go for her. But whatever it is, we'll go through it together."

She had to voice her fears to her husband. "But if it's bad enough, even if it's not bad, it could remove her from the line of succession." Astrid whispered the words, unable to speak them aloud.

Jordan just grinned. An odd response. "Then I'll adopt her because it won't matter."

Astrid managed to give him a half-smile. "Do you always see the silver lining?"

"Sometimes you just have to, but I truly believe it won't come to that."

Gretchen, still distraught over the near miss, slipped in now that the doctor had left. "They're ready for the two of you to make your statement downstairs." Martina had come by earlier to help Astrid look more presentable.

Astrid sighed. "Let's go."

She and Jordan were escorted to a service elevator and then to the room used for press conferences. Astrid waited for the signal then walked out, Jordan behind her.

"Thank you all for being here. I will make a statement. I will not take any questions at this time." She couldn't handle it. "As you are aware, there was an incident on the beach at the San Minorian Palace two days ago. Though the name of the child involved has not been officially released by the police, the widespread speculation that the child was our daughter, Princess Sofia, is correct. I cannot comment on how she came to be on the beach unsupervised as that is still under investigation. My husband, the rest of my family, the rest of his family, and I have cooperated fully with police. We expect the investigation to show it was a series of unfortunate, nearly tragic, but ultimately innocent events that led to the situation. We look forward to completely clearing our names and those of our staff. Princess Sofia is doing well and will be released from the hospital shortly. We will be taking her home to finish her recuperation. Jordan and I will be resuming a limited schedule of engagements in the near future while we focus on taking care of our daughter. Thank you for your patience as law enforcement does their job, and for your prayers. We appreciate them more than you know. Thank you."

She stepped away from the microphones and left the room, ignoring shouted questions, with Jordan a half step behind, his hand resting on her back. Though the corridors were clear, she waited until they reached Sofia's room to relax a bit. Jordan held her in his arms and let her soak up his strength.

Before she was ready to let him go, a nurse, Astrid's favorite from the last two days, walked in with a stack of papers. "Let's get this little princess out of here."

Her father had made arrangements for a helicopter to take them back to San Minoria. Once the paperwork was signed, Astrid settled into a wheelchair, Sofia in her arms. They were taken to a service elevator then up to the roof with Jordan beside them the whole way. The royal helicopter waited for them. In just a few minutes, they were on their way.

As they took off, Astrid could see a small crowd on the street. "Are they here for us?"

Jordan looked out his window. "I think so. I saw some when I got here, but I wasn't close enough to really tell. I can't imagine a crowd for any other reason though. If we want, we can check the news. I'm sure there's coverage. Otherwise, ask Jade or Thomas to check."

"That sounds like a better idea." She wasn't ready to see what some of the commentators or royal haters were saying. She'd probably said it enough to herself already.

It wasn't true. On one level, she knew that. On another, it didn't matter. Mental self-flagellation didn't care if it was true or not.

Now that her daughter was headed home, and she would be out of the sometimes chaotic hospital environment, maybe she could find the peace she desperately needed. Some quiet time in the chapel would be good as would a good night's sleep, though Astrid wasn't sure she'd be able to get that. Measures had been taken to ensure Sofia wouldn't be able to climb out of her crib again - she did know that was how her little girl had escaped her bed. It wasn't the most elegant, but a net over the top would keep her in place.

As much as she longed to make sure Jordan knew all was right in their world, Astrid was pretty sure she'd be sleeping in Sofia's nursery at least for a few days. She prayed he'd understand.

It was time to get back to some semblance of normalcy, but Jordan found it hard to do. They'd been home for days, but Astrid still slept in Sofia's room - something Jordan completely understood. He'd thought about moving the crib into the room he was supposed to share with his wife just to make it easier on both of them. In fact, he still might suggest it for a few weeks.

Beyond that, Astrid seemed to be having difficulty sleeping as did Sofia, though Jordan hadn't seen it himself. Astrid said she'd been waking up crying every night since the incident. He wondered if there was much a therapist could do to help a twenty-month-old process the trauma. He guessed not, but he'd find out.

Sofia's personality had also changed. Instead of the happy, playful little girl he'd fallen in love with, she'd become much quieter and clingy. Also to be expected, probably, but he hoped she'd find her way back to the carefree child she should be. She refused to let go of her turtle or moose most of the time.

His cell phone rang, even though he was in his office. He didn't check to see who it was before answering. "Jordan."

"You answer your phone with your name now?" Betsy's teasing lightened his spirits immediately.

"Please tell me you're not in your bedroom."

Dare's laugh joined Betsy's. "We are," his friend said. "But only because then we could tell you we were, and it would annoy you."

"We wanted to check on all of you," Betsy told him. "How's everything?"

"Good. Mostly. There's aftereffects, obviously, but it could have been so much worse." He didn't tell Dare that Astrid wanted to see him knighted for service to the Crown or something to that effect. Once the police investigation was officially closed and cleared all of them, she'd make it happen.

"Agreed. We want to come back down sometime soon," Dare said. "Can you let us know when would be good? Mom and Dad want to come, too, of course."

"Mom and Dad? Since when do you call them that?" It didn't bother Jordan, but he hadn't heard it before.

Dare just laughed. "They said I could. It kind of came naturally."

Jordan turned and stared at the sliver of ocean he could see out his office window. "Bets, can I talk to Dare for a minute?"

"Sure. Love you, brother."

"Love you, too." A minute later, it was just his best friend on the phone. "How did you know?" Jordan asked.

"Know what?"

"Know to follow me like that? To go left when I went right?"

"How long have we known each other?" Dare's stern tone surprised Jordan.

"First grade."

"And in those twenty or so years, until the last few months, how many days have we *not* spent at least part of together?"

"None, give or take." Jordan started to see Dare's point.

"Exactly. We've spent at least part of almost every day together for the last..." Dare had to be doing mental math. "...7300 or so days together. We've played hockey together for at least half of those. Why do you think we won that last game? Because you, and I, and everyone else had played together so long we could read each other's minds. So even though I wasn't sure what was going through your head the other day, when you bolted, I followed. No questions. That's what we do, remember? Why did I go left? Because you always go right. Or you always go right because I always go left. I'm not sure which, but the point is, that's how it's always worked."

A memory flooded Jordan's mind. "Except that one game."

"Exactly. And that's why it worked. Because you gave me a signal, we switched it up and surprised them. You're my best friend." Dare's voice softened. "You're closer to me than a brother. It's a good thing you're not my brother, because I married your sister."

Jordan groaned.

"You're closer to me than any brother I could have," Dare continued. "I will *always* have your back, just like you'll always have mine. That includes your wife, your daughter, and any other kids you'll have. Just like I know you'll take care of my wife and kids, and not just because she's also your sister."

"I don't ever want to have to."

"I don't either, but it's part and parcel of being besties."

Jordan half-groaned, half-laughed. "When did you start saying *that*?"

Dare chuckled. "When I knew what kind of reaction it would get out of you. Now, why are you in the office?"

"Because I'm supposed to be working."

"Are you accomplishing anything?"

"What do you think?"

"Then go find your wife, find your daughter, and be together, even if you just sit on the couch and watch Sofia sleep."

Jordan turned that idea over. "That sounds great."

"Do you know what Betsy's gushed over the most, besides Sofia being all right?" Dare's voice had lowered to almost a whisper.

"What?"

"Being on a first name basis with a whole royal family. The king actually sounded almost offended when she called him 'Your Majesty' and curtsied."

That made Jordan laugh for several reasons. "Remind me to tell you what I was wearing the first time I met him. Right now, I'm going to take your advice and go find Astrid. I'll let you know when it's good for you to come visit. Wait." He actually snapped his fingers like they did in the movies. "I know when. There's an event..." Jordan outlined his whole plan to Dare and said he'd try to get tickets for the four Canadians.

"That sounds perfect. We can make a weekend of it. Let me know."

They said their good-byes, and Jordan hollered one over speaker phone to Betsy, then hung up. He told Thomas where he'd be then went to the kitchen. He found a fresh batch of chocolate chip cookies, wrapped up a few, and headed to the nursery where he was sure to find the two girls in his life.

32

Astrid wasn't prepared for the crowd that greeted her outside the Garden Club. At least not their numbers. A small group outside a luncheon like this wasn't unusual, but there had to be several hundred people. She and Jordan had attended one event together a couple days earlier, but neither one of them had been fully comfortable with it. They trusted Gretchen, but there could be no substitute for being there themselves.

At least the police had finally announced publicly that they expected the investigation to be finished in the next couple days. As police investigations went, it hadn't been that long, though it seemed an eternity to Astrid.

Glancing at the signs and faces of the crowd, it seemed to be mostly friendly. Thank God for small favors.

Someone opened the door for her, and she took the offered hand to climb out of the car.

"Thank you," she murmured. Did she work the line? Or wave and walk through?

Mostly cheers greeted her ears. Very few angry voices came through. Okay. Short visit.

She walked along the line, shaking hands, taking pictures,

accepting flowers, answering questions superficially. Yes, Sofia was doing well. That was about the extent of her answers regarding the incident. The other questions she ignored. After about ten minutes, she stepped back from the line, arms overflowing with bouquets she promised to take to Sofia. She could only manage a small wave with her fingertips because there were so many.

Rather than going inside, she turned and went back to the car. Her driver, not her usual one, but a man she didn't know well, waited by the door. He helped her lay them neatly on the back seat.

"Thank you, all!" she called. "That way they won't get dropped or misplaced inside!" She gave a real wave and walked through the doors.

The luncheon was as enjoyable as it could be with her mind still planted firmly in the nursery a few miles away. Jordan had promised he wouldn't leave Sofia while she was gone. The company was polite, asking about Sofia but not pressing, and certainly not shouting invectives like a few people outside had been.

In less than two hours, she was headed back to the palace. A good event for her to get her feet back under her on her own. After thanking her driver, she took one of the bouquets and headed upstairs. She'd already texted Jade to make sure the others were spread around the palace.

Familiar sounds greeted her as she neared the door to the family quarters. Were those happy shouts? Little girl squeals even?

"Look out Hayley! Sofia's coming!" Jordan shouted.

Astrid looked in the nursery to see Sofia waving a sparkly pink hockey stick in the air and doing her little hop in place thing.

"My win! *'Gin*, Papa!"

"This time I'm going to try to stop you." Jordan, on his knees with a navy blue hockey stick the same size as Sofia's knee-walked in front of the goal. "See if you can get it past me." Were those knee-pads?

Sofia hit the foam ball gently a couple of times then whacked it.

Right between Jordan's knees.

He gaped and looked down like you see in movies. Astrid slid further back out of sight and stifled a laugh.

"My win *'gin*, Papa!"

A four-word sentence? Look at her go!

Jordan laughed and picked her up. "You did, sweet girl. You're getting the hang of it. We'll go skating with Mama soon, okay?"

"Yay!"

Astrid knew the second her daughter saw her. Sofia wiggled out of Jordan's grasp and ran to Astrid. "My win, Mama!"

"I saw." She swept her daughter into her arms. "Great job beating Papa." It felt natural to refer to him that way.

But when she looked at him, he seemed to struggle to stand up. When he made it to his feet, Jordan groaned and stretched his back. "I'm not as young as I used to be. Playing on your knees is for kids."

Astrid laughed. "You're not exactly old."

He grinned as he walked toward them. "No, but I made you smile." After a quick kiss, he took Sofia from her. "Why don't you show Mama?"

Sofia ran off to pick up her stick as Astrid leaned into Jordan's one-armed embrace.

"Who's Hayley?" she asked.

"Hayley Wickenheiser. She was the first woman to play professional hockey and not be the goalie. A Canadian, of course, but she had to play in Europe. The game's not quite as physical there, and there weren't as many barriers to her playing in a men's league. She was one of *Sports Illustrated*'s twenty-five toughest athletes in 2008. She has four Olympic golds and a silver."

Astrid leaned her head on his shoulder as they watched a very serious Sofia try to get the foam ball to stay where it was supposed to. "You have all that memorized?"

"Every Canadian kid has that memorized. Our San Majorian kids probably will, too."

Her conversation with her father came back to her. "Papa told me something today. Once the investigation is over, they're going to propose a change to the law. As long as the member of the royal family is the living parent, regardless of gender, the non-royal step-parent can adopt a child without the child losing their place in line."

He moved slightly away. "So I could adopt her?"

"If you still want to."

The grin on his face gave her the answer before any words could. "I won't love her any more if it does pass and I can, or any less if I never do. You know that, right?"

"I know. I think everyone knows that, but still. The way the law is written now is stupid."

He chuckled and pulled her close again. "I can't say I disagree."

Sofia finally got the ball to sit still and swung at it, smacking the floor behind it.

Astrid winced.

"We'll work on form as she gets older," Jordan whispered. "We've got all the time in the world."

"Are you sure we should do this?"

Jordan turned to see Astrid lagging behind, Sofia in her arms. "We don't have to, but I think it would be good to see how she does."

They'd been home over a week. They were meeting with the investigators in a few hours.

"If she freaks out, we'll go back, but we need to know."

Astrid sighed and started walking again. "I know."

"This is how we get places," he reminded her.

Sofia reached for him, and he took her from Astrid.

"I know." His wife brushed past. "That doesn't mean I have to like it." She pushed the heavy door open. It now sounded an alarm if left ajar longer than a minute.

Jordan followed her down the stairs, paying close attention to the body language of the little girl in his arms. She didn't stiffen or cling. She just looked.

They weren't going in the water. The most they'd do is let the water get Sofia's toes, but only if she seemed comfortable or wanted down.

Crossing the sand didn't take long, but still seemed to take forever. Jordan kicked his sandals off before reaching the water's edge.

Sofia lunged for the ground. "My *s'im*!"

Jordan closed his eyes and breathed a sigh of relief. "We're not swimming today, sweet girl. We're just going to get our feet wet." He set her on the ground but kept a firm grip on her hand. Astrid took the other one. "Here comes the water!"

Sofia giggled and kicked with one foot as the small wave came in. She did the same with the next one and the one after that. A few minutes later, a little bigger wave, this one slightly "rogue" for the area, came at them. Without needing to talk to each other about it, he and Astrid lifted her, swinging her over the wave. She giggled as it splashed around Jordan's upper shins. Then he realized what had likely happened to cause Sofia's near drowning. He'd have to tell Astrid later.

After a few more minutes, Astrid told Sofia it was time to go inside. She didn't want to, but agreed when Astrid offered to play hockey with her.

"This I gotta see," Jordan chuckled as he leaned over to pick up his sandals. Barefoot, they walked back to the stairs. "Hey, Sofia," he started, picking her up. "Can you do something for me?"

"Yeah, Papa." She fiddled with the ribbing at the neck of his t-shirt.

"I need you to never, ever go down these stairs by yourself, okay?"

Sofia nodded. "'Kay, Papa."

He used his free hand to tilt her chin so she could look at him. "I mean it, superstar. You can't ever go down the big beach stairs without a grownup. Mama, or Papa, or Gretchen, okay?" There were others on the list, but that would work for now.

"My not." She pointed at stairs. "Yockey, Mama!"

Jordan trotted up the stairs with her in his arms, thanking God the whole time that she wasn't scared of the beach. It would have curbed the beach-y lifestyle they enjoyed and made it more difficult to get off San Minoria, but mostly it would have bothered him that Sofia was so scared.

Back in her nursery, she gave Astrid the pink sparkly hockey stick.

"This one is yours." Astrid tried to hand it back.

"Mama's."

Astrid shrugged. "Thank you for letting me use it."

"You can use my knee pads if you want," Jordan told her, picking up his camera and sitting on the floor.

Her nose wrinkled. "I'll be okay."

"Suit yourself."

Watching the two of them was the most fun Jordan had had in a long time. Neither of them had a clue how to play, but Sofia had clearly made up rules in her head. Those rules, of course, benefited her each time.

After they played for a while, the three of them ate lunch someone brought up. Sofia laid down for her nap. Gretchen stayed in the room with her, though out of sight of the crib. No one was taking any chances.

They walked to the conference room in Astrid's office and watched out the window as her family walked up the beach.

"We should put a sidewalk or stepping stones of some kind there," he told her. "I'm kind of surprised there isn't already."

"I think there used to be, but no one's lived here full time in a long time. When my parents would come visit, they'd go to the dock and drive over." Her hand slid through his arm. "What would you think about putting a desk in here for you? As long as

I'm not on the phone with state business or we're both on the phone at the same time, it would work. We'll get you a cordless phone so you can take it to your office if you need to."

Jordan wrapped his arm around her waist. "You mean so I can lose track of it?"

She shrugged, her face the picture of innocence. "You said it, not me."

"I love the idea if we can make it work."

"My parents do, and I know you'd love this view."

"That's not why I'd enjoy having a desk in here."

"I know."

Before he could kiss her, they heard her family entering the office. Jade walked in behind them. "The investigators have arrived, ma'am. They'll be up momentarily." Nerves made small talk impossible until they arrived.

They shook hands all around, introductions made where necessary, then the lead investigator suggested they all have a seat. He hooked his laptop up to the projector as Jade lowered the shades to make it a little easier to see.

Finally, he turned to face all of them and nodded to one of the other men. That man set a recorder on the table.

"For the record, please state your name, title if appropriate, and that you know this meeting is being recorded," the second man told them.

One by one, they went around the room, each giving their name and title.

"Jordan Haines, Prince of San Majoria and Duke of Bevingdale," Jordan said when it was his turn. "I know this meeting is being recorded."

"Before we get started, Your Royal Highness. Last time we spoke, you told me you weren't sure what your legal last name was, but you presumed it was still Haines, though no one used it any longer. Have you confirmed that?"

Jordan looked over at the king who didn't give any indication one way or the other. "I have not. With everything else going on, checking into it slipped my mind. I will look into it this week."

"Very well. This meeting is to report on the findings into the near drowning incident that took place at the San Minorian Palace on October 23, 2016 at approximately 1400 hours. I won't go over the details of the incident as I'm sure you're all more aware of them than I am since the child is your daughter, stepdaughter, granddaughter, and niece. What we're going to outline here is the findings about *how* Princess Sofia came to be on the beach unattended and whether or not any criminal charges will be filed."

One whole side of the table held their collective breath and willed the man to get on with it. To tell them whether there would be charges before he laid out what they believed happened. The longer he went without saying there would be no charges, the more afraid Jordan was that there would be some.

And his wife was the most likely target.

Jordan reached over and took her hand, trying to convey to her his belief that it would all be okay.

He hoped she believed it, because he wasn't sure he did.

33

Astrid forced herself to breathe normally, or as close to it as possible. She loosened the death grip she had on Jordan's hand, otherwise he'd lose circulation.

But rather than just getting right down to it, the guy blathered on.

"There are several nanny cams in the nursery. One faces the door, which was left slightly ajar. The nanny, Ms. Lynch, is seen sitting in a chair, presumably with the book she mentioned reading. She doesn't move from her seat, nor does anyone enter the room through that door."

As they already knew.

"Princess Sofia was laid down by Ms. Lynch at approximately 1215." They showed that portion of the video. "After several minutes of activity, Princess Sofia settles down, and goes to sleep." The video was fast forwarded over an hour, allowing them to see that nothing of interest happened anywhere near the crib. "Around 1340, Princess Sofia wakes up. Using her blanket and two stuffed animals later discovered to be a turtle and a moose, she managed to get her leg over the side of the crib railing. From there, she climbed out. Quite well, actually."

The video forwarded through Sofia wandering around her room, playing with this toy and that one, though none of the noisy ones.

"After several minutes, she started walking around the room, running her hand along the wall."

Something Sofia did all the time and drove Astrid crazy while they were walking through hallways. More than once, she'd had to pull her daughter away from some priceless artifact or other.

And then the Sofia on the screen peeked behind a tapestry hanging in her room. Astrid meant to have it removed, but hadn't yet.

Sofia disappeared behind the tapestry, but didn't emerge.

"Where'd she go?" Astrid asked, scared, though she already knew the outcome. She looked over at her father to see his ashen face.

"There's a tunnel there." His strangled whisper tore at Astrid's heart. "I forgot all about it. I knew it was there, but I never explored it. If you had asked me if there was one in that apartment, I'm not sure I would have remembered."

"Which is basically what you told us in your interview." The investigator clicked the button and the video on the screen changed to the hallway near the door to the beach. "The other end of the tunnel is right..." One of several tapestries on the walls moved and out came Sofia. "...there."

From there the video was unnecessary. Sofia walked out the door, was caught going down the stairs, but the color of her outfits and the shadows meant she was difficult to see. The camera didn't catch the actual incident, and for that, Astrid was grateful.

And then Jordan, with Dare hot on his heels, barreled through the door. If she didn't know better, Jordan had to have gone down the stairs four at a time. She'd never been able to go down even two at a time, but he certainly seemed to be skipping some.

The rest of the family hurried after them, though not as fast since they were trying not to trip over each other and had no idea what was going on.

Jordan and Dare disappeared off the side of the screen only to reappear thirty seconds or so later with Sofia in Jordan's arms.

The real Jordan's hand tightened around hers. When she looked at him, she noticed tears flowing down his cheeks while the Dare on the screen began CPR.

A flash of white appeared in front of her, and with her free hand, Astrid took the handkerchief her father offered.

"The conclusion we've reached is that, though nearly tragic, there was no negligence or criminal liability in the matter of the near-drowning."

Relief flooded over Astrid and the palpable tension in the room began to dissipate.

He nodded toward her father. "Leaving the door open, though against palace protocol, doesn't meet the legal definition. Our understanding is that the person who propped the door open is no longer an employee?"

"Correct. He is no longer employed at the palace. When he realized what he'd done, he was mortified and offered his resignation immediately. He has otherwise been an exemplary employee for many years and has taken a demotion and relocation to another home that seldom has the family in residence. When the family is in residence, he will be given unpaid leave until such a time as it is determined that he has paid his debt to the family." The tone of his voice told Astrid her father doubted that would ever happen.

"I think I know what happened," Jordan told them. "On the beach. We were out there earlier and a rogue wave came in. Not very big by an objective standard, but compared to most of the ones we get here it was. I think it probably caught her off-guard and knocked her over."

The lead investigator nodded his agreement. "That's the conclusion we came to as well."

The discussion moved on to the press conference that would be held the following day. What video or stills would be released to the public and which ones wouldn't. Though her father hadn't been seen in public much, his black eye had definitely been noticed.

This meeting with the press would be different. Several of them, including the police inspector, her father, Jordan, and herself would be seated at a table and would take question after question.

Finally, the meeting ended. Everyone left the room except Astrid and Jordan. She sank into his arms. "It's over," she whispered.

"And the outcome was what we knew it should be. You're not a bad mother or neglectful mother. Anyone with half a brain knows that."

"My head knows that, but..."

"Your heart's a different matter."

"Exactly."

She wanted to avoid the press conference, go on vacation somewhere far away from cameras that followed them everywhere, from speculation that would never quite go away, all of that.

But no matter how much she wished she could avoid it, the press conference came anyway.

As she followed her father into the room, the press acted very different than the last time, likely because they knew they would all be here quite a while and most of their questions would be answered.

The investigator started off, giving the same rundown as he'd given the family but with fewer visuals, saying that many of them were classified.

Because the outside of the palace wasn't classified, the video of Jordan and Dare coming out of the door was shown, stopping as Kensington and Harrison emerged after them.

The investigator concluded with the statement absolving them of criminal liability and that the person who'd left the door propped open had immediately offered his resignation. He didn't include the further details.

"And now, the panel will take your questions."

Jordan wasn't sure how this would go, but could feel the tension radiating off his wife.

The investigator called on the first reporter.

"How is Princess Sofia? What is her long-term prognosis?"

"She's doing well," Astrid answered. "She had nightmares for a few days, but those seem to be behind us. The doctors say there's no reason to expect anything more than the most minor cognitive impairment at worst. They emphasized that given the amount of time she was in the water, the rapidity with which CPR was administered, that she never lost her pulse, and how long she went without breathing there is every reason to expect no impairment or delays at all."

"If there is impairment," the reporter continued, "would that affect her ability to be queen someday?"

The king answered. "Fortunately, that day is a long time off. I don't intend for my daughter to take over for some time and my granddaughter far longer. However, given that we have every expectation that there will be no impairment, that is a discussion not currently worth having."

The reporters all raised their hands. The king chose one.

"Prince Jordan, what made you and your brother-in-law realize something was wrong?"

Jordan leaned slightly forward and explained what he'd seen.

"And your brother-in-law didn't realize what was happening?" the reporter pressed.

"I don't believe so."

"Then why did he, who's only been married to your sister a few months, charge after you like that?"

The guy clearly hadn't done his research. "He's been my brother-in-law for a few months, but he's been my best friend since we were five and first wobbled on the ice together in TimBits. We skated together, played hockey together for nearly a decade and a half. We can almost read each other's minds. When I needed to move fast enough that I knocked the king..." He shook his head. "That I knocked my *father-in-law* over and gave him a black eye, Dare doesn't need to know why. He just has my back."

"You're the reason the king has a black eye?"

Jordan shrugged. "I told them to move. He didn't get out of the way fast enough. It's not something I'd normally do, but when the choice became knock him out of the way and get to my daughter faster or waste a few extra seconds, it was a no brainer."

"But she's not your daughter," another reporter called.

Jordan glared her direction. "If it was legal for me to adopt her, the paperwork would have been started the day after the wedding."

The king stepped in. "We will be working to change that legislation beginning next week. As the law is written, it assumes any heir to the throne is through the paternal line making it illegal for a stepfather to adopt an heir without the heir giving up the line of succession. Clearly that isn't an issue here since Princess Sofia's mother is the one in the line of succession. We will also be finding an appropriate way to reward both Prince Jordan and Darren Weaver for their service to the Crown."

More questions rained down, but Jordan didn't have to answer any of them. Finally, the thing ended, and they all left the room. They all shook hands with the investigator who went on his way. Jordan put his arm around Astrid's shoulder as they walked to her office and talked to her father.

"Your answers were perfect," his father-in-law told him. "That reporter can be kind of obnoxious. He clearly either didn't do his homework or didn't care. You answered just right, and it was a great way to bring up the black eye while making sure it wasn't a big deal."

They spoke for a few more minutes, and then the king left to return home.

"I'm worn out," Astrid told him, turning so her arms wrapped around his waist. "I think I may go lay down."

"You should. I'm going to do some work here."

He sat back down at his desk and tried to figure out a way to honor everyone he wanted to at the Women in Medicine banquet. Maybe he'd talk to his father-in-law about it.

That decided, Jordan went back to editing the pictures of Astrid and Sofia, but the last week caught up with him. He went upstairs and went to bed nearly as early as the rest of his little family.

34

Astrid didn't really want to attend the Women in Medicine fundraiser, but for different reasons than she'd anticipated.

Life was finally settling back into normal, and she wanted to stay home with her two favorite people.

Instead, she and Jordan had returned to the palace in Cabo Juan-Eduardo to get ready for the evening. His family joined them and her family was attending as well. She had no idea why unless they wanted to make sure her mind was off what happened the last time she attended.

Jordan had been talking with her father so she met all of them near the garrison. Several cars were being taken as there were too many of them to be comfortable in one.

Her parents and Jordan's climbed in one car and it drove off. Her siblings rode in the next one.

She gasped when the next car pulled up. "Jordan! It's yours?"

He opened the door to his prized car for her. "I had it brought over here. I won't drive it often and this garage has better climate control."

"I don't know what else is going to happen at this banquet, but I have a feeling your car will be the talk of the town." She settled into the seat, her stomach suddenly churning. Maybe this wasn't the best idea. The car she and Andrei had been in was one of the most well protected in the country. If this car were to be hit, they'd all be in trouble.

No!

She wasn't going to dwell there.

Fifteen minutes later, when they pulled up, she was back to normal. They greeted well-wishers on the sides of the red carpet. She heard a number of them thanking Dare for his role in Sofia's rescue.

Inside, they mingled, ate dinner, chatted with family and others seated with them.

Finally, the head of the organization stood to make her speech of the evening.

"Your Majesties, Your Royal Highnesses, honored guests, ladies and gentlemen," she began. "Normally, this is where I give a big speech, but tonight, I'm turning that honor over to someone else. Someone a little surprising given that, well, he's not a woman. But I think by the time he's finished, you'll understand why we've chosen to go this route this evening. His Royal Highness, Prince Jordan, Duke of Bevingdale."

Only then did Astrid realize Jordan had slipped from his chair.

The crowd applauded as her husband stepped to the podium. He repeated the doctor's greeting, then moved on.

"I asked Dr. Lyttleton to allow me to give the address this evening for several reasons. In fact, she doesn't know all of them." He looked at his notes. "Normally, there is an announcement made about a bursary, or scholarship, for a deserving young woman to attend medical school. This year, the bursary is being expanded from a nominal amount for one year, to a full scholarship for four years. It has been renamed the *Duchess of Bevingdale Award for Outstanding Future Female Medical Personnel.*"

Astrid managed not to gasp.

"As I've gotten to know my wife over the last months since we met, I've also talked with others. I've learned something she only hinted at in conversation. If she could be anyone but who she is, she would be a pediatrician. We recently met Dr. Jonah Fontaine, Duke of Parkenham, and husband of Princess Anastasia of Montevaro. He balances his life as a pediatric hospitalist with life as the husband of a princess. I overheard Princess Astrid say something to the effect of she would have loved to be able to do that, but knew from a very young age it wasn't the path she would take. She decided instead to help other, deserving young women reach that goal. This award is a way to further that goal." Another look at his notes, and he announced the name Astrid recognized as a candy striper from the hospital a few weeks earlier.

Cheers were especially loud from one corner of the room. The young lady walked to the stage and accepted a certificate and plaque from Jordan. They posed for a couple of pictures, and she returned to her table. Astrid would make sure to talk with her later.

"This year, another award is being added to those given by the Women in Medicine Organization. It is my privilege to hand out this first one. The other award we're announcing tonight is the *San Majorian Excellence Award for Women in Medicine*. With this award comes a donation to the charity of the recipient's choice, as well as a monetary prize. Each year, there will be a winner and a runner up. This year, the choice was particularly difficult."

"The runner up for the inaugural award is Dr. Marie Chaucer."

Applause filled the room as the doctor made her way the stage.

"My wife and I met Dr. Chaucer a couple of weeks ago after Sofia nearly drowned. She is the neurologist who assured us that, in all likelihood, the long-term effects on our daughter would be minimal and very possibly non-existent. But we needed to delve further into Dr. Chaucer's history. Though young, Dr. Chaucer is already making her mark." He read off a list of things Astrid didn't really understand, but meant the doctor was a leader in her field. Jordan handed her a certificate and plaque. The checks would come later.

Dr. Chaucer stepped to the podium and gave a few words

about how unexpected it was and how glad she was Sofia was doing well. She returned to her seat.

"As a result of our conversations with Dr. Chaucer, my wife and I are announcing a fund that will provide free water safety courses to the families of all children under the age of six. Details will be available in the near future, but we pray it prevents another situation similar to ours but with more tragic consequences."

Astrid watched him shuffle his note cards and take a deep breath. "Before I announce the winner of this award, I have a story to tell."

She knew what was coming. They'd talked about an announcement soon, but she hadn't expected it tonight. Not like this.

"A little over two years ago, this banquet was held in July. That night, on the way home, Princess Astrid and Prince Andrei were in a car accident that, in the next forty-eight hours, would take his life. It is public knowledge that he gave one last gift to the people of San Majoria. His wife aided him in that gift, and his organs were donated to those in need."

Was he about to out Andrei as his donor? Astrid couldn't breathe.

He held up a card. "I don't have names, but there were several people who donated organs in the hospital in the days after that accident, including four from the accident itself. A total of five kidneys were given to a ten-year-old boy, a twenty-year-old woman, two men in their thirties, and a teenage girl. Two are San Majorian. One is American, and one Sargossian. Corneas were donated to a Canadian and a San Majorian." He continued down the list saving the hearts for last.

"And one of the hearts went to a Canadian who had been vacationing in San Majoria. A young man in his early twenties, his heart just sort of gave out on him out of nowhere. His friends practically pulled him off his windsurf board and into the emergency department. Once there, he didn't leave the hospital for months. In the hours after that July banquet, he received the gift of life because someone made the heart-wrenching and gut-wrenching decision to give it to him."

Tears escaped Astrid's eyes. She peeked at her family and Jordan's at the tables around her. Betsy and her mother weren't even pretending to hold back.

"That Canadian would go home, heal, learn to live his life, and eventually windsurf in San Majoria all over again. This time, though, he accidentally stumbled onto a private beach where he met the woman who would become the love of his life. On the most difficult day of her life, she had made the decision to donate her husband's organs. Someone else, nearby - possibly, or even probably, from the same accident - at nearly the same time, made the same decision. And now, I get to spend the rest of my life loving a woman who could make that selfless decision."

He looked straight at her, though Astrid was sure he couldn't see her through the spotlight.

"As I'm sure you've surmised, I'm the Canadian." A picture of him windsurfing then one of him in the hospital before surgery came on the screen.

Astrid couldn't stop more tears. She'd never seen any of those pictures. Seeing her husband in the hospital bed, swollen from medications and fluids, and so helpless, was nearly too much.

"I never planned to spend more than a couple of weeks in San Majoria." The picture changed to one of him walking down the hospital hallway after the transplant, dragging his IV stand behind him. Dare was at his side. "Because of that one choice someone made, I get to spend the rest of my life with someone else who made that same choice."

The picture changed again, then again, and again. She'd seen some of the pictures on his computer, but she had no idea he basically stalked her with the camera.

But she couldn't be upset.

The pictures of her with Sofia rocking, playing hockey, on the beach were priceless. The photos of her at her desk in San Minoria, kneeling next to a little girl and accepting flowers, dressed in an evening gown and laughing at something at a fundraiser.

So enamored was she with the slideshow that she didn't realize what else was happening until Dare nudged her.

Jordan hadn't expected a standing ovation for Astrid, but there was one. After a minute, everyone sat back down. He looked back down at his notes. This was, by far, his longest speech ever. Even in high school speech class. And he wasn't nearly done yet.

"My wife would be the first to tell you that despite how hard it was to make that decision, she would make it again in a..." He gave what he hoped was a self-deprecating smirk. "Well, in a heartbeat. I told you this story for a reason, and not just in the hopes you would consider being an organ donor yourself. Dr. Catherine Lyttelton is the head of cardiothorasic surgery at Cabo Juan-Eduardo General Hospital. As such, one thing she does when necessary is heart transplants. She cut open my chest, removed my barely functioning heart, and replaced it with one that gave me a new lease on life. When I found out she's the president of the San Majorian Women in Medicine Foundation, I did some research."

Another long list. How bored were these people? Or were they as fascinated as he had been? "She is the first San Majorian woman to perform a heart transplant. In fact, she's the first native San Majorian surgeon, male or female, to do one. Dr. Lyttelton is the youngest doctor ever promoted to the head of a department similar to hers." The list of other accomplishments he read off were equally impressive. "She is renowned not only for her skill with a lancet and Finocheitto retractor." He leaned closer to the microphone. "For those of us who've never been to medical school, those are a scalpel and a rib spreader."

The laughter helped him relax.

"Dr. Lyttelton doesn't just know her way around an operating theater, but the bedside as well. Her bedside manner is one to be emulated. I don't know how many times I talked to her during those months at San Majorian General, but I do know that every time she left, I felt reassured. She donates her time to organizations around the world, visiting third world countries, doing procedures and performing surgery, free of charge. She is an example of what a great doctor, male or female, should be." Jordan grinned. "And she had absolutely no idea this was coming."

He picked up the certificate and plaque. "Ladies and gentlemen, Dr. Catherine Lyttelton, recipient of the first annual *San Majorian Excellence Award for Women in Medicine*."

Dr. Lyttelton walked up onto the stage and took the certificate and plaque then gave him a big hug.

Jordan hugged her back, this woman he owed his life to. "Thank you," he whispered.

"My pleasure, Your Royal Highness." The smirk in her whisper made him smile.

They took a couple of pictures, and she stepped up to the podium. There was a note there telling her to end the banquet as planned when she was done. Jordan wasn't sure where he was supposed to go so he slipped off the other side of the stage, in the shadows and went to sit by his wife.

"I don't usually see my former patients all dressed up," she started. "And I really don't expect them to hand me something like this. To say I'm shocked is an understatement." She made a few remarks thanking her family, the foundation, her team, and several others. She then closed the dinner and mentioned that the recipients needed to come to the stage for pictures.

The stress of getting ready for the event finally bled off. Jordan wanted nothing more than to return to San Minoria with his family, get some sleep, then enjoy the day tomorrow with his family.

But they had to mingle. It seemed like an eternity, but eventually, Jordan drove his car back to the local palace. They boarded a helicopter, and flew to the other island. After a round of hugs, his parents and Dare and Betsy went to their rooms.

Astrid had disappeared, likely into her dressing room to change out of the gorgeous dress that had been perfect for her. He tugged off his tie and dropped it onto a chair. His tuxedo jacket came off and went over the back of the same chair.

The door opened behind him, but he didn't turn around. "How do you think tonight went?" he asked, unbuttoning his top button before starting on his cuff links.

"I never did give you your other birthday present."

Jordan still didn't turn but worked on the other cuff link. "I'm not too worried about it. The ones you gave me were fantastic. I can't wait to go ice skating with you two." They hadn't yet had a chance.

"I asked your mom to send me some of your other things, too."

With his second cuff link off, he finally felt a bit freer. Jordan turned, but froze when he saw her leaning against the door frame to her dressing room. "Is that what I think it is?"

Astrid looked down and uncrossed her arms, holding the hem like a dress. "This old thing?"

"Is that my hockey jersey?"

She spun. Sure enough. *Haines* was spelled across the top. "Is it?" As she started toward him, he realized her smile could mean only one thing.

His hands rested on her hips, and he kissed her. Without breaking contact, he murmured, "I think I'm going to need that back."

His wife giggled and kissed him.

Jordan forgot everything but her. Time stood still and the two of them once again discovered the dance as old as time.

Later, with his wife curled at his side, she traced down the scar in the center of his chest. "I know 'heart' is metaphorical as well as physical. I know your metaphorical heart is the one I can trust." She pushed up on her elbow and leaned over to kiss the center of the scar. "But it seems this physical heart was just meant to belong with me. Do you think that's how God planned it from the beginning?"

"I don't know. Probably. If He knows what's going to happen long before it does, before we're even born, then I would imagine He knew this was where we'd both end up."

She seemed to turn that over in her head. "Well, just don't go forgetting this heart is mine."

He chuckled and pulled her closer. "Not a chance. I'm pretty sure it's been yours since I first saw you on the beach. Somehow I knew."

She leaned up and whispered in his ear. "Me, too."

When Astrid kissed him, everything else fled, but he knew.

He'd found the one his heart loved.

EPILOGUE

"Good morning."

Jordan's husky voice in Astrid's ear didn't startle her. Neither did the arm pulling her backward and into the hollow created by his body.

"Morning."

"Merry Christmas."

"Merry Christmas to you, too." She rolled away from him and then turned to face her husband. "Want your first present?"

A slow grin crossed his face. "We have to meet our families before long."

Astrid smacked his arm. "Not that." She rolled over and opened the drawer of the table next to the bed, pulling out a card before rolling back. "This."

Jordan lay on his back and opened the envelope, pulling the card out. On the front were a few words and three pairs of ice skates - hockey, figure skates, and a smaller pair. He read it aloud. "While it's just the two of us laying here, before we go see the family and more..." He glanced over and opened the card. "The three of us will soon become four." The three skates were replicated with a fourth tiny pair next to them.

His head twisted to look at her. "Four?" He blinked a couple of times. "Wait." With one finger, he traced the skates on the inside of the card then turned to look at her again. "Are you...?"

Astrid's vision blurred as she nodded. "You're going to be a daddy."

Jordan dropped the card and cradled her face in his hand. "Are you serious?"

She laughed as the tears spilled over. "Do you really think I'd tell you if I wasn't? I saw the doctor yesterday, just to make sure before I told you. They did a test. I wanted you to be the first to know, but I had to be certain, and I can't exactly go buy a pregnancy test without the whole country knowing."

He kissed her, a long slow kiss. "You have no idea how happy that makes me," he whispered.

Astrid thought she did. She loved Sofia with her entire being, but this time there was none of the trepidation there had been when she first found out she was pregnant last time.

She trailed her finger down the scar on Jordan's chest. "You know, when I found out I was pregnant with Sofia, I didn't tell Andrei. He didn't know before he died, and I was nearly ten weeks along. I wasn't very sick, just tired, so it's not like I was throwing up every morning or anything. But I didn't want to tell him. I was going to a few days later, but I never had the chance. I almost told him in the car that night. I was going to just say it, but I knew he'd be upset I had known so long. He'd told me I wasn't smart enough to make it in medicine. It annoyed me, so I didn't tell him."

Anger flashed from Jordan's eyes, but she covered his mouth with a finger.

"I don't think he was trying to be mean, just that he didn't think I would be able to do it. And that's okay. I'm not sure he was wrong. Not everyone is cut out for every job they think they might want. I'm okay with it now, really." She kissed him softly. "This time, I'm only about five weeks. I only started to suspect a few days ago. I just needed to be sure."

Before they could talk any further, a yell from the other room caught their attention.

Jordan's arm around Astrid's waist pulled her close. "She'll be okay for a minute," he murmured against her lips. "The big question is do we tell our families today?"

"We can." She kissed him. "I'll show you the cards I printed up for them. If you want to, we can, or we can wait. Your family will be here for a week."

"We'll see." Another shout from the other room sent Jordan rolling away from her. "Stay put, Mama. I got her."

Astrid grinned and wondered if she'd be allowed to do anything for herself any time soon.

A couple of hours later, they were all gathered in her parents' sitting room. Jordan's family, along with Dare's mom, was there. Presents were handed out. Jordan's gift of a photo album, including pictures of her and Sofia experiencing a virtual white Christmas, something she'd mentioned once in passing that she'd never had, made Astrid cry. Not too surprising given her other news.

As everyone was about to disperse, Jordan nodded and winked.

"There's one more," she told them as her sisters both started to stand. She reached into a bag and pulled out the cards. "There's one for everyone." She handed the stack to Betsy who sat on the floor next to her. Betsy took the ones with her name and Dare's on them before handing the stack off.

When everyone had one, Astrid told them to open it.

She could see over Betsy's shoulder. The cards were similar to the inside of Jordan's. Personalized for each family member, with four pairs of skates and the phrase, "New Recruit for Team Haines arriving late summer 2017."

Dare got it first. He pumped both fists in the air. "I knew it!" He wrapped an arm around Betsy's neck and tugged her toward him. "Didn't I tell you?"

Everyone laughed and swarmed Astrid and Jordan. Hugs were

given all around, even Sofia, though she didn't understand what was going on. Astrid wasn't ready for Sofia to know. She'd be in the public eye several times in the next few weeks, and her secret keeping ability was questionable.

By the time Astrid crawled into bed next to her husband, she was exhausted, but happy. The Christmas before had been the loneliest of her life. Single mother. Starting to get pressure from outside her family to marry again.

But this year, her heart was full. Overflowing. With her head on Jordan's shoulder, they talked for nearly an hour about everything and nothing until he dozed.

She shifted until her ear rested on his chest. With the steady rhythm in his chest as her lullaby, Astrid drifted off.

To the beat of the heart of her prince.

LETTER TO READERS

Dear Reader,

Thank you for joining Jordan Haines, Princess Astrid, and Princess Sofia in *Heart of a Prince*! I appreciate you and hope you enjoyed it! This is the first book in the new - likely long running - series, *Crowns & Courtships*!

This series title will accommodate the royal families of Eyjania and San Majoria (and beyond?) through the use of subtitles - *Heart of a Prince* is *Crowns & Courtships, Book 1: Royals of San Majoria*. Just replace the country name when necessary ;).

Next up should be the sequel to *Grace to Save* - tentatively titled *Grace to Stand*! It should be out /fingers crossed/ in late August or early September. Then... a Christmas novella in the *Serenity Landing Teachers* series!

Last time, I said *Crowns & Courtships, Book 2: Royals of Eyjania* - King Benjamin would be next but... Well, one of Astrid's little brothers has informed me his story takes place first. So has one of her sisters. And then Prince Isaiah let me in on what he was doing and it all fits SO WELL... :p. I can't wait to get to Benjamin's story - but it'll work better and make more sense to put it off a bit. That said... It will likely pick up when Benjamin returns to his palace after his confrontation with his uncle, Prince Isaiah, at the Mevendian Founders' Ball.

Organ Donation

I don't remember how the beginning of this story came to me, but I'm pretty sure it was when my oldest daughter ran in Liv's Run for Life in Spring 2016. A teenage girl was in a tragic car accident, but had told her parents she wanted to donate her organs should anything happen to her. They followed her wishes and started an organization to raise awareness, etc.

In my research, my first thought about heart recipients was that they probably had to take it pretty easy. Then I read about Joe Matthews. He took his new heart and decided he owed it to his donor to live life to its fullest. He runs marathons, played rugby, and all kinds of other things. He was gracious enough to answer a few questions for me along the way. (Though I feel like I probably should have gone to interview him in person... business trip to Great Britain anyone?! ;)) You can read more about Joe's story here (2014) or here (2016) - and watch a video produced by Stanford here. If you'd like to follow him, you can on Facebook. Though I left many of Jordan's details vague, his story is very loosely based on Joe's experience with idiopathic cardiomyopathy.

HUGE thanks to Joe for answering my questions and helping me out! A portion of the proceeds from this book will go to one or more of the groups he recommended - Transplant Sport, Stanford Hospital (specify organ donation), and Donate Life California.

HEA-TV

I mentioned this last time. It's still VERY MUCH a work in progress, but I'm working on some of it behind the scenes and then it'll all show up publicly in short succession.

It's found at www.hea-tv.com (that's the name of the Hallmark type channel in this universe, remember?) you'll find "Everything You Ever Wanted To Know About Carol Moncado's Fictional Universe... & More"! There's a "universe" timeline where you can see how everything fits together. Each book will have (or already has) it's own timeline. There's book wikis with character and location/business lists (what was that restaurant again?! ;)) with each entry as a glossary term so you can hover over it to find out more about that character/place, along with summaries of what that book was about. Hello, SPOILERS! :D

There aren't any character or location/business wikis - yet. For now, there's book wikis for both *Lifeguard* books and, by the time this actually reaches your Kindle, hopefully all of *The Brides of Belles Montagnes* and the other two books in *Serenity Landing Second Chances*. I'm working on it!

Previews

In just a few swipes, you'll find chapter 1 of *Grace to Save*, the first book in the Serenity Landing Tuesdays of Grace series! It's the story of Travis Harders and his daughter, Cassie. Travis is the theater teacher at Serenity Landing High School and both have shown up from time to time in other books. It's a story that's very near and dear to my heart, to the core of who I am.

It's a story of prodigals, and redemption, and mercy, and oh-so-much grace.

You can find it available now on Amazon.

The sequel, *Grace to Stand*, introduces new characters who know Travis and Cassie (though they're likely just meeting Abi), so if you haven't caught up with them yet, you totally should!

In just a few more swipes, you'll find chapter 1 of *Good Enough for a Princess*, book 1 in the Montevaro Monarchy series which is FREE on all retailers! Though it was two series ago, that book is the beginning of the events that lead to *Reclaiming Hearts*. Many of you have likely already read *Finding Mr. Write*, but if not, it too is FREE on all retailers!

Other Stuff

I see a meme floating around Facebook from time to time that tells readers what they can do to help their favorite authors. Buying their next book or giving a copy away is kind of a no-brainer, but the biggest thing you can do is write a review. If you enjoyed *Reclaiming Hearts* would you consider doing just that?

I would LOVE to hear from you! My email address is books@candidpublications.com. To stay up-to-date on releases, you can sign up for my newsletter (there's fun stuff - like a chance to get *Dare You* free for a VERY limited time! You'll also get notices of sales, including special preorder pricing! And I won't spam!) or there's always "What's in the Works" or "What I'm Working On Now" on my website :). You can find my website and blog at www.carolmoncado.com. I blog about once a month at www.InspyRomance.com. And, of course, there's Facebook and my Facebook page, Carol Moncado Books. But... the way pages work, sometimes very few people (often 1-5% of "likes") will see anything posted. I keep trying to find the best way to get to know y'all and "spend time" together outside of your Kindle - at least for those of you who want to!

To that end, I've recently started a Facebook reader group! I'd love to have you there! It's easier for you to see what's posted, etc. and where we do fun stuff! There will be discussion questions after the release of a book, spoilers for the next one, general discussion, as well as chances to win copies of books and other goodies! I'd love to have you there!

Thanks again!

ACKNOWLEDGMENTS

They say writing is a solitary endeavor, and it absolutely can be. Sitting in front of the computer for hours on end, talking to imaginary people.

And having them talk back ;).

But the reality is no one walks alone. Since I began this writing journey over six years ago, I can't begin to name all of those who've helped me along the way. My husband, Matt, who has always, *always* believed in me. All of the rest of my family and in-loves who never once looked at me like I was nuts for wanting to be a writer. Jan Christiansen (my "other mother") has always believed in me and Stacy Christiansen Spangler who has been my dearest friend for longer than I can remember.

Ginger Solomon, author of *One Choice* and a bunch of other fantastic books (but *One Choice* is still my favorite!), has been invaluable with her proofreading services. Check her books out!

Then there's my writer friends. Jessica Keller Koschnitzky, Joanna Davidson Politano (her debut comes out this fall!), Jen Cvelbar (the best case of misidentification *ever*, not to mention best conference roomie - and has a new book coming next summer! YAY!), Kristy Cambron, and Stacey Zink are BritCritters, too. We do a lot more living than we do critting, and I wouldn't have it any other way. All five of them are beyond gifted as writers, and I thank God they're in my life. There's my MozArks ACFW peeps who laugh with me, critique, and encourage to no end. Then there's the InspyRomance crew, the CIA, my Spicy peeps (you know who you are!), and all of the others who've helped me along on this journey.

And Jennifer Major. And Emily N. who are both INVALUABLE to my writing process! I have NO IDEA what I'd do without the two of you! And Mikal Dawn (her debut, *Count Me In*, is FABULOUS!) who is so bossy! In a good way ;).

I said I could go on for days, and I could keep going. On and on. I know I've forgotten many people and I hate that. But you, dear reader, would quickly get bored.

So THANK YOU to all of those who have helped me along the way. I couldn't have done this without you and you have my eternal gratitude. To the HUNDREDS of you (I'm gobsmacked!) who pre-ordered and encouraged me without knowing it as that little number continued to climb, you have my eternal gratitude. I hope you stick around for the next one!

And, of course, last but never, *ever*, least, to Jesus Christ, without whom none of this would be possible - or worth it.

GRACE TO SAVE PREVIEW

SEPTEMBER 11, 2001

A ringing jolted Travis Harders from a deep sleep. He cursed as the phone knocked to the floor with a clatter. "This better be good," he snapped when he got the handset in place.

A glance at the clock nearly made him groan.

4:07.

"You'll be hearing from the police soon."

He rubbed the sleep out of his eyes with the heel of one hand and tried to process the statement. The words didn't really register as the guy, whoever he was, kept talking until Travis interrupted. "What? Who is this?"

"Mark's dad." Right. Travis's best friend. "You remember us? The ones who treated you like family? Let you live with us?"

Travis's stomach sank. Mark's family had practically adopted him when he moved from southwest Missouri to the Big Apple. They had filled the gap in his life left by parents who disapproved of Travis's choice to move to New York. Mark's parents let him spend holidays and birthdays with them, with Travis making only the obligatory phone calls back home.

But none of that explained why Mark's dad would be calling the police.

"Who is it?" a sleepy Jennifer asked.

Travis covered the mouthpiece and whispered to his girlfriend, "No one." His feet hit the cool floor, and he headed for the other room. At least he had a place to escape to. Being an out-of-work-actor-turned-barista didn't pay much, but he'd lucked into a fabulous apartment. Closing the French door behind him, he tried to focus on the voice yelling from the other end of the line.

But he only caught "my daughter" and "spring break" and "drugged."

If possible, Travis's stomach clenched further as that night flooded back to him. Memories of bringing her back to this very apartment when she was in no condition to go home without risking the wrath of her parents. But after what happened between them...it was only right for him to be on the receiving end of her dad's anger. "I don't know what she told you sir, but…"

"I know all I need to know," he bellowed.

Even though he was in the other room, Travis lowered the volume on the handset. "I take full responsibility for…"

"You're right, you do!" He let loose a string of obscenities. "You'll spend years in prison! Drugging a girl! Sleeping with her!"

"What?" His whole world spun. Travis regretted every minute of that night after they got back to the apartment, but he hadn't drugged her. He didn't even know where to get those kinds of drugs. They weren't in love, never had been, but to place the blame solely on him? The next morning, they'd talked about it enough to know she hadn't blamed him.

What changed? Feeling sucker punched, Travis hung up on the man. What he said didn't matter. Travis would find out when he was on trial for something he didn't do. On autopilot, he dressed for his five a.m. shift. Coffees of the World wasn't the best job, but it had flexible hours and had led to finding this sublet. There was no shortage of interesting characters to populate his imagination. Like the skinny brunette with the shoulder length bob who worked for Morgan Stanley and always ordered a short nonfat mocha, decaf, no foam, no sugar, no whip. She could be the heroine in one of his screenplays even if he never knew her name.

He kissed Jennifer's hair and told her he'd call after work. Five flights of stairs later, the sounds of the city waking up greeted him as he walked toward the train that would take him to the Trade Center. Standing at the top of the subway steps, he changed his mind. Travis headed for his car parked a couple streets over and called in.

Two hours later, he stopped in McLean for gas about seven thirty, filling up the tank of his Toyota Corolla hatchback. Three hours after that, he could still drive for a while longer before he'd need to stop again. He contemplated leaving the state, but decided not to, instead turning northward before leaving Allegany County.

He'd gone through more emotions than he knew he had, none of them good. Anger. Fear. Frustration. Blame. Worry. Intimidation. In western New York, things were more peaceful than they ever were in downtown Manhattan, but his insides were in utter turmoil at the thought of an arrest and trial.

His favorite heavy metal CD blared from the speakers. During the lull between songs, Travis could hear his cell phone vibrating on the passenger seat where he'd tossed it. After an hour and a half of the stupid thing ringing nearly nonstop, he finally snatched it up.

"What?" Travis growled.

"Are you okay?" Though he only talked to her twice a year, there was no mistaking his mother's voice.

Or the panic in it.

The tremor set him on edge. "Yeah. Why?"

"Thank you, Jesus," she whispered, though Travis couldn't figure out what she was thanking Him for. "Where are you? You got out okay? Were you working? There was no answer at your apartment."

Why was Mom calling just to ask if he was okay? Why was she

frantic? "I'm in western New York State. Out for a drive. Get out of where?" Could Mark's dad have called already?

"You don't know?" Frenzy changed to disbelief.

"Know what?" Travis held the phone against his shoulder as he downshifted into a turn.

He could hear the tears over the static-filled line. "Two planes, Trav. They hit the Towers. Both of the buildings are on fire."

His heart thudded to a stop. "What?" Hadn't a bomber hit the Empire State Building in WWII? But two planes? On a brilliantly clear day? No weather in sight. "How bad is it?" he croaked.

"They're saying it's a terror attack. The Pentagon is on fire. There's another plane out there somewhere. Big jets, Travis. I saw the second one hit. The explosion. Papers flying everywhere. The people..." Her voice broke. "You really weren't there?" she confirmed.

"No, Mom. I'm not anywhere near there." But he needed to find a place to stop. A television. He had to see for himself. Tens of thousands of people would be dead and dying. Did he know any of them?

"There are people jumping, falling, out of the upper stories. I can't imagine." He could almost see her pacing around the kitchen alternately running her hands through her hair and wringing them together. "They're jumping from a hundred stories up. What could be so bad to make that the better option?" Her voice caught. "I don't know how I can watch this, Trav, but I can't turn away. All I can do is pray."

Pray. Right. A face flashed before Travis. The uptight former-football-player-turned-businessman from the 102nd floor of the North Tower with his caramel macchiato and corny joke of the day. Was he one of those jumping?

She gasped then whispered. "Dear God, no. No!" Her scream made him move the phone even as his stomach sank.

He pulled into a café parking lot near Danville. "What?"

"The tower. It's gone. Just gone. The south one, I think." Her voice trailed off in prayer.

The shock he'd felt after the phone call from Mark's dad paled compared to what he felt now. "Mom, I gotta go." Jen. His friends. His coworkers. He needed to make calls of his own. Find out if they were okay. And Mark. His best friend had been a firefighter for a year. He'd be down there. Inside one of the Towers. Travis hadn't talked to him since that night, the March before, but part of him, the part that still believed there was a God in heaven, whispered a prayer that Mark was somewhere safe as faces of customers and friends flashed through Travis's mind.

The blonde. The cute, petite one who ordered a crunchy, cinnamon pastry and half caf, double tall, easy hazelnut, non-fat, no foam with whip extra hot latte on Tuesdays. She flirted shamelessly, though he knew she was recently and happily engaged to some guy in Tower Seven. Her family lived near his in Serenity Landing, Missouri, and she worked at the Marriot World Trade Center in the shadow of the Towers. Could it have survived the collapse? Was Joanna now buried underneath the rubble?

"Be safe, Travis. Do you have somewhere you can go? They're evacuating Manhattan."

"I'll be okay." He hesitated. "I love you, Mom. You, Dad, Jay. I love all of you. I'll call when I can, but I have to try to find out about my friends, about my girlfriend. I'll talk to you soon."

His mom's "I love you," came through the line as he clicked his phone off.

He started his first call as he walked into the café. Call after call failed as he stood with others, watching the screen in horror as the second tower crashed down. His problems. Mark's dad. Mark's sister. All of it fled as the enormity of what was happening sunk in.

The whole world had changed.

December 18, 2001

"It's a girl."

Abi Connealy collapsed back onto the bed, tears streaming down her cheeks as a newborn squawk filled the delivery room.

A girl.

A million thoughts flew through her mind, few of them happy, as a nurse laid the baby on her chest. So small. So scrunched up and red. Dark hair. Abi couldn't see her eyes as she wrapped her arms around the tiny bundle. "Hi, baby," she whispered. "I'm so glad you're here."

"How are you?"

Abi looked up at Brenda Wardman. Her brother's girlfriend had been a rock the last few months. She didn't need to clarify, because Abi knew what she meant. "I don't know." The voice mail she'd left her parents on the way to the hospital remained unanswered unless Brenda knew something she didn't.

Her fingers brushed over the cheek of the tiny girl. "She's perfect, Bren." Another tear fell, this one landing on her new daughter's face as Abi closed her eyes.

The nurse took the baby to the warmer and did whatever it was nurses did, but Abi didn't see any of it. Her eyes remained closed, and she clasped Brenda's hand as more hot tears streaked into her ears. Just under twenty-four hours of labor meant she didn't have the energy to wipe them away. She knew she didn't have the will to do so even if she could have.

"Do you know what you're going to do?"

Abi wanted to yell at her friend for bringing up the most difficult decision of her life just moments after the birth of her daughter. But since Abi hadn't made up her mind beforehand, Brenda needed to know to help make the arrangements.

Except Abi didn't know.

Not for sure. She knew what the smart decision was, though her head and her heart didn't agree. But she had to put her baby first. "I'll have them call."

"It's going to be fine," Brenda tried to reassure her, but Abi heard the doubt in her friend's voice.

Right.

Fine.

Once the social worker arrived, she'd never be fine again.

Somehow, Abi managed to doze for several hours during the afternoon, but after listening to the message from her parents, the one that told her all she needed to know without really saying anything, her eyes refused to close. Instead, she stared at the bracelet encircling her wrist, rotating it around time and time again.

A knock sounded half a second before the door pushed open. "Hi, there, Abi. Someone's looking for her mama." The nurse compared the baby's bracelet to Abi's before lifting the blanketed bundle out of the clear bassinet. "The card says you're giving her formula?"

There was no judgment in the woman's voice, but Abi felt her own condemnation eating away at her. All she could do was nod.

After a few minutes of helping them get situated, the nurse started to leave, but stopped before walking out the door. "The emotions are normal, honey. They get everyone at one point or another."

Abi nodded but didn't take her eyes off the little cheeks sucking in and out. She memorized the sounds, the smells, the essence of the tiny bundle in her arms. Or tried to. Even as she did, she knew it would never work. In the morning, a social worker would come and Abi would sign the papers put in front of her.

And she'd never see her daughter again.

But when the social worker sat in the chair by the window, asking the questions, one tripped Abi up.

"Do you know who her father is?"

The night was burned in Abi's memory banks. Part of it anyway. When she hesitated too long, the worker prompted her again. Abi nodded. "Yes. I know who the father is."

"Then we'll need his signature, too."

"He doesn't know," she whispered. "I haven't talked to him since. I was going to, but then 9/11..." Her voice trailed off.

"Was he in the Towers?" the social worker asked as gently as she could.

Abi shook her head. "I don't he was. I mean, I know he wasn't one of the three thousand, but I don't know if he was there or not." She'd called his apartment from a pay phone a few weeks later. When he answered, she hung up.

"If you know who he is, we have to have him sign away his parental rights, sweetie."

Something she hadn't considered when she made this plan.

The nurse walked in, once again pushing the bassinet. Her face fell when she saw the social worker. "I'm sorry. I didn't realize you were..."

With a swipe of the overused Kleenex, Abi wiped her face. "I wasn't sure, but now I can't anyway."

The social worker left a couple of fliers and walked out with a sympathetic smile. The nurse awkwardly helped Abi get situated to feed her daughter one more time.

"Do you have a name you like?" The woman sat on the edge of the bed holding Abi's empty water bottle.

"Cassandra."

"That's beautiful."

"It was my grandmother's name. She died this past summer." The grandmother who would have adored meeting her great-granddaughter, who would have taken Abi and the baby in when she needed somewhere to turn. Had given Abi hope she'd do just that before succumbing to a sudden, massive stroke.

Abi didn't have anyone else like that in her life. Brenda would if she could, but there was no way. Abi had no other family. No one else in her life who would support her no matter what.

Darkness descended, but Abi refused to send little Cassie back to the nursery. She didn't know what she planned to do about adoption, but she wouldn't give up another minute with her baby.

Yet another round of tears leaked down her face as Abi cuddled the tiny bundle against her chest. With all but one light turned out, the desperate whisper ripped from her throat. "God? Are you there?" She'd never prayed before, but this seemed like the time to start if there ever was one. "I don't know what to do."

Baby Cassandra yawned and blinked her eyes open, staring up at her mother. The light caught them just right and struck Abi with the bright blue.

Then it hit her.

The one place she could take her daughter where she'd be safe. And loved.

December 23, 2001

Two days before Christmas, Abi sat in a coffee shop on Long Island and waited. Calling him had taken every ounce of courage she had. Leaving the voicemail took more.

Sitting there, Abi didn't know if she could go through with it. The stroller with her little girl sat to her right. On the other side of it, Brenda sat with her back to the door. Diners nearby sipped on gourmet coffee, but Abi focused on the stationary in front of her. She arrived early so she could write the note, but the paper remained nearly blank.

When she'd arrived at her parents' Long Island home after leaving the hospital, a note reiterated her father's threat. Since then, Abi had planned what to say, but realized she'd never make it through even the shortest speech. She'd planned the words to write, but now the time had come to put pen to paper, and she only managed his name. A glance at her watch told her she didn't have much time. If she didn't write it now, she'd have to make the speech. No way could she do that.

She picked up the Mont Blanc knock-off she'd received for graduation from her grandmother and scribbled a few lines. Her heart squeezed as she reread the note. She couldn't be a student and a mom. But *this*? Abi had her suitcase packed. She wouldn't return to her parents' home but would crash at Brenda's for a few days while her friend went out of town. Brenda knew most of what happened, but not everything. Abi's fingers furrowed through her hair, and she turned to stare out the window. There he stood. His six-foot frame seemed shorter with his shoulders slumped and hands shoved deep in the pockets of his coat. He looked at his watch and trudged across the street.

The bell over the door jangled. Abi crossed through the unfinished sentence, scribbled a last sentiment and her name, and shoved the note in her purse as he sat down across from her.

"Hi." At the sound of his voice, the knots in her gut tightened.

Abi looked up, knowing he'd see the remnants of her tears. She twisted the napkin in her hands and tried not the think about the weight she'd gained. And if he'd notice.

"Thanks for coming. I wanted to try to explain, but..." Abi shrugged. "After 9/11, after Mark..." The thoughts of her brother nearly overwhelmed her already overwrought emotions. "Daddy isn't going to pursue anything. I tried to tell him you weren't guilty, but he didn't believe me at first. He found your name in my journal on 9/11-before it was '9/11.' I'd left it lying out by accident." This time the shrug was a mere halfhearted lift of one shoulder.

"Mark?" he interrupted. "I read the list of firefighters a bunch of times to make sure he wasn't there."

"He wasn't on the lists. He was killed at a fire on 9/11. Not at the Trade Center. Another fire where they didn't have enough manpower because of everything else. They think he died right around the time the first tower fell."

Were those tears in his eyes? He and Mark hadn't spoken in months. "I'm so sorry."

Cassandra let out a cry. The disguised Brenda made a shushing sound, but Abi didn't look. She couldn't. It was too much. She had to get out. "Can you excuse me for a minute?"

She didn't wait for a reply but motioned toward the back, leaving before he had a chance to stop her. Brenda went out the front door. Abi dug the paper out and waved the barista over. "Can you give this to that guy?"

The woman nodded. Abi fled to the other side of the street and collapsed in Brenda's arms.

Travis read the note three times before it began to sink in.

Dear Travis,

She had to have written it earlier. There hadn't been time since she excused herself.

I hate doing this to you, especially like this. I tried to handle it on my own. I thought I could, but this semester was so hard. Even more than just everything on 9/11 and Mark. I can't do it. I can't be a college student and a mom.

It took several minutes for that to really register.

A mom?

He read on, his disbelief growing with each word.

The baby in the stroller is yours. From that night. I hate that I haven't told you sooner, but I didn't know how. I couldn't tell my parents what happened, not all of it. They would blame you, and it wasn't your fault. I know this is the coward's way out, but I can't tell you to your face. Everything you need for a couple of days is in the diaper bag and the duffel on the bottom of the stroller. So is her birth certificate.

Her name is Cassandra. She's only a few days old. Please take good care of her for me. I won't be home for a while so you can't reach me. My parents left for vacation out of the country, so they wouldn't be here when she was born.

I wish things had worked out the way we planned. The way we talked about all those times. ~~*I wish*~~

Whatever she wished, she didn't finish the thought before scribbling through it. About like their relationship had been. A wish that was never finished. He went back to the letter.

Tell Cassandra I love her.

I'm sorry.

Abi

He read it two more times, starting to come to grips with what it meant.

And then the baby began to fuss.

Taking a deep, steadying breath to fortify himself, he turned to the blanket tented over the handle of the car seat. Lifting up one corner, he saw pink. Fuzzy bunnies on the toes of a sleeper. A tiny foot kicking those bunnies in the air. He looked further and saw the bluest eyes he'd ever seen staring back at him, almost as though she knew who he was.

Her father.

Her daddy.

The one responsible for her from here on out.

And in that moment, he fell helplessly in love.

December 25, 2001

Christmas night, the little gray Toyota turned off I-44, south towards Serenity Landing, as the wailing in the backseat reached a new level.

"I'm sorry, Cassandra. We're almost there. I'll get you something to eat in a ten minutes, I promise." Jennifer kicked him out the moment he tried to explain his arrival at the apartment with a baby. Instead, he'd boxed up all his worldly belongings along with the things Abi had left for the baby and packed it in his car. They headed for the only place he knew he could get the help he needed until he had a better handle on things.

Over twelve hundred miles. Stopping every two or three hours to feed his daughter or change her diaper. Sometimes more often than that. Always taking much longer than it should. Failing to take into account how many things would be closed on Christmas Day, he ran out of the bottled water when he needed to make one more meal for his daughter. He pressed the pedal a little closer to the floor in an effort to reach Serenity Landing a little faster.

The newborn squalling had quieted a bit when Travis finally pulled to a stop in front of the house where he'd grown up. In the front window, a Christmas tree stood, multi-colored lights twinkling. In the window next to it, he could see Mom and Dad sitting at the dining room table, though he knew they wouldn't be able to see him. His brother walked in with a platter, piled high with a turkey way too big for the three of them. They'd be eating leftovers for a month.

Another squeak came from the back. "Okay, baby. We're here."

Somehow, Travis managed to get the diaper bag and the baby seat out of the car and headed toward the door, snow crunching under his boots with each step. The smell of oak burning in the fireplace both comforted him and heightened his anxiety. What if they turned him away? Then what?

Should he knock?

He hadn't been home in two and a half years. Did he just walk in?

Even with his hands full, Travis managed to press the doorbell. He took a deep breath and blew it out slowly, finishing as the door opened.

Mom stood there, her jaw hanging down for a second before her hands covered her mouth. "Travis!"

He tried to smile but failed miserably. "Hi, Mom." In the space of a heartbeat, he saw what he needed to in her eyes. Forgiveness. Acceptance. Love. Grace. With a prayer tossed heavenward, he tried again to smile, this time successfully. "There's someone I want you to meet."

Available Now!

Travis Harders has been a single dad since the day he learned he had a daughter with his only one-night stand. Fifteen years later, he and Cassie are getting along just fine and he's even fallen in love. The last thing he expects to find on his doorstep one Tuesday morning is Cassie's mom - the one person he thought he'd never see again - and she's asking the impossible.

Circumstances, including her firefighter brother's death on 9/11, forced Abi Connealy into a decision she's spent years regretting and her daughter grew up without her. But now, a family crisis compels her to do the one thing she swore she never would: find the daughter she'd abandoned just a few days after birth.

Shocked when Travis doesn't send her packing, Abi prays to a God she doesn't believe in that her relationship with her daughter will be restored. Travis plans to propose to his girlfriend, but their relationship hits the rocks as he and Abi both struggle with the long-dormant feelings that never had the chance to develop.

When Cassie demonstrates incredible grace toward the grandfather who refuses to acknowledge her existence, Abi begins to learn the love of a Savior - a Savior who has more than enough Grace to Save.

GOOD ENOUGH FOR A PRINCESS PREVIEW

Charlie Brewer pushed the hood of his heavy winter coat back with one gloved hand. A fender bender? Really? Like he didn't have anything else to do? Like get home to... Screaming interrupted his thoughts. He rapped on the window and prayed for it to stop. "Ma'am. Are you okay?" Stinging bits of ice pelted his face and peppered the car as he prayed she wasn't hurt.

Abruptly, her mouth clamped shut.

Bits of sleet pelted his face as he knocked again. "Are you okay?"

The girl looked up and the first thing he noticed was her big hazel eyes, filled to overflowing with tears.

"Are you okay?" Broken records had nothing on him. He cupped his hands and peered in the window. She didn't look hurt. He flinched. Except maybe for the gash on her forehead.

She nodded but didn't say anything and didn't roll down the window.

"I need to give you my contact information."

The window creaked down half an inch or so.

"No. I do not need your information. I will take care of my

own vehicle, thank you." Even with the frantic note in her voice, he knew it would be almost melodic in a calmer situation. The window scratched its way back up and slid into the rubber casing.

He tried to take a deep breath but the frigid air pierced his lungs. "Let me buy you a cup of coffee. You'll need a tow. Your wheel well is all messed up and you've got two flat tires."

She bit her bottom lip as her eyes flickered to the café across the parking lot. The look in her eyes suddenly reminded him of a scared little girl.

With both hands held up, Charlie tried to look less threatening than he must have when she first saw him with his hood up and face shadowed. He gave the best smile he could with frozen cheeks. "I promise I'm a good guy."

Finally, with a nod, she grabbed her purse from the front seat of the SUV, and turned the engine off. She reached for the handle on the inside of the driver's door. It didn't budge.

Bright lights caught him in the eye. A semi-truck passed a little too close for Charlie's comfort. If she had that door open and slipped...

"This side," he hollered at her and pulled on the handle.

She nodded and climbed across the center console while he pulled again.

Frozen shut.

Ice continued to fall, sliding down the back of his neck and into his shirt. If he wasn't already frozen through, that would have done it.

"You push from that side," Charlie yelled. "I'll pull."

Another nod and she pushed with one hand but it didn't move. He closed his eyes and breathed a quick prayer. "Put your shoulder into it."

Tears flowed, but she pushed against the door with her shoulder as he pulled. The door popped free and she tumbled out.

He caught her by the elbow to steady her on her feet, caught off-guard by the whiff of sunshine in her hair. "Are you okay?"

She nodded, her chin quivered just a little and Charlie gentled his hold on her. "I am. Thank you, sir."

There was something in her voice, or maybe her perfect posture, that brought visions of Mary Poppins to mind. He shrugged them off and closed her car door behind her. With a slow steady pace, he continued to hold her arm as started toward the inviting warmth of the café.

Warmth? Yes. He couldn't feel his nose anymore.

"You do not need to help me." The dismissive note in her voice bothered him until she jerked her arm away.

And slipped, wobbled, then righted herself. But she didn't fall.

Charlie contained his smirk and a dutiful bow. "I'm sure I don't, miss, but I'd feel much better if you'd allow me. I already crashed into your car. If I let you get hurt in the parking lot, I'd never forgive myself."

She sighed. A puff of white air blew out in front of her but she didn't pull away again. The thirty-second walk took nearly five minutes. Slow, half-steps, muscles tensed, toes bunched inside his boots trying to grip the slippery surface on top of the asphalt. They finally made it to the door. Hot air and the smell of sizzling bacon blasted him.

"Have a seat anywhere, kids!" a woman's voice called.

Charlie turned toward a row of booths along the front window. "After you?"

The woman pulled the knit cap off her head. Golden brown curls tumbled around her shoulders. She looked around carefully before walking all the way to the far end and sliding in the seat against the wall.

He sat across from her and held out a hand. "I'm Charlie."

One corner of her mouth twitched up before she shook his hand. "Adeline."

"A pleasure to meet you, Adeline. I just wish it was under other circumstances."

"Agreed. A car accident..." A flash of awareness crossed her face and she set her large black bag on the table. She flipped open one flap and dug around. "Where is it?" she muttered as she searched. Somehow, even that action seemed delicate. She wasn't from here.

"What are you looking for?"

"My phone. I need to call..." She stopped abruptly, gaze traveling to the café window. "Do we need to move the vehicles?"

Charlie shook his head. "We're far enough out of the main lane and the cars are stuck together. We'll have to wait for a tow. It could be a while." He pulled out his own phone to call roadside assistance.

"Should we call 911?" Adeline asked as she took a sleek black phone out of her purse. He tried to control an eyebrow quirk but failed. There were cell phones. There were nice smart phones. There were really nice smart phones. Then there was this one.

"No. They're on emergency status only. As long as no one's hurt, you deal with it yourself."

"Of course," She whispered and stared at her phone for a long moment. "I do not have a card for roadside assistance. Perhaps you could ask your service to send an extra tow truck for my vehicle?"

Something in the way she asked made him wonder if she'd ever called for auto help. The tilt of her chin and honest curiosity in her eyes reminded him of the children's fairytales he used to read. Did fairies come into the real world during ice storms? "I'll take care of it." It made him feel protective. Almost manly. When was the last time he'd felt the need to protect a woman? Ever? He found the right entry and pressed the screen. After listening and going through the process, he finally got a real person. Holding up one finger to Adeline, he stood and walked toward the front door to explain the situation.

Crown Princess Adeline Julianne Elizabeth of Montevaro

relived the sickening crunch of metal as her car slid to a stop in the ditch outside. She could still feel the steering wheel as she'd gripped it, trying to keep the tears, and the panic, at bay. Her unsuccessful attempts now showed on her face, she was certain. Red, blotchy eyes. Tear-stained cheeks. Moisture still leaking out from time to time. Her mother would be mortified.

She knew when she left the house an accident could happen. No one ever dreamed of letting the Crown Princess learn to drive on ice, of all things. But she had taken matters into her own hands. Adeline, the girl who never did anything wrong, who always did what was expected of her, had slipped away from her security detail, taken the safer of the two vehicles at her disposal, and left. All because she wanted a few moments of freedom before the ice storm settled in.

A shaking hand had pushed the hair back from one side of her face as she ran through her mental checklist.

No airbag deployment. Good.

Pain in her head meant she likely hit the steering wheel. Bad.

Slow speed at time of impact. Good.

Impact. Bad.

As long as she did not have a concussion or bruising from the steering wheel or seat belt, she would be able to convince Mark and Todd she was fine. They would read her the riot act. Debate long and hard about calling her father. Eventually, they would call their superiors, debate some more and, sooner or later, her father would find out. She had rested her head on the steering wheel. He did not need the additional stress. The last two times she visited Montevaro, her father had seemed off. She feared what he would tell her when she returned home for good in a few months.

She had contemplated digging her cell phone out and giving a preemptive call. Cut them off at the pass. Reassure Mark she was rattled but fine and his relief would overwhelm his anger and concern.

She took a deep, shuddering breath and dug her phone back out of her purse. Addie closed her eyes and finally turned her phone back on. Three times, her finger slipped off the "on" button. It went through its start-up procedure and buzzed with missed calls and text messages. Every one of them came from Mark, Todd, or the house. Before she could listen to any of the twenty voice mails, the phone rang again.

With a deep breath and a whispered prayer, she pressed "answer." "Hello?"

Mark's bellow did not help her headache. "Where are you?"

She sighed. "At the Serenity Landing diner on Highway 60 about two miles from town."

"What are you doing there?" His voice softened slightly as she heard the garage door open in the background.

Just saying the words made her wince. "I was in an accident."

His bellow returned. "What?"

"I am fine, Mark. A gentleman ran into the back of the SUV. He helped me out of the vehicle and to the restaurant. He is calling tow trucks right now."

"We're on our way." His words were clipped and nearly cut off by the sound of a slamming car door.

Once the connection severed, Addie set the phone on the table and rested her face in her hands, biting back the groan threatening to escape her throat.

"Tow trucks will be here when they get here." Charlie scooted into the seat across from her. "We're way down on the list since we're not on a major highway. We're somewhere safe and warm, we're not blocking traffic, and no one's hurt."

"I will likely be gone long before they get here." She put her phone in the side pocket of her purse and snapped the flap closed.

"At least let me buy you that cup of coffee." He turned to look for a waitress.

Addie looked at Charlie for a moment before deciding she could trust him. Something about his curly, dirty blond hair and mocha eyes convinced her to give a curt not. "Very well."

The waitress, stereotypical for a restaurant of this kind, bustled up. "Sorry, kids." She handed them each a menu. "What can I get ya?"

With a smile, Addie looked at her. "Hello, Melony."

A wide grin split Melony's face. "Well, hey there! How are ya, sugar? Where's Mark and Todd? What're they thinkin' lettin' ya out here in this weather?"

Addie nodded toward the street. "Mr. Brewer and I had a bit of an accident. We are fine. Mark and Todd will be here shortly." She tucked her hair behind her ear. "Could I get a cup of tea?"

Melony gasped. "You're bleeding." She grabbed a napkin, sending a fork and spoon clattering to the floor.

"I am fine, Melony. I promise."

"Nonsense." Charlie watched as Melony pressed the napkin against Adeline's forehead. "You need to go to the hospital."

"No. Mark and Todd will be here soon. Mark has medic training. If I need stitches, he can do it." The girl took over holding the napkin to her own head, leaving Charlie wondering who Mark and Todd were and why she seemed both annoyed and comforted by the idea of the two men.

Her brothers maybe?

But if they were on their way, he needed to get to know her and fast. Because he'd never met a woman who intrigued him so much from the first moment he heard her speak. Was it the accent? The lilting tone? He didn't know but he wanted to find out. Charlie turned his best smile up to the waitress. "Melony, is it?"

The dark curls bounced up and down as she nodded. "Sure is."

"Melony, would you get Adeline that cup of tea? I'd love some coffee if you've got it. Do you still have breakfast?" He'd driven by the diner many times but had never stopped. Most of these places had breakfast all day, didn't they?

"Sure do, hon. Twenty-four seven. Why don't you two decide

what you want and I'll get those drinks?" She looked pointedly at Adeline. "Keep pressure on that."

More than anything Charlie wanted to reach out and brush the hair back, away from the cut in the otherwise smooth skin. He tilted sideways and pulled a handkerchief out of the pocket of his pants. He dipped it in the water glass Melony had set there. Half-standing, he leaned over the table. "Let me see?"

Adeline nodded and pulled the napkin away. "It feels as though the bleeding has stopped."

The cut didn't look good, but it didn't look too bad either. "Here." With slow movements, he did his best to wipe off the dried blood. "I think you'll be okay."

"Thank you, Charlie." Her eyelashes lifted enough for him to see the gold-flecked hazel of her eyes then moved downward again.

He finished cleaning around the wound, refolded his handkerchief, and held it to her head. "You might still want to hold that, though."

Her fingertips brushed his hand as she reached up, sending chills, the good kind, down his spine. "Thank you, again."

He settled back in his seat. "You're not from around here, are you?"

The silky brown hair shifted as she shook her head. "No. I am not."

"Where are you from?"

Melony set two steaming cups in front of them. "Just like you like it."

"You are a queen among women, Melony." Her voice drew Charlie further in.

"Don't you know it?" Melony winked, covering one of her pale green eyes. Charlie couldn't help but compare them to Adeline's. Though they were both primarily green, they were as different as the Amazon rain forest and split-pea soup. "Now, what can I get you to eat?"

Charlie ordered pancakes and bacon. Adeline decided on her "usual," whatever that was.

Once Melony headed for the kitchen, Adeline resumed their conversation. "Have you ever heard of a country called Montevaro?"

With his brow furrowed, Charlie tried to think, but came up mostly blank. "I think I have but that's all I can say."

One corner of her mouth tipped upward. "It is a small nation, sandwiched between Mevendia, Switzerland, and Italy."

"Mevendia?"

"Yes. It is even smaller than we are, on the southeastern border of Switzerland. We have cultural and historical ties with Mevendia and Ravenzario. Ravenzario is..."

"Two islands off the coast of Italy and France in the Mediterranean. I think I visited there as a kid."

Adeline nodded. "Yes."

"And you're from Montevaro, is it?"

She nodded. "Yes. Three of us were chosen to come here and study International Relations at Serenity Landing University."

"Chosen?" He quirked an eyebrow at her. "Did you do the best on some sort of test?"

This time the smile was a bit more full-fledged but still didn't reach her eyes. "Something along those lines, yes."

"I'm sorry I hit you, but I'm glad you're here so I could meet you." Deep inside, he cringed. That sounded like such a line.

"You did not hit me, Charlie. You hit my vehicle. And given the weather conditions, it could hardly be considered your fault."

"Still. I'm glad we've met. But what exactly does one study in international relations?"

"The relationship between countries. The relationship between countries and all kinds of different organizations: intergovernmental organizations, nongovernmental organizations, multinational corporations. Things like that."

"So will you work for the State Department of your country?"

Charlie wrapped his hands around the mug to warm his fingers and sipped his coffee.

"We do not have a state department like America's, so no. But yes, I will be involved in foreign relations between Montevaro and any number of other entities."

"Is it interesting?" He didn't see how it could be, but different strokes for different folks and all.

She gave a bit of a half shrug. "It is not uninteresting. International relations is the family business."

Family business? Like the Kennedys? Or what was the local family he saw in the tabloids while stuck in the checkout lane? The last name was Langley, he thought, because it always made him think of the CIA.

"So it's expected of you."

"Something like that."

Melony chose that moment to come back and set their food in front of them. "Here ya go. If you need anything else, just holler."

They ate in silence for a few minutes until lights flashed across them. Charlie looked outside. A dark sedan with tinted windows pulled up.

Adeline set the rest of her sandwich on her plate and picked her napkin up from her lap. "That is my ride. Thank you again for your assistance."

Charlie chuckled. "I hit you. It's the least I could do to offer to help."

She reached for her gloves and hat before setting them back down and reaching into her purse. "Here is my card if you need to reach me." She left it on the table.

The door jangled open behind him and he heard boots stomping.

"Adeline, let's go."

Turning his head, he saw a giant hulk of a man standing near them.

"Of course." She slid out of the booth and stood.

Charlie followed suit.

"Thank you again, Mr. Brewer."

He took a deep breath, ignored the man towering over him, and plunged in. "Can I call you? Once this storm blows over?"

Adeline smiled, this time showing perfect rows of pearly white teeth. "I suppose that would be all right."

Charlie watched as she and the man walked toward the front door. He wondered if he'd see her again. The thunderous expression on the face of the man in front of him said, "no."

Available FREE for Kindle!

Crown Princess Adeline of Montevaro has her life planned out for her: get her Master's in international relations, marry nobility, produce an heir, inherit the throne. There's no room for romance with the single father she meets when their cars collide on an icy winter night. Parliament - and her father - would never approve.

Charlie Brewer grew up without roots. The son of an archaeologist father and anthropologist mother, he either traveled along or lived with his aunt and uncle in the States. He's determined to give his daughter the stability he never had. He also wants to give her a mom, but the beautiful European he's falling for refuses to move to Serenity Landing, Missouri permanently.

He won't move. She can't stay. What will happen when they try to forget each other by dating someone "acceptable"? They find themselves drawn together by one of the girls in the after school program Addie supports - a girl who happens to be Charlie's daughter. How will Charlie, and his daughter, feel when they find out the woman they've both fallen for is a... princess?

A trip halfway around the world shows Charlie and Addie how much they long to be together - and how impossible it is. Is there any way he can prove he is *Good Enough for a Princess*?

ABOUT THE AUTHOR

When she's not writing about her imaginary friends, USA Today Bestselling Author Carol Moncado prefers binge watching pretty much anything to working out. She believes peanut butter M&Ms are the perfect food and Dr. Pepper should come in an IV. When not hanging out with her hubby, four kids, and two dogs who weigh less than most hard cover books, she's probably reading in her Southwest Missouri home.

Summers find her at the local aquatic center with her four fish, er, kids. Fall finds her doing the band mom thing. Winters find her snuggled into a blanket in front of a fire with the dogs. Spring finds her sneezing and recovering from the rest of the year.

She used to teach American Government at a community college, but her indie career, with over twenty titles released, has allowed her to write full time. She's a founding member and former President of MozArks ACFW, blogger at InspyRomance, and is represented by Tamela Hancock Murray of the Steve Laube Agency.

www.carolmoncado.com
books@candidpublications.com

OTHER BOOKS BY CAROL MONCADO

The CANDID Romance Series

Finding Mr. Write
Finally Mr. Write
Falling for Mr. Write

The Monarchies of Belles Montagnes Series
(Previously titled The Montevaro Monarchy and The Brides of Belles Montagnes series)

Good Enough for a Princess
Along Came a Prince
More than a Princess
Hand-Me-Down Princess
Winning the Queen's Heart
Protecting the Prince (Novella)
Prince from her Past

Serenity Landing Second Chances

Discovering Home
Glimpsing Hope
Reclaiming Hearts

Crowns & Courtships

Dare You
Heart of a Prince

Serenity Landing Tuesdays of Grace 9/11 Tribute Series

Grace to Save

Serenity Landing Lifeguards Summer Novellas

The Lifeguard, the New Guy, & Frozen Custard
(previously titled: The Lifeguards, the Swim Team, & Frozen Custard)
The Lifeguard, the Abandoned Heiress, & Frozen Custard
(previously in the *Whispers of Love* collection)

Serenity Landing Teachers Christmas Novellas

Gifts of Love
Manuscripts & Mistletoe

Mallard Lake Township

Ballots, Bargains, & the Bakery (novella)